CHASING TOMORROW'S NIGHTMARES

CHASING TOMORROW'S NIGHTMARES

O. G. DIAZ

Copyright © 2022 O. G. Diaz

Paperback: 978-1-63767-676-9
Hardcover: 978-1-63767-678-3
eBook: 978-1-63767-677-6
Library of Congress Control Number: 2022900063

All rights reserved. No part of this publication may be reproduced, distributed, or transmitted in any form or by any electronic or mechanical means, without the prior written permission of the publisher, except in the case of brief quotations embodied in critical reviews and certain other noncommercial uses permitted by copyright law.

This is a work of fiction.

Ordering Information:

BookTrail Agency
8838 Sleepy Hollow Rd.
Kansas City, MO 64114

Printed in the United States of America

CHAPTER 1

What on God's earth am I doing here? This is not a place where I would have ever conceived to end up, much less die.

Never once have I contemplated that I would one day die, much less so far from home. But, my nineteen-year run at life terminates in minutes, rather than decades or even years. All that I am, and all that I could one day have been will soon cease, brutally violent, and far too early to have accomplished anything notable. It will all end, not as a big bang felt throughout the cosmos, but rather as a footnote to a miniscule addendum, of an after-action report of the March 1, 1969, operations in Binh Dinh Province.

Who do I dare lay responsibility for this travesty about to unfold on my first exposure to combat? Can I blame it on young, pretty women that lured me away from my studies? What about my parents who made the check for the fall 1968 tuition to my name, rather than to Louisiana State University? No, those were nothing more than an irresponsible means to what had been a headlong, hedonistic dive into manhood; of which, I was the lone culpable figure.

It was a time of liberation from a stagnant cultural and old moral constraints. The music, the arts, the fashions, and the self-anointed elites, all screamed, 'Off with the shackles of the old ways,' and I fell victim to the times.

Yes, the truth is that I have no one to blame for what is about to befall me, other than myself. It wasn't my "friends and neighbors" at the local draft board that were responsible for my being here, either. They were merely delighted to have me join of my own volition, saving them the guilt of conscripting and sending some other hapless nineteen-year-old to this murderous paradise.

Morose from guilt at my lifestyle landed me here. My conscience ached at having squandered the folks' hard-earned tuition money on selfish indiscretions. Those funds, for a bright future that they were intended to provide, went so quick that I failed to comprehend the long-term consequences of my frivolity, until it was too late.

The same is true of young women. I initially took them as playthings to be welded to my desires through mere tender, passionate words. It was easy, and they participated ever so willingly that I now question, if I was the one toyed with.

A single, daily dose of synthetic estrogen and progestin liberated them of sexual fears and restraints. They demonstrated their new found independence through unabashed, tantalizing behavior. Braless, exotic blouses and sweaters, and short, revealing mini-skirts were the uniform of their new found liberation. But in fact, they were not fully emancipated of their sexual morality. They were still wed to a notion other than mere outright, lustful pleasure.

During that early phase into manhood, so often referred to as sowing one's oats, I was too blind to see my female companion's long-term expectations of me, especially with so many other pretty things, thinking themselves liberated, and needing someone to ply them with those incantations they longed to hear. The pain at the disappointment inflicted on abandoned, carnal partners, eventually took a heavy toll on a Catholic conscience, already overwrought with guilt.

I had navigated through life without a moral rudder. There was little purpose to my existence; lustful desires and immediate gratification were my life's pursuit, but even a prodigal son has to eventually face up to his wasteful ways.

A penance of sorts was required to ease my guilt over that reckless lifestyle, and a means to alter and steer my life toward a more productive direction also seemed vital. At the time, enlistment into the U. S. Army appeared the answer. A chance to mature in a disciplined environment seemed the simple solution to all my problems. As it turned out, that was flawed judgement. My quest for absolution and maturity through a temporary military career came at a time of an unpopular war.

I enlisted during an ongoing war in Southeast Asia. It was a war based on economic ideology, led by World War II era generals, and micromanaged by faint-hearted politicians, secured in their safe confines of Washington DC. Less than six months after enlistment, I was catapulted over all stages of manhood, directly into the warrior class and cast into a war zone, at the far side of the world.

The consequence of that search for atonement is about to commute my light penance, to that of a death sentence.

"L J," it is my tracker team's cover man, Carl Talmadge, whispering to me, but showing no signs of apprehension on his fair and lightly, freckled face. "You ever seen hills like that?" the lanky, sandy-haired Tennessean asks.

He points to four monstrous protrusions of earth scattered over a wide sandy, coastal flood plain to our front.

The expanse of shoreline to where he points is a half-mile deep, ribbon of sugary white with sparse, ankle level ground vegetation. That sand strip is hemmed in to the east by the South China Sea. Thick foliage that runs as far as the eye can see, fences the broad beach to its west. Four, towering, mesa-like pillars, capped with tall hardwoods, stand helter-skelter a mile of each other along that coastline. The earthen rises, with their base eroded by semi-annual inundations off the sea, soar upwards from the sand, to a height of seventy meters. They appear like great bastions standing guard over a sandy domain.

We crouch in a tree line of dwarf trees and not so dwarf shrubbery, facing the broad beach. Our eyes are focused on the first earthen outcrop, two hundred meters to our front, searching for signs of rice farmers with automatic weapons. Dozens of Viet Cong tracks from a previous evening's ambush of a platoon, lead in the direction of that outcrop. A wisp of blue smoke, discernible to frightened, but well-trained eyes, show they are still there.

"They're not hills," I pensively answer, while carefully studying each bush, each boulder and each small crag on the heights for a sign of an enemy that awaits our approach. A quick deep breath that sounds more a gasp, replaces air inadvertently held for far too long. That gulp of air exposes a tightness at my chest. "I think they may be salt domes. We have them at home near the Gulf of Mexico, but ours are far larger than these four pups."

"You're pulling my leg, ... aren't you?" he questions with his boyish, Tennessean drawl that brings some calm to my apprehensions. "Those piss ants from the nearby village would have dug out the salt by now if there was any. Vietnamese don't let anything go to waste."

"They're small domes," I offer, finding the talking therapeutic for diverting a mind racing with thoughts of death, waiting on that height. "Maybe the salt is not worth the effort to get at, or maybe they don't know what's under there. At home, they use heavy equipment to burrow deep caverns to extract the salt from under the domes. That hot sauce you douse your food with at the mess-hall comes from Tabasco Peppers grown and distilled atop one of the domes."

"How do you know all that?" Talmadge appears to be challenging my words.

One or two members of our unit tend to exaggerate their home lives and their personal accomplishments; so, I understand, but yet dislike the notion of his questioning me.

"I grew up in a small town, Lafayette, Louisiana, just north of many such mounds," I reply.

"Thought you said that you were from the capital city of your state?" he continues his probe.

"My dad is a civil engineer with the highway department," I answer somewhat in a snit over his continuing testing of my veracity. People seldom question what I say. They often claim that I am far too candid, to the point of being brutal with the truth, when I do have something to say. But his questioning takes my attention away from what lies to our front, and I find a sense of calmness in talking. "Dad took a promotion and transfer to his department's headquarters in Baton Rouge, at the end of my eighth grade."

"Well, this place is hot as hell, a lot hotter than that sauce from your state," Talmadge complains, seeming satisfied with my explanation. "I intend to go home to Pigeon Forge, Tennessee, and live a simple, pious life, so I don't spend an eternity in such a damn place as here."

Suddenly, he contorts his facial muscles. He slaps at a mosquito, leaving a gob of fresh blood smeared on his freckled cheek. With that same hand, he swats at gnats, impervious to swats, as they cluster about his boyish face. Between futile swipes, he points to two approaching soldiers: one wearing clean, tiger camouflage fatigues and matching cloth boonie hat, the other, a helmet and baggy, standard issue, jungle fatigues, filthy with weeks of dirt and crusted body salt.

Our team leader, Walter Newsom, hurries toward me, brushing away branches that hamper his way. He has a somber look on his striking black face that ends all talk of salt domes. At his side, is a short, blond, blue-eyed sergeant of an eight-man squad of paratroopers. He and his men have been assigned to our team, to engage the enemy once we locate them. Though the young man's uniform and face are gritty from weeks in the field, there is no mistaking that grave look under his steel pot.

"Man, we need your team," the teen insists, tugging at Newsom's arm to halt him. "If they're waiting and ready for us, they will waste my squad before we reach the base of that damn thing. The extra fire power from your weapons may make a difference. You have to help us!"

"Oh, hell yeah, they're waiting on you," Newsom spins about, shakes off the squad leader's grip, fury showing on his face.

Anger is uncharacteristic for the soft-spoken man and most experienced member of our team. Sweat, that now drips off his chin, which I had presumed the Florida native was immune from, adds to an uncharacteristic behavior.

"If not, they will once they see you start across that open ground. Listen closely," Newsom takes a short step toward the young sergeant to ensure the boy's attention. "What waits on top of that hill is more than one or two simple paddy farmers that occasionally venture out of their huts and take pot shots at us. There are likely dozens of those bastards up there, and the only way to root them out is by going up to the top. I told that lieutenant of yours that his entire platoon was required to support us, but he was too smart to listen. That Prick took the rest of your platoon around the village to the opposite side, certain of intercepting your ambushers there. Hell, he's three hours away, chasing ghosts, and what awaits your squad up there are hardcore Victor Charlies. Our job is to track the bastards down and then have you guys move forward to waste them. Our job is done!"

Newsom turns his back to the squad leader. He takes a long, angry look toward the earthen rise, a gaze that must be imagining a meager eight paratroopers crossing open ground while under the scrutiny of patient, Asiatic eyes. "I can be court martialed for deliberately leading my team into a firefight, and if one of us, especially our dog, Prince, gets killed, I will be in a shit storm."

Hanson, our dog handler, and Prince, our black Labrador tethered to a twenty-foot leash, approach. The talk of his Australian/Malaysian trained, canine partner possibly getting killed got the best of Hanson's curiosity. The make-shift gathering also draws our fifth teammate, Brandon Whitman, our visual tracker, who toils at dry, caked blood up his nose.

"L J, any word from that platoon leader?" Newsom asks without taking his eyes off the dome.

"No, and I've radioed for him twice the last ten minutes," I reply. "Each time, his radio operator says that he is indisposed and will call back when he's available."

"That goofball is probably in the bush doing his Monday morning thing, blowing a liquid stream out of his ass," Talmadge chuckles. "Ya'll forget today is Monday?"

It suddenly strikes me that Carl Talmage has no idea of the dilemma facing the team. While he detected the faint wisp of smoke rising from the dome ahead of others, he has not discerned the ghastly position that we are in, or the difficult decision weighing on Newsom.

Our team leader is in an unwinnable situation. He can violate unit protocol by joining in an assault and thus face severe, disciplinary repercussions, or he can bring shame and discredit to our unit's two teams, by standing down and allowing the eight-men squad to undertake the confrontation alone. Other than Talmadge and apparently, Newsom, who persists on mulling at a decision with but a singular, inevitable outcome, the rest of us have a clear understanding of what that answer will be. Only the arrival of the rest of the platoon will save our five-man team from a murderous engagement, and they are hours away.

"Yeah, I did forget today is Monday," the teen squad leader mutters. He digs into a breast pocket and pulls out a small, reddish-brown colored bottle. "I got to hand out the weekly malaria tablet to my guys. You guys need some? I got plenty."

"What the hell you worried about malaria for?" I explode, flabbergasted by his offer. It is insane to worry about getting malaria, just now, and my fears at having to engage in an attack over open terrain have me ill-tempered and lashing out. "You're more likely to catch a chunk of lead this day than a parasite."

"Yeah, but if you crap all over yourself while going across, you can blame it on the pill," Talmadge injects his levity, grinning ear to ear.

The radio crackles; it's the platoon leader, finally calling. "He wants you," I rudely utter and give the transmitter/receiver hand set, to the squad leader.

"What do you think?" Newsom turns to Hanson.

Prince's handler is the only other member of our team with combat experience. Talmadge and I, along with another member, Sam Cooper, arrived twelve days earlier from in-country Combat Tracker Training school at Bien Hoa near Saigon. Whitman, is equally green. He arrived from Visual Tracker School at Fort Gordon, Georgia, a day after we did. Our inexperienced opinion, it seems, is of no consequence to Newsom's decision making. Only the dog handler's consideration matters, yet another uncharacteristic behavior for Walter Newsom, given that Hanson is generally invisible to us.

Henry Hanson is a very quiet person who keeps to himself. He spends more time with Prince than the other guys in the unit. Theirs is not a man/pet relationship or anything resembling that; it's a professional partnering. Our dog handler devotes his time at Dog Patch, our name for the kennels and compound we share with the German Shepherds of a Scout Dog Platoon, keeping Prince's cage spotless and a water bowl filled with clean, cool water. In return, Prince will find and follow a track, and when all visible evidence of tracks made by the enemy are lost, the dog sniffs out and sets our visual tracker back on course. It is also Prince's actions that alert Hanson to enemy ambushes or nearby booby traps. Unfortunately, when Hanson does speak, it's always curt, and his speech sounds as if his tongue gets in the way. A brief shrug of the shoulders that looks more like a spasm is all he offers to Newsom.

The squad leader gives back the hand set. Beads of sweat trickle off a melancholic face as he stares down at his feet. "Lou wants me to check out the top of that damn thing. He's heading back to last night's bivouac area and will support us from there if we run into trouble."

"A lot of good that will do!" Newsom angrily speaks out. "He'll still be forty-five minutes away when he gets to that camp site."

"Well, we have to jump-off," the young sergeant adds, looking resigned to a ghastly fate. "There looks to be a winding path going up over to the right. That'll be our objective for heading up."

"Our dog and handler will follow behind your squad," Newsom softly states. "There looks to be a narrow trail over on the far left. I'll take the rest of my team up from there."

Someone gasps. It may have been me, but more likely, Talmadge. The constriction to my chest returns with a vengeance. Getting air into the lungs becomes labored and a knotted stomach feels as if it needs to hurl out what little is trapped there.

I am about to engage in an enterprise that I see little opportunity at surviving. It is a venture with which I have no experience, and it terrifies me. Never would I have thought myself a coward, but the anticipation of a whirlwind of brutality and death that I will soon engage in, has me panicking and yearning to be elsewhere, anywhere, but here. I am also enraged that a reprieve fails to arrive to save us. I hope that someday, someone will avenge us by fragging that prick lieutenant.

CHAPTER 2

Prophylactic pills dispensed and swallowed under watchful supervision, we set an assault line in front of the trees and bushes. As we form, I find time to reflect on all that has transpired since our early morning's arrival at the platoon's bivouac.

Much has occurred since that dawn arrival. First, a disagreement with the platoon's lieutenant, ignorant of our having been assigned to track down his previous evening ambushers, and a call from his company commander, rebuking him and ordering him to just let us do our job. Second, our halt on the way to pick up the trail at the ambush site, to gawk at a pretty, young woman, brazenly disrobing to bathe out in the open. That was followed by pain and bloody noses resulting from concussion by a booby trap. The explosion inflicted noses to bleed and ears to ring, but little else. It was triggered by a paratrooper at the head of the column. Without doubt, the explosive was hastily planted and poorly set by a cohort of the bathing beauty. Finally, my abhorrence, as a screaming Brandon Whitman runs to me after the explosion, hands drenched in blood covering his small baby like face, crying out, begging me to look, if he still had one.

The metallic clatter of rifle bolts, chambering 5.56 caliber rounds, break my thoughts. It is about to commence. That lock-and-load sound signifies a resolve to engage an enemy at the other side of open ground. Youth is about to be offered up for slaughter, and I dread that I will not be spared from that butchery.

I take another look at the hill, but it is the flat ground to my front that suddenly catches my eye. The terrain to traverse is far longer than it appeared from the tree line. An open space, some two-football fields long, clearly separate us from the base of the rise.

My heart now races faster as the knowledge of the length of our exposure over open ground sinks deep. Each rhythmic pulse of surging blood causes arteries along temples to pound. Muscles in my chest tense further; their tightness crushing the chest, leaving me once again needing to gasp for breath. Suddenly, a strange sensation overtakes me: my head spins and confusion seeps in.

A World War I documentary that I once saw on television suddenly pops to mind. I recall hundreds of thousands of poor Frenchmen leaping from the safety of their trenches to storm across the fallow grounds of no man's land. They threw themselves at opposing German trenches that were protected by interlocking fields of murderous, machine gun fire. Aware of the butchery that awaited them, they bravely charge, to be mowed by the thousands.

Suddenly, a far stranger sensation overtakes me. My head spins with far too many thoughts now coursing through my head. My cognizant mind appears in panic at the stupidity that I am about to engage.

Someone calls out to me from the tree line. It is a woman's anxious voice, and it sounds faintly familiar. I turn to look back as she implores me to come and join her among the bushes. My eyes tear up, as I struggle against the temptation.

Fear is not unknown. I survived an undertow at a Florida beach through calm application of wit, and I have miraculously walked away from a nasty automobile wreck. But this, this is more than fear; this is self-inflicted terror. This is not some inadvertent catastrophe to suddenly strike out at me that I must somehow overcome. This is a folly that I am about to consciously commit myself to participate in, and it appears to terminate in certain death. It is against my better judgment, and though I am deeply opposed to this endeavor, I find myself, for some unknown reason, compelled to go along and to pass on that luring invitation from the tree line.

One of the paratroopers starts forward. We all follow as pre-arranged. We keep a walking pace for a long fifty meters, nervously eyeing the top of the mound for signs of the slightest movement. Once that distance is traversed; we commence to double-time.

We agreed to maintain a jogging pace as a singular line for the length of a football field, with the understanding those still able, would sprint the final stretch to the base of the mound.

Time passes slowly as our line runs that length of a football field. I find the stress easing with the exertion of energy. Each stride loosens taut muscles and slackens that grip, crushing at my chest.

My mind somewhat less apprehensive, I become cognizant of stimulus picked-up by hyper-charged senses. The heavy thump of jungle boots pounding sand, the clanging of the paratroopers' loose equipment, a faint Hail Mary prayer, an occasional whimper rolling out a paratrooper's young lips, and the short, heavy panting of those at either side come to my ears. An overhead sun, now feels blistering hot on this March morning. It heats the black, plastic cover guards over the M-16 barrel, making them hot to the touch. A flock of green parakeets appear out of nowhere. They fly between us and the rise, before disappearing to the safety of the tree line. A briny smell, blown in by a sea breeze is in the air; it stirs memories of summers at beaches along the Gulf of Mexico.

There is no gunfire during our steadfast pace across the sand and no sign of the enemy. Though we are in range of enemy weapons, we expect that the Viet Cong will wait until their chance for a kill improves. Then they will unleash horrendous, rifle fire and mow us down as if it was the very trenches of 1916, France.

Someone from the right of the line panics and bolts, far too early. It doesn't matter; we all join in that race. We sprint for our lives, certain that at any second, a thunderous chaos of automatic fire will erupt. We run on shaky limbs, waiting on the stings of death to strike.

To my horror, as I near the mound, it takes on a far different makeup. I now see its true composition, a massive, vertical rock. That slow, rising slope that is the team's objective is nothing more than a geological crack on a plumb rock surface. How am I to climb this damn wall? The skills of a mountain goat are required to scale the height, and I have no such skills. Full panic sets in as I try to grapple with this unexpected dilemma.

The rock hill suddenly appears to move before me. To add to all my fears and concerns, the darn mountain seems to be slipping and sliding away. It moves, toying with me, slinking further with each progressive stride I take. *Is this fear, playing with my mind?*

I cannot gather my wits long enough to formulate an answer to this new quandary. My brain is now racing with far too many thoughts. It is fleeting from one cognizant, mental deliberation to another, without fully completing any one contemplation. Though my body continues its quest forward, independent of conscious thought, the mind is in full panic of its own. Suddenly, a sensation of a mind wrenching itself free of the flesh overwhelms me; worse, it appears to succeed.

The body is forsaken in little time. The spirit breaks with the flesh, and the body acts fully independent of the mind. A sense of surreal tranquility overtakes me. It is a miraculous transformation of feeling, one that frees me of fear and stress, and cloaks me in a god-like quality: unassailable and obscure to other fleshy beings.

I am no longer a part of the terrifying death race that the body continues to pursue. I am a spectator, hovering and watching the silly thing chase after the monstrous earthen rise, and yet, I find nothing odd or unusual with this turn of events. I am free and excused of all responsibility over the flesh and suffer no deep attachment or loyalty to it. At least, I, or perhaps the mind, am safe of the body's folly. I contemplate, whether this is nature's way of preparing for the effects of a traumatic end to the poor, fleshy creature.

I watch four bodies catch and take hold of that vertical wall. With no slope to walk up, they mount the rocky surface. They grasp and pull their way upwards, jutting rock by jutting rock, looking like green geckos, scurrying up a wall. And yet, not one shot has been fired.

What are the Viet Cong waiting on? Have they not seen the quartet, or have they planned something more diabolical for them?

Countless thoughts now race through my mind. They are of meaningless questions and equal meaningless likelihoods, most not of my conscious formulation. Short-lived lucid periods, occasionally break through the insanity, further complicating thinking and adding to the confusion. I am aware, during those rational moments, that I have to regain mental control to concentrate on the task of reaching the summit. But my mind appears to have taken a life of its own.

The body progresses without aid. It has found a six-inch ledge that slopes upward. It is side-stepping, hugging the rock surface and brushing aside shrubs protruding from cracks, but steadily inching upward along that narrow shelf. Twelve meters from the crown, the ledge abruptly ends. The body halts to examine the task facing it. A sheer, rock wall is all that stands between it and the hill's crest.

I now find myself a cheerleader, urging the silly flatlander from Louisiana to scale that damn wall. "*Climb, climb, climb,*" I implore, but wonder if it is in the nineteen-year-old to get it done. A fall from this height will prove fatal and a rock slide will draw attention, proving equally grave. Nevertheless, I continue to urge the silly thing to climb, and to my surprise and horror, it does.

Weary hands reach up and grasp at rocky points and shrubs that barely protrude from the rock surface. Lacerated and bleeding, the hands grasp and pull, while legs quivering from exhaustion push off other rocky knobs. Inch by inch, the body struggles upward, pushing and pulling, a herculean task that seems endless.

The summit is attained. The exhausted creature crawls forward and shelters against a massive, granite boulder at its right. It lays there, quietly, chest heaving, too tired to move, oblivious, or perhaps uncaring, as to the perilous purpose of the climb.

It is then, while at rest, and the immediate area appears innocuous, that a reluctant mind abandons its refuge to rejoin the body.

The dangerous ascent accomplished, it is time to recuperate and to labor on the purpose of the climb. I take to my knees, sit back on my heels and inhale deep to recover as much strength as I can, while surveying the area.

Beyond the enormous boulder, the visible surroundings show little other than four tall trees, shrubs and a handful of other large boulders. Seeing and hearing no signs of life, I glance to my left and rear. Again, no one, just a wonderous expanse of beach, the nearby Vietnamese village, and a thick, green canopy that spreads beyond a far-off mountain range. On any other occasion, this panoramic view, would make the climb worthwhile, but not this day.

Where is the rest of my team? Newsom, Talmadge, and Whitman should be here. They bore no radio to weigh them down and should have been here far ahead of me. Are they trying to catch their breath behind some tree or boulder, or perhaps, hiding from the VC? Hanson and Prince were to follow the Grunts up the trail; they should be here, as well.

I am deeply conflicted and confused. I struggled and risked all to reach this summit only to find myself alone. *Have they returned to the tree line without informing me?* No, I just as quickly conclude. The team would not abandon me. They are here, sheltering and surveying the area for danger, as I am.

It is time to venture forth and find who or what is to the right of the massive boulder. I rise, stoop, and inch my way along the rock, careful to not make a sound. At the boulder's edge, I straighten and pause to gather courage, before stepping out.

A man, all in black, with weapon in hand, pops into sight. I freeze. I hold my breath. I do not dare to so much as blink. I am so petrified that my feet feel rooted to the bedrock. There seems little else to do for now, but to wait for him to turn and kill me.

Never, during my military life, did I ever presume to one day come so close, while so precariously exposed, to the enemy. But here, a mere thirty feet away, a short husky man saunters across my front, and he carries a rifle.

My heart pounds hard; so hard, I fear it will burst out the rib cage, or worse, bring attention to me. My mind explodes once again with a multitude of thoughts, none of which center on what evasive action to take, only on a horrific outcome to this hap encounter. I continue holding my breath, praying he goes away without seeing me.

I watch as he strolls past me, unaware of my presence. He walks, nonchalant, toward the base of a tree where canvas backpacks lie. The Kalashnikov automatic rifle that he carries keeps me petrified.

A thunderous fusillade of M-16 and machine gun fire erupt to the man's rear, making him snap his head around. He sees me. We lock eyes. Black Asiatic eyes stare at terror-stricken, brown occidental eyes.

It cannot be but a split second that we stare at one another, though it seems hours. My frightened mind spontaneously notes all that the eyes see and concludes that which it cannot of the man. He is five foot three inches tall, in his late thirties or early forties, well-fed, and of stocky build. An unbuttoned shirt shows a muscular upper torso. A deep, ugly scar from a bullet that tore across his left cheek gives him a hard, menacing look and shows that he is a seasoned fighter. But wide-open eyes on an ashen face scream shock and horror at my presence.

I sense the man's fear through that gaze, just as he must mine. Action is required, and quickly, but I am too terrified to act through that long, split second.

His full body suddenly hurries at a turn to eliminate his threat. The barrel of his AK 47 rifle rises and turns with him. Like a graceful ballerina performing a pirouette, his left arm and leg gracefully initiate a sweep through the air ahead of that spin, but his grounded foot snags on something as he hurries his turn. That simple glitch, causes him to slightly totter, all the while, squeezing at the trigger of his weapon. Kak, kak, kak, kak sounds.

Out of the corner of an eye, I see dirt leap and dance into the air as bullets burrow into the ground. It is then I realized that I am also firing. Short flashes of flames spring and die at the end of my M-16's barrel. Instinctively or through training, I am unconsciously firing, though my eyes are yet locked in a duel of their own with those of an enemy, just feet away.

The man recovers from his falter. His body suddenly snaps abruptly upright, and his torso jerks to the right. He now stares at me with squinty eyes as his facial muscles tighten and snarl. His entire right arm, yet grasping hard at the weapon, slides out its long black sleeve. It strikes the ground, drawing black eyes away from me.

Volleys of automatic rifle fire join in, striking the man. It sends him to the ground. He lays there, motionless, his facial muscles still constricted from the initial pain, and his chest ripped open. Free of all fear and pain, of memories and thoughts of a future, he lays there with accusatory eyes wide open, their gaze boring deep into the memory banks of my mind.

Newsom, Talmadge, and Whitman appear. They approach at my left, inching cautiously forward.

Nausea overtakes me. An urge to vomit forces my eyes shut; I struggle against the inclination at such an inopportune time. I hold my breath, fearing release will result in a hurl of acidic bile. A thumping sound comes to my attention. A quick glance down to the source of the thumping shows my right leg quivering and boot heel repeatedly tap-tapping at the ground like some nerve tic. There seems no stopping the leg, so I scan the area for further danger and to ease my mind of all the physical conditions plaguing me.

No voice sounds, no birds flitter, and no breeze rustles leaves on trees. Nothing moves or sounds, just an errant leg. At this point, I realize the fighting is over. That tumultuous chaos of weapon fire begins and ends in seconds, four to five seconds that obliterate a lifetime of human experience and forever scars the memories of others. That pandemonium of a struggle for survival is now replaced by graveyard silence. It is a quiet that pricks at arm hair and appears as terrifying as the chaos of the just concluded firefight.

"Clear, here," comes a loud but shaky voice from the far side of the hill top. That voice startles me. I recognize it as the paratrooper's sergeant. His two meager words are meant to query the status on our side, as well as to inform us of the condition on theirs.

A reply is expected. I am far too numb and too spent by all that has transpired to care to reply.

No one else on my side of the hill top seems eager to answer. Talmadge stands in the open with his weight on his right leg and the barrel of his weapon cradled in the nook of an arm, staring at the lifeless body. Newsom sits on the ground. His weapon rests across his lap, and his arms behind him, propping his torso. Whitman has taken a knee, nervously scoping the area, as if expecting further encounters. "We're…. we're okay," he stammers a response.

The nineteen-year-old sergeant soon approaches. Enlarged, blue eyes on a tired, melancholy face tell much. He stands, viewing the corpse, as if waiting for the body to miraculously move and rise. A slow turn toward me, he softly asks, "You waste him?"

I take angry exception to his query and refuse to answer. After all, what difference does it make who took the man's life? He is down, rib cage ripped open and his right arm feet away. There is no point in staking claim to having committed the dastardly deed, and I find his question accusatory.

The grungy teen turns his attention back to the corpse. He does not wait for an answer, seeming to know none is forthcoming. He walks to the severed arm. With callous disregard for the appendage, he plants a foot on it and wrenches the weapon loose.

"We took three other AK 47s and two SKSs from the five we wasted," he says, looking at me with eyes dead as those of a serpent. "They were cooking lunch, rice and dry fish. The rest from last night must have didi maued earlier," he adds, carrying on as if he needs to converse.

I want him out of my face. I point to the ruck sacks and web gear laying against the tree, in a selfish act. I need time, time alone to recover and to work through all that has transpired, and I find his very presence irritating.

The young sergeant looks about at the other team members. Finding no one appearing willing to talk, he moves toward the VC equipment.

"Watch out for damn booby traps!" Newsom snaps at the poor kid.

No sooner gotten rid of one irritant, another appears. Hanson approaches, hurrying with a reluctant ward in tow. A look of wild exuberance is on the man's face; a look counter to that of all others. "Hold this," he mumbles. He throws me the dog's leash and pulls his bayonet from its scabbard. "Going to make a necklace," he utters.

His words fail to rationally resonate. The notion of making a necklace is absurd, considering our immediate environment. Perhaps, his tongue has somehow altered the intended words, but then, my mind has not functioned sensibly since we started across the sand. I take Prince's leash and just watch.

Hanson wastes little time getting to the dead VC. He kneels next to the carcass. With the free hand, he tugs at the left ear while his bayonet neatly slices downward along the man's temple. There is not the slightest, bit of objection from the dead and little discernable bleeding to dissuade the dog handler from continuing. Hanson repeats the grotesque process to the other ear. He stuffs both severed parts into a breast pocket, before scurrying off to the other enemy carcasses.

I am not appalled by what I just witnessed. I sense that I should have a strong revulsion to Hanson's actions, but I suffer no sense of disgust or horror. Perhaps it was the body's lack of a struggle at surrendering body parts that has me insensitive to the sight. But then, my mind is so numb, so muddled that it cannot properly account for what just occurred.

I begin to suspect this prodigal son will never be the same after this.

CHAPTER 3

He lays there, staring up at exposed ceiling rafters. Motionless and silent as the dead, he rests atop his bunk, shirtless, hands laced behind his head, looking up as he so often does. But on this singular occasion, Carl Talmadge's eyes are not darting about in their sockets, searching for large, black rats scurrying across the two by four joists of our hooch. They are void of life, seemingly staring into the vastness of oblivion. That homemade sling shot used to propel steel bearings removed from anti-personnel mines is not in hand. He just lays there, staring up at nothing, giving the vermin unmolested passage.

Brandon Whitman is also on his bunk. The latest issue of *Mad Magazine* is in his hands. No pages turn and no smile or laughter lights up his small, babyish face, a physical contrast to his muscular six-foot frame. As Talmadge, he is unflinching to the loud chatter and heavy laughter of Team 2's members, as they play cards.

I know that there is something wrong with me. I have sat at my bunk for an hour or two, steeped in dark thoughts. The stock of my weapon rests on my lap. Four other pieces are scattered about my bunk, factory grade clean and smelling of gun oil. It is past time to reassemble the damn thing, but I am not inspired to do so. Something mental prevents my joining the pieces together.

The tautness in my chest remains, and my mind races with endless thoughts of the events of the morning and mid-day. I bathed, and I changed uniform, but the memory from atop that mountainous pillar did not wash away. I am left struggling with paranoia and apprehension at what has happened to me.

Of foremost concern, have I gone mad, or did panic play bizarre tricks on my mind? Who called to me from the tree line at that beach? The voice sounded vaguely familiar and seemed to know my inner most fears. My mind was far too muddled back then, to clearly know who called to me, and yet, in the safe confines of our hooch, I still do not know. Also, how was I able to view myself from a distant vantage point? It is physiologically impossible to have done so. Nothing like this has ever occurred to me, and I have scoured my memory of anyone having gone through such a weird phenomenon. I suspect these and other such strange experiences are the behavioral hallucinations of a deranged mind. The persisting, self-psychoanalysis adds to my questioning the veracity of my sanity.

Of secondary concern, is the sudden revelation of the sort of ugly creature that I truly am. A tsunami of introspect struck me on that beach, exposing an ugly fact in its wake. I discovered something horribly shameful about myself; I am a coward. Fear of the magnitude which I suffered this day can only be experienced by one lacking any semblance of courage. Through my nineteen years, I have been conditioned by movies, television and books as to what constitutes bravery. No man can exude the fear that I have and not view himself a shameful coward.

The devastation left by that wave of awareness has struck at the core of my being. It washed away large chunks of my self-assurance and esteem, leaving me mired and wallowing in self-loathing.

A part of me is forever lost. That childish, fun seeking, and happy-go-lucky part of me was amputated and mutilated by fear and violence. The horrors of today's event are forever etched in memory, and I realize that there is no going back to who I was before this day. I am left to debate who I now am and how to live with any residue of who I once was. To add to all my woes, I realize that my very existence depends on sorting things out, and doing it quickly.

I am a member of a five-man team assigned to hunt down experienced, hit and run jungle fighters. The team relies on the unwavering performance of its five members, to accomplish each mission and to survive in the process. Swift but undetected movement through hostile terrain, constant diligence to surroundings and to signs inadvertently left behind by elusive guerrilla fighters, and a calmness to withdraw, unobserved, once the enemy is located, are required. What if I crack during the next engagement? What if someone is killed as a result of my actions? Afterall, only a coward would suffer the degree of fear that I felt this day, and I dread that it may always recur. But worse, I dread the others suspect that as well, and now think less of me.

The unit's two five men teams have had four replacements with my arrival and await another to make both whole. The leader of Team 2's tour of duty in Vietnam ended days after my coming. His is the only departure since. New guys like myself have no clue as to what became of the members we were sent to replace, and the older members are disinclined to speak of them.

My first mission ends in a firefight and my tour in Vietnam has forty-five weeks left. At a rate of one, maybe two missions per week, it does not require a statistician to quantify the odds of survival or to figure out what happened to the trackers we were sent to replace.

All of these thoughts racing through my head leave me mentally exhausted. I feel as if I can sleep for days. But how am I to lie down to rest without putting aside what occurred on that beach? I have tried, and I have failed. Asiatic eyes haunt me whenever I shut my eyes.

It was either he or I that had to die this day. So why must I be tormented by that vivid image of those horror-stricken eyes, begging to comprehend, why him? On several occasions, I have come close to convincing myself that it was one of the other team members that killed him. After all, during those chaotic seconds on that hill top, who can be certain. Why then, must I be the one to bear this onerous memory?

My two team mates remain on their bunks. Not so much as one word has been offered to assure me of my sanity or to indicate that I yet retain some level of competence and of respect among them. I anxiously await the two to rise and speak, and their failure to comply with my telepathic biddings, infuriates me. I fight back a powerful urge to up and flip their bunks over, with them in it.

Hanson suddenly enters the hooch, distracting my current ire. He wears the same sweaty, dirty clothing and that earlier look of crazed enthusiasm. He has been busy satisfying Prince's needs and appears ready to commence taking care of his own.

I watch him pull out a bootlace from a trouser pocket as he straddles his footlocker. He meticulously stretches the string and lays it over the chest.

Observing Hanson's actions offers a viable excuse for not assembling my weapon, should anyone care. As I watch the man, it dawns on me that I have little interest at how this one member of the team may perceive me. A legitimate reason escapes me for the moment, but perhaps it has to do with his limited association with others. His time spent with Prince and his poor verbalization skills place him on the fringe of our core of comradeship. Perhaps, once officially ostracized for my cowardness, that fringe is where I will find myself exiled.

Hanson returns to digging in a breast pocket. He dumps twelve severed ears on the locker.

Strangely enough, I am finally appalled. It mattered little when he took those ears from their owners, but their sight, I now find horribly repugnant. Anger also encroaches, as I watch him string and tie the ears. His actions bring on a fresh flood of unwanted memories that I have not had time to recall, but which I suddenly find myself now dwelling into.

It was near two o'clock, the hottest part of the day, when we climbed down the mountain and returned to the Vietnamese village. I recall the unfortunate paratroopers, in grimy clothing, trudging cautiously into the village. Torrents of sweat flowed from under their hot, heavy, metal helmets.

The offensive odors of human existence at the fishing village permeating the air also come to mind. Heat and humidity seemed to excite and propel communal ground stenches upward to assail unaccustomed nostrils. Olive Drab jungle fatigues, drenched in sweat, and the unwashed bodies of the paratroopers, added to the foul reek as we entered the coastal village.

Villagers squatted in clusters, silently observing our approach. They soon noticed the Viet Cong weapons and equipment in our possession. The sight of that cargo alarmed them. They had to have heard the distant gunfire from the killings atop the beach mound. Our possession of enemy weapons and equipment must have screamed at the outcome of that firefight. They soon glared at us with greater facial animosity than they had, when we first passed by that morning. From their silent rage, it was easy to conclude they knew or were sympathetic to the casualties atop the mound.

The leader of the paratroopers instructed two of his men to follow and posted the others to stand guard. We remained behind with the rest of the squad, uncertain as to his intentions. He and his two men moved with the cagey demeanor of carrying out a routine, but dangerous task. They entered the hovel of the bathing beauty of earlier that morning. Female sing-song voices abruptly sounded in angry protest at an intrusion. Their voices were quickly drowned out by loud grunting and shouts of a physical altercation, which included that of a male Vietnamese. A burst of M-16 rifle fire sounded. Those of us outside dropped to the ground, while the villagers took to their feet. The voices of two females soon screamed in anguish. A familiar "Clear here," sounds out. Shortly after, the paratrooper trio exited the hut, a distraught female bather in custody.

Andrei Nieman, our acting sergeant in charge of our two teams, pops into the hooch. He wears his typical apprehensive look, a lone look, occasionally replaced by one of anger, but never one of joy. His entry offers a welcome distraction to the stringing of ears and memories of earlier today. He walks to the center and looks about. No one, but I appear to pay attention. He clears his throat, but no one else so much as looks up.

Unlike Hanson, Nieman is not even within the fringe core of the teams' comradeship. He desires to be, but his temporary position of authority over the unit and his quartering at the headquarter hooch, keep him distant. His acting as a lacky, for the Scout Dog Platoon lieutenant we report to, does not help win the hearts and the minds of the unit's members. He is also older than the rest of us and of southeast European birth, complete with a dark, gypsy like appearance and accent.

He clears his throat again, but gathers no curiosity. "Can I have your attention?" he calmly begs when he should be forcefully demanding. He shifts his focus to Team 2's members playing poker at the back of the hooch. He squints his left eye and tilts his head away from them as if expecting a violent, physical attack for his words. "Seagram," he calls. A square faced young man with curly blond hair and crooked front teeth acknowledges with a flip of an arm, without taking eyes off the cards. "Once the Lieutenant finishes chewing Newsom's ass, drive everyone over to the mess hall. Take truck CCT 1. After this morning's action by our gunslingers, I expect a renewed demand from Brigade for our service. I want everyone well fed and ready for action."

"I'm not going," Talmadge angrily interrupts from his bunk. "I'm not hungry."

"Didn't ask if you were hungry," Nieman snarls at him. The new guys are the only members he dares to enforce his authority on. He takes pleasure with his rank on Talmadge, Whitman, and I of Team 1, as well as Cooper who in three weeks will replace Tom Cardona as the radio operator for Team 2.

"Team 1 goes back on standby tomorrow," Nieman explains. Talmadge props his torso up on his elbows, but Nieman moves closer to him to head off further protest. "My guess is that a call is likely to come in before breakfast."

It is Whitman who challenges the standby assignment. "We had a rough go on the mission! I would think a day or two to recover is due."

"Newsom thought so too," Nieman snickers, "but our lieutenant lacks combat experience and the only thing he knows about tracking is that we stay out of firefights. He told Newsom that had he followed that procedure; you guys would not have had a tough going. Besides, I am the only person available to lead Team 2, and the Lieutenant wants me at hand."

"You're right about one thing," I speak with a heavy, but angry heart, while returning my assembled weapon to the rifle rack. "This lieutenant doesn't seem to know dick."

The poker players chuckle at the remark. "I have been here ten months and don't recall having ever seen that man," Chuck Seagram shouts out, piling further on the lieutenant.

"Anyone know his name?" Joe Tillman, our other dog handler, suddenly wants to know.

"Ratchet, Pratchet, Cratchet, something like that," Tom Cardona answers.

"I saw him once coming out the crapper back at An Khe," the tall cover man, Bert Thompkins, injects with his typical, serious, puritanical look. "He is a little fellow with red hair and thick military eyeglasses. He couldn't see enough to retrace his steps in the wet sand if his life depended on it."

"Well, the blind man wants to see the inside of the berm around the kennels lined with double rows of sandbags, six feet high," Nieman interrupts the insubordinate discussion. "He worries that the quick job by the 173rd Engineer Company may collapse under a mortar or rocket attack. The sandbags will reinforce the dirt berm from the inside. That should take a few days to complete. Those not on standby will have something to keep them occupied, starting tomorrow morning," he adds, and makes a hasty retreat for the Headquarter hooch, having completed his assignment, but failing to make friends.

"Why the hell do we get all these shit assignments!" Cardona, the other team's radio operator, screams out the door. "There are twenty pens out there, but only two are ours!"

"Man, you are leaving for the land of the big PX in three weeks after a year here, and you haven't figured out why we get the shit assigned to us?" Thompkins asks.

"Yeah, step-children," Cooper answers for Cardona.

"More like bastard children," Cardona replies for himself.

The 173rd Airborne Brigade is finalizing its relocation from An Khe to LZ English on the outskirt of the small town of Bong Son. The pressure from Brigade to complete all construction at the new base has to be overwhelming. A second lieutenant of a platoon of German Shepherd dog handlers has to be feeling the heat. His handlers stay predominantly in the field, walking point for infantry patrols, and the only labor force available to get things done around a compound of five hooches and twenty dog kennels is an attached unit that resents him.

A light, short barrel, collapsible stock version of an M-16 has been returned to the rifle rack with a clip still in the magazine well of the weapon. There are four of these CAR-15s at the rack along with six M-16s. At one time, each of the ten trackers was assigned one of these carbines. The Scout Dog platoon leader reassigned most of the prized, lighter weapons to his scout dog handlers. The trackers don't mind; the weight factor is negligible, and we get along well with our counter-part German Shepherd handlers.

"Hanson, you left a loaded weapon in the rack," I yell out, still annoyed at the man.

He approaches, all smiles, obviously unaware of my current temperament. He loops the string of ears over his head. He grins at me as he adjusts the severed body parts and asks, "Well, what do you think?"

"I think you should stay downwind of me in the future," I snap at him.

"No need. They're cartilage," he mumbles, looking bemused.

"Yeah, cartilage covered by skin and capillaries to bring in blood," I respond, caring little as to how he may take my dry reply.

Nieman suddenly returns, this time carrying a clipboard. Team 1 members close their eyes and take a deep breath.

"Seagram, bring CCT 1 around," he orders, using his mission statement tone. "Newsom will be ready to go in five minutes."

He then proceeds into the meat of his announcement. "Brigade called as I expected. They were pleased by the outcome of today's mission and they want our services again. An hour ago, a mechanize company engaged a large force at the base of mountains thirty kilometers to our southwest. They recovered over two dozen dead NVA and spotted boo-coo blood trails leading away. They want us there at the crack of dawn, to see if we can find additional bodies or where they may have disappeared."

"Hell, those mech guys likely trampled over all signs left by the North Vietnamese Army regulars," Seagram, Team 2's visual tracker, smiles from experience. "Grunts are experts at mucking up signs while following up blood trails."

"If they haven't, their armor personnel carriers have certainly chewed up the ground," Thompkins joins in. "You Cherries are going for a short, early morning ride in a Huey, while we get stuck behind, filling and stacking sandbags all damn day."

"It's beaucoup, not bo-coo, and why must it always be so damn early," I protest to no one in particular.

Nieman looks displeased by all the commentary to his announcement and tries to recover control by pretending to be authoritarian. "Seagram, get the truck. Lejeune, Talmadge, and Whitman, with today's firefight, the lieutenant has put in the paperwork for your Combat Infantry Badge. Everyone on Team 1 is also being put in for the Army Commendation Medal."

"Damn good that does inside a coffin," Talmadge spouts off.

"Does it mean that Newsom is off the hook?" Whitman wants to know.

"Higher-ups call, highly pleased over results," Thompkins answers for Nieman. "You bet your sweet Cherry ass. That little blind bastard is fantasizing captain bars right this minute, and you, young whippersnappers, need to show appreciation for the medals Fearless Leader is bestowing on you."

"I read on *Stars and Stripes* that over half of all medals are awarded to officers," Tillman injects. "That small group of people who write the after-action reports for other officers to read, are award half of all the medals. Consider how fortunate you are to have a team leader to actually write up reports and not garner all the heroic credit for himself."

"That's right," Cardona adds. "Think how the babes at home will swoon at seeing those pretty medals pinned to your chest; but of more significance, on your next firefight, show Mr. Charles those medals. He'll be mighty impressed and didi the area out of fear."

Nieman tries to regain control once again. He moves his head away from Cardona as if expecting a sucker punch while speaking. "Everyone outside to the truck. Oh, by the way, Lejeune, the lieutenant plans to keep that pistol you traded with that squad leader for the AK. In the future, turn over all enemy weapons to the infantry support. That hand gun taken from the dead VC in that Vietnamese village or any captured weapon should never be used in trade."

"He's welcome to it," I say. "Next time he goes to the crapper, tell him to take it with him and shove the business end up his...."

"Enough," Nieman cries out. "Go get in the damn truck."

CHAPTER 4

"Look, I'm sorry we messed up the terrain," the mechanize infantry commander speaks, offering not an apology, but rather the facts, as he sees them. He is in a hurry, but feels compelled to offer explanations. "We were not aware you guys were coming until hours after our contact with the NVA broke off. My men were following up blood trails of which there were several, looking for wounded or dead North Vietnamese regulars; so, I'm sorry. Also, Brigade authorized my use of your chopper to run errands. I'm looking at five hours, so keep looking, you guys may get lucky and find a clear track. Should you find something, Lieutenant Harbor and his second platoon are standing by. I have already explained things to him. His men will follow you, dismounted, keeping a hundred meters to your rear. His boys are a bit green, but they're eager for action."

We watch the captain hop into our transport. No doubt, the man is delighted with our arrival. He has use of a Huey assigned to transport us, to run his errands, beating those at the top of the que of field commanders, waiting on helicopters to run housekeeping chores. As our ship lifts off, I find myself feeling strangely abandoned in the middle of nowhere. A sinking sensation hits my midriff as my gut seems to implode. I want to reach out and touch someone to assure myself that I am not alone. From the looks on the faces of the others who also watch our ship lift off, they appear deserted as well.

Prince manages to pick up on a scent a short time afterward. He found the spoor, during a deep sweep of the area, on what turned out to be an old, overgrown path, leading into the jungle interior. It is eight thirty in the morning when he picks up the smell, and visual signs confirm its enemy tracks. In no time, we are fast on the move, brushing through the confined space of a forgotten footpath.

Though it is not even mid-morning, the heat and humidity retained by the thick vegetation is stifling. No breeze worms through the narrow, overgrown trail to offer any relief from the oppressive conditions. By nine thirty, my jungle fatigue jacket is drenched with sweat, and perspiration burns at my eyes. At times, it feels as if I am swimming in a hot tub, trying to breathe while underwater, and the worst of the oppressive heat is yet to come. I cannot recall ever encountering such a horrid combination of temperature and humidity at home in Louisiana, although the foul conditions appear to have no effect on our dog's well-trained nose.

The path widens a kilometer from where we started. It runs south, parallel to foothills of tree covered highlands to our far right. Prince sweeps either side of the trail with his nose, but keeps a steadfast pace forward. The path's heading along flat ground allows Prince speedy movement, but two to three hours later, he pants, and his tongue hangs to one side.

We covered several kilometers, trying to catch up to an enemy with a fourteen-hour head start. Unfortunately, canines do not have the level of stamina that nineteen-year-old human males have, and a dog's panting can alert the enemy to our presence.

Brandon Whitman moves to the front of the formation and takes over tracking. The visual tracker hurries up the jungle path, moving from one sign post carelessly left by the NVA to others further up the trail. Talmadge follows close behind to cover him from danger. A partial sandal print here, a broken sprig there, has Whitman moving as if he is in a race to gather eggs at an Easter egg hunt, rather than in pursuit of a dangerous, armed quarry. Talmadge occasionally moves forward to tug at his web gear to slow him, if only for a minute or two.

It is fascinating to see the tracking process at work. We all trained to perform this very task, but it is something totally different to witness a tracking team in action. Like young Grim Reapers, the process has us quickly descending upon unsuspecting victims to harvest their lives.

Tracker School taught us all to see and discern things the mind of others tend to overlook as superfluous. We learned to see everything, even the most mundane of details, things necessary to stay on track or vital to survival. It also taught us to move quickly, silently and undetected through all sorts of terrain and water features. What they failed to teach, is how to conquer one's terror while on the chase. Nevertheless, I marvel at a process that brings us closer, and closer to someone's death.

We move fast for hours, in silence, like apparitions in the wind, far too vigilant with the jungle surroundings to dwell into fears or to continue contemplating the oppressive heat and humidity. Eleven to thirteen NVA, hauling five to six wounded, left clear signs that a blind lieutenant can follow. They appear to have no idea that anyone is in pursuit.

Every kilometer or so, trampled vegetation and pools of dry blood show where the enemy rested and cared for their injured. Those rest stops serve as reminders of yesterday's confrontation at the beach, though we are assured that this time, a full infantry platoon will spare our involvement in any killing. After locating each of those pit stops, we progress cautiously, at least the first quarter of a kilometer, before Whitman resumes a quick pace to the NVA's next stop.

Our team leader, Newsom, finally calls a halt. It is past one in the afternoon. We have spent some five frenzied hours trying to catch up with a small band of slow moving NVA. The stop is a welcome breather from our constant diligence to safety, as much as for our bodies to recover from exertion.

Newsom points to coordinates on a map to relay our location to lieutenant Harbor. I finish woofing down a small can of fruit cocktail and make the call. The lieutenant voices reservations with the great distance covered and our speed of travel. They lag far to our rear and have tired. I softly inform the platoon leader that we are closing with the quarry. Broken vegetation on the trail has wet sap, and the last NVA pit stop had blood, still moist to touch. The platoon leader comprehends, and says he and his men will make up the distance.

Ten minutes later, Whitman has us back on the chase. Vigilance is at its height. Talmadge presses closer to Whitman as a constant reminder to the enemies' nearness and to better regulate the visual tracker's speed. The pair approach every sharp turn of the trail as if expecting to see someone around that bend. We all scan through the thick vegetation and far up the trail, looking deep into the surrounding foliage for anomalies, or the slightest movement, just anything appearing out of kilter. After all, advantage for survival goes to the party that first detects the other.

I find myself far more anxious as we close with the dozen plus men ahead of us. At times, I find that I am holding my breath and have to make a conscious decision to release the spent air and breathe. When I do, it is a deep intake of muggy air, laden with mildew of rotting vegetation. Those deep breaths lessen my anxiety for only seconds, precious seconds nevertheless.

My body is also tense. All muscles are wound tight, ready to launch me into the safety of the shrubbery at the outbreak of gunfire; all typical reactions to what you would expect of someone lacking mettle.

Whitman and Talmadge take a knee some fifteen to twenty minutes after resuming track. Talmadge gives the hand signal to halt. Something to their front caught their attention. Whitman stoops his way back to explain the problem.

"Broken branches near the trail are covering something," he softly whispers, pointing at what appears to be an inconspicuous bush, showing early signs of wilting.

"Any idea what it may be?" Newsom softly asks.

"Not sure, but I think I saw fingers poking out," he whispers back.

"Probably a dead NVA," I pensively suggest.

"Hanson," Newsom faintly calls to the man at our rear. He jabs two fingers toward his eyes before sweeping them from the back of the trail over and across the left flank. "LJ, you and Talmadge cover the trail to our front. Tell him Whitman and I will approach the darn thing from the right."

A dead North Vietnamese soldier in his teens is soon stripped of his shroud of leaves. Harbor is alerted to expect seeing him. Whitman resumes point. He and Talmadge lead us up the trail with greater diligence, expecting to encounter the dead man's friends at any moment.

Foliage along the trail begins to thin out. Visibility deepens further. The path has entered foothills and takes the direction of the lush highlands that had been to our right. It leads toward mountains, where massive, fortified, enemy encampments lie concealed under thick canopies of trees. Obscured to detection from above, those camps lie in teasing challenge to lure in young men on the ground to their death.

My fears heighten further at this sudden change in direction. The hunt is nearing conclusion. The slow climb toward the highlands impedes our quarry carrying wounded, more so than a fast-moving team of trackers. My eyes hurriedly scan everything to the left, front and right as we move, while I panic that in my haste, I may overlook a critical sign. For forty odd minutes, I scan and re-scan, studying each shrub, boulder, mound of dirt, and fallen tree, praying that I catch sight of our prey, before they spot us.

Out of the corner of an eye, I catch Whitman and Talmadge drop to their belly. No hand signal is offered, but the rest of us comprehend and follow suit.

My vision is hindered by ground level vegetation. I close eyes to reinforce my sense of hearing. Faint moans and barely audible Vietnamese voices come to my attention. I reopen my eyes to the near-by sound of Whitman and Talmadge, crawling backwards toward us.

We make our way to the rear. After a distance of back pedaling, we shelter behind a fallen tree along the trail.

The stump of the log rises five feet next to the path. What remains of that stump is covered by dirt and debris from a termite colony. I radio lieutenant Harbor and hand the receiver to Whitman to explain in detail the number and layout of the enemy.

A sense of relief encompasses me. Our mission is accomplished, this time by the book, and I have managed not to discredit myself in the process. A deep breath starts to loosen muscles tensed for far too long. I am comforted by the fact that forty well-armed grunts are on their way to engage the NVA, sparing our involvement in another horrific firefight. Whitman hands me the receiver, a Mona Lisa-like smile on his cherub face shows his relief as well.

I toy with the fallen tree as we await the arrival of Harbor and his troops. The bark comes off with little effort, exposing plump grub worms, nesting there, or doing whatever it is those fat little buggers do. The wood is eaten throughout the inside. I almost laugh out loud at the notion of our having sheltered behind nothing more than cardboard.

Reclining behind the log to await Harbor and his platoon to sweep forward, lulls my senses. An overwhelming urge to shut my eyes and think about nothing strikes me. It then occurs to me just how mentally exhausted I am. My guard has been at peak attentiveness for seven hours. I have scanned and examined trees, bushes and rocks at either side of the trail, searching for possible danger for far too long. That effort has me now wanting to shut down and sleep, and from the looks on other faces, it seems they do as well.

The sounds of a platoon's approach come to our attention. We all take stock of the noise. It revives us; it lifts our spirits, much like the cavalry charge, breaking through to a besieged wagon train in old western movies. We look back along the trail for sight of the column. Though we cannot see them through the undergrowth, we clearly hear them. Someone in their group falls and curses. Others softly giggle, followed by an authoritative, "Shut the hell up." Their bungling movement through an enemy infested jungle, highlights the need to keep them a far distance to our rear. It is nevertheless, welcome noises.

Loud rifle fire erupts. Instinctively, I dive to the ground. The termite mound at my side disintegrates as bullets rip it apart. That rifle fire lacks that distinct hammer rattling on metal sound of an AK that I heard at the beach. It has me confused, but it does not take long to realize that the gun fire is from an M-16, and it's coming from the rear. *One of my own is shooting at me!*

That thought now resonates over and over in my head. Someone, whose arrival I have looked forward to, is now trying to kill me. The rest of the team is also cognizant of the source and the target of the gunfire. They likely reached that conclusion ahead of me, and have dived to the other side of the log, unaware of the paper-like quality of its composition, while I bury my face in termite dust.

I raise my head and spot the terrified face of the teen culprit. The point man of Harbor's platoon is running for a tree while continuing to indiscriminately fire. I want to shout out to him to stop, but I am unable to form the words, much less yell out.

What should I do? Leaping to the opposite side of a paper log, as others had, is ludicrous. Horrified by the inconceivable turn of events, I continue to observe the frightened kid fire, and I find myself struggling against an urge to kill him.

The jungle suddenly erupts in a spectacular explosion of color and noise. Red tracers rip through jungle foliage in all directions. Explosions sound, and tree limbs crack and fall. The rest of the platoon is blindly shooting into the jungle around them.

"Cease fire, cease fire!" I scream into the radio's transmitter.

A frantic call to cease fire emanates from down the trail. Other shouts to cease firing join. The noise and tracers subside and soon cease all together.

A platoon sergeant and a squad of nine, including the point man, sheepishly approach to investigate. They halt on the trail and watch anxiously, as we take to our feet.

Furious faces greet them. Our looks clearly exhibit a loathing for their pathetic existence, and our weapons, menacingly pointed at them, are ready to liberate them of their hapless lives.

Whitman unexpectantly springs over the log. He charges at the irresponsible point man. A bloodthirsty look on that fleshy baby face is as terrifying as the friendly fire itself. All watch in disbelief as he runs, unhindered, weapon raised overhead and stock forward, set to bludgeon the careless teen's head.

Lieutenant Harbor intercedes. A short man, not much older than any of us, but with a stature of command of someone far older, calmly steps in front of Whitman, halting him. He gives us all a quick look over, and calls to his platoon sergeant, map in hand. "Sergeant Arroyo, take the first two squads and cut through there," he calmly orders, pointing to the left of the path. "I'll take the rest of the platoon up the trail. You should find a stream about a hundred meters in. Cross it and sweep the opposite bank till you intersect with the trail or see us," he orders.

"Maybe we can still salvage something from this long day."

Arroyo has his group moving into the undergrowth in no time. Whitman angrily eyes the reckless grunt until the nervous, young man disappears into the vegetation.

Harbor orders the remainder of his platoon forward. He looks at us for some time before speaking, "I'll radio when it's clear." With that said, he joins his column.

"When it's clear," Hanson mumbles, mocking the lieutenant, but not until the platoon disappears from sight. "As if the NVA are going to sit around and wait after that disaster. Yeah, they are just going to hang around to be shot and killed by a bunch of Fucking New Guys!"

It is the longest string of verbalization to come out of Hanson's mouth the three weeks since I joined the team. In fact, it may be the most words that he has uttered in my presence. We all stare at him, stunned and in disbelief, but not surprised after narrowly escaping death by friendly fire.

Hanson moves to the log and plants his butt hard on top. The log crumbles to dust under his weight. I and others laugh. Perhaps we laugh at having survived the friendly fire episode, more so than the comic incident of the log crumbling under him. Even the angry Baby Face manages a grin, as he lends Hanson a hand up.

A small, chartreuse-colored snake emerges from the rubble of what had been the log. Smiles vanish as the creature crawls between Hanson's feet. We all dance a safe distance, allowing the creature wide berth to slither past us. We watch, as it takes its time to brazenly enter a nearby bamboo thicket.

"Holy crap, that's a damn two-step," a terrified Hanson cries, forgetting his whereabouts.

"Two-steps are different in color and have black bands," Newsom challenges.

"A what?" Talmadge demands, his eyes, as the rest, focus on the bamboo thicket the snake disappeared into.

"Two-step snakes," Newsom repeats. "It bites you; you take two steps and die."

I suddenly have greater respect for the little serpent. The notion of such a speedy death, by such a small viper, suddenly propels it to the top of all my new fears. Knowing its location is now of the utmost interest, and I strain to locate its whereabouts in the thicket. I spot it, curled up like a ball around a bamboo shoot, blending well with the color of the stalk.

A firefight with the enemy, then, friendly fire from my own, and now, I am exposed to other murderous ways to die in this land. How am I going to survive this hellish Garden of Eden?

Once again, I question the insanity that has brought my life to this point. Those thoughts always end with the same conclusion, I need to go home. I so desperately want to leave this place and return to a location of safety and familiarity with its surroundings that it strains my gut tight. But how do I get there, with yet forty-four weeks of penance, before the Army ships me back.

Kak, kak, kak, kak suddenly sound. I drop to a knee, forgetting all thoughts of self-pity. That horrendous, deafening commotion that had engulfed us minutes earlier erupts once again. M-60 machine guns and M-16 rifles from Harbor's platoon are responding somewhere nearby. They are soon joined by the thumps and explosive sounds of grenade launchers. The noise resembles fireworks at the commencement of a New Year, but it is truly, an awesome, audio display of infantry firepower.

Minutes later, the sounds of the mêlée end, just as sudden as it started. I and the other members are left to wonder at an outcome.

Though I am grateful at not having been involved in that firefight, I find myself apprehensive and tense at unknown results. Live rounds have been discharged, bullets with intent to kill, fired. Who, if anyone, has been hit or killed? Have any of the enemy escaped to make their way toward our direction? These are concerns that now plague me.

Lieutenant Harbor eventually calls on the radio. "Your helicopter is on its way. It will retrieve you at an open field just across the stream from our current position." He pauses, briefly, perhaps to allow me the opportunity to speak. "Once we cover your departure, we will head back. Don't mind saying, wish we had a ride back. I don't expect to hook up with the rest of my company till past dark."

"And the firing?" I hurry to inquire.

"Yeah," he pauses. "Sergeant Arroyo and his two squads engaged the NVA. They bagged eleven, and the rest skedaddled to the mountains. No friendly casualties, though."

CHAPTER 5

Team 2 is on standby the following morning. They are ready to depart at a moment's notice, to chase after armed and dangerous enemy, should a call come in. Surprisingly, they are elated at having to do so. They are spared back-breaking labor of digging at hard earth to fill sand bags, if only for this one day.

Though less than a hundred bags were filled and laid out over a ten-hour period, ugly blisters on palms and fingers attest to their previous day's effort. "The problem is with the dirt on this hill," Seagram offers up blistered palms as emblematic proof. "It's been stripped of top soil to build the berm around the kennels. Hard clay is all that is left, and you need a jack-hammer just to break it apart. Also, we have no damn gloves."

"The lieutenant is not pleased with yesterday's effort," Nieman inserts himself, his head and upper torso shying from Seagram. "He expects better results. He says at yesterday's rate, it will take thirty days to complete the task, and he wants it finished far earlier."

"Oh, the Great Oz wants it done earlier," Tillman, Team 2's dog handler, mocks, using a deep, bass tone, an uncharacteristic act for the mild-mannered fellow. He moves to his bunk and plops himself down. "My hands are ripped up, and I have to handle Zeus' leash if we get a mission. Just how many bags does he expect us to fill with these blistered hands?"

"What if we take one of our three-quarter-ton trucks to the river at the other side of Bong Son?" I ask, dismayed by the blisters and open skin of Seagram's palms. "There's loose sand there. Four of us can fill and return with more bags in one trip than we can fill here in ten hours. We should be able to get two, maybe three loads in a day."

"If we use CCT 1 and CCT 2, we can do more," Talmadge proposes, looking pleased with the concept. "Once one of the trucks is loaded, two of us can deliver the load while the other two stay behind filling more bags. We should be able to get an extra load or two in the process. Hanson and Cooper can stay here to help unload the bags when a truck arrives and afterward to stack them."

"How are we to get to the chopper pad if a call comes through?" Nieman guffaws at Talmadge's idea.

Our Tennessean's joy is smitten from his face by the outright rejection. Downcast eyes and slouching facial muscles say it all. But something else on that fair face, suddenly strikes me as looking oddly different. Perhaps, it has been that way all along, and I just never took clear notice of it, but Talmadge looks to have aged since that day along the beach, where we discussed salt mines in Louisiana and Tabasco sauce. The taut facial muscles under smoothly layered, pale skin on his youthful face appear to have changed. Those muscles now show slack, and lines are now visible on his once smooth skin. Years seem to have been heaped onto a youthful, freckled face since that firefight on that beach.

"We can use the Scout Dogs' deuce and half-ton truck," Bert Thompkins comes to the rescue.

Staff Sergeant wannabe, Andrei Nieman ponders the idea. From the thoughtful expression on his face, it is easy to surmise that he has an interest with what has been proposed. But he pauses to contemplate for far too long, mulling over a simple, logical suggestion to all our problems. His long deliberation worries me he may reject the recommendations and leave my team to suffer hands as the others had.

I never considered Nieman as bright. His aptitude seemed perfectly suited for obeying orders in the military, but little else. The older members extend him little respect, and it is unclear, if it has to do with his mental acuteness or some incident from the past.

A nudge is needed to sway him. "The lieutenant wants the work completed sooner rather than later, right?" I inject into his deliberation process.

Twenty minutes later, both trucks are on the main road, approaching the business sector of Bong Son. Fear and anxiety have diminished. The trip is a welcome diversion to our lives at Dog Patch and from the hazards of field work. I take in sights, sounds and smells of the small town, feeling like a tourist, on a sightseeing holiday. As we approach what constitutes downtown, I marvel at all the exotic wonders of a Vietnamese town.

The little business strip is a bee hive of activity on this morning. Narrow, but elongated, multi-storied buildings with their ground floor, metal, front walls hoisted up over sidewalks, butt up to each other. Signs above the outlets, with exotic lettering in a multitude of colors, vie needlessly for attention. Small but well-maintained retailers demonstrate their owners' success through spick-and-span, brightly lit interiors. Scattered among the retailers, the less successful industrial shops of basket weavers, sandal makers, and metal workers detract from the economic success of their neighbors. Mothers and grandmothers, towing small children, dive in and out of mom-and-pop grocers, as well as other sundry shops, some which openly display baskets of spices, rice, nuts, fruits and produce along the walkway. Young women in their traditional Ao Dai, white, ankle length shirts, split on the sides at the waist, with white or black silk slacks underneath, walk in pairs, arms looped between them. A man, wearing black business slacks, white shirt and dark tie, stands in front of an empty pharmacy observing his neighbor, a pot maker, sawing at a 155mm artillery casing to create brass cookware. Across the street, an animated couple haggles over a thin mattress with the owner of a bedding store, whose sole inventory appears to be cheap, light blue, striped mattresses.

Talmadge, in the vehicle to the front, has recovered from Nieman's rebuke of earlier. His head and upper torso stick out the passenger side window of the truck. He waves his boonie hat at two attractive young women to garner their attention, "Good morning, babes," he hollers to the pair. But like a philandering cheat, he no sooner repeats the process to another pair, further up the road.

Seeing Talmadge carry on as he does, brings a smile to my face. The poor guy's father died three years ago in a highway accident. He dropped out of high school afterward and worked construction to support his mother and five younger siblings. His entire meager, Private First-Class salary, including his sixty-five dollars of Combat Pay, goes to his mother. There seems little in his life to make it a joyous one; so, the few rare occasions when he finds a little pleasure, we all take notice.

"L J, how long you think before these hot babes get wrinkly, leathery faces and black teeth and gums?" Whitman asks, referencing the young attractive women on the sidewalk. "Five, ten years before they turn into Mama Sans?"

I never cared for the nickname that I was saddled with by the other members, much less understood why, L J; Baby Face for Whitman makes far more sense. But pragmatism dictates I keep my mouth shut; my handle could be far worse.

Whitman abruptly brakes to allow a trio of young beauties to cross the road. His action comes as a surprise and prevents my answering his question while I contemplate his unexpected purpose. I never thought of Brandon Whitman as a gentleman, maybe it's because of his small, childlike face. Perhaps, I now assume, he just wants to prolong viewing the three pretty things as they stroll past the truck. But, no sooner stepping off the curb, the truck lurches forward, forcing the trio to leap back to the safety of the walkway. Whitman waves for them to cross, his baby face appearing apologetic. They proceed again, cautiously, staring hard at the truck's driver, distrust clearly showing on unblemished almond faces. He lurches the truck forward again, his cherub face now wickedly lit up with laughter.

The young beauties once again leap back to the refuge of the walkway and commence with a long dissertation of the angriest and yet so pleasing to the ears sing-song words. As we drive off, I hear the last of their tirade, all in hideous English, "G.I. number ten."

I am uncertain why Whitman harassed the young ladies. Did he tease them because they were girls and attractive ones to boot, or did he deliberately aggravate them because he viewed them as inferior Asians? "Mama Sans," I say with calm reserve in answer to his earlier question, "have wrinkled, leathery faces because of the long, hard hours toiling in rice fields, trying to feed their families. The blackened teeth and gums is due to discoloration from the betel nut that they chew to lessen the affects and conditions of medical ailments and pain due to years in those fields. The pretty young ladies in town are urban women, and not likely to deteriorate as their poorer, agrarian counterparts."

"Good to know, professor Einstein," he replies, his cherub face impishly grinning.

The river we seek intersects the road just past the little, capitalistic, downtown section of Bong Son. The road continues on south across the Eiffel Bridge. That nickname was given to the bridge built by U. S. military engineers, because of the many metal spans used in its construction that somehow are supposed to resemble the Eiffel Tower's construction. Our destination, however, is down to the wide sandy banks of the river it spans.

We strip off our jackets and gather shovels and armfuls of bags as a dozen or more Vietnamese children descend upon us. The kids are five to thirteen, maybe fourteen, fifteen, or sixteen, as it is hard to determine the actual ages of these bantam teenagers. With the exception of two, sad looking, small girls, the rest are boys, seemingly bored and eager to be entertained by their larger and older American counterparts.

Talmadge walks across the sand to the two little females. Sad black eyes on grimy faces of the waifs watch his approach with suspicion and apprehension. He bends down inches from their faces to visually inspect both heads with overdramatized, curiosity on his face.

Looking horribly shocked at spotting something strange, he reaches behind an ear of a child, appearing to pluck out a Hershey bar hidden there. Before the amazed child can reach for her ear to confirm that all there is well, Talmadge has a go at the neck of the other, slightly flipping her chin with a Mars bar, miraculously extracted from there. He extends his findings as friendly offerings to the pair of waifs.

Sadness and suspicion evaporate, replaced with bright, joyous smiles on pretty little faces. The boys quickly approach, but Talmadge raises open palms at them.

We all watched Talmadge's interactions with the two waifs. It touched our hearts and brought warm smiles. It was an act of kindness that made us feel human. His playfulness with the pair of little girls are the first signs of decent, compassionate, behavior extended to locals, by any of the guys since my arrival; but then, our only other associations in this province have been with adults that want to murder us.

Work proceeds quickly and smoothly. Whitman holds the bags open while I scoop and dump in sand. The boys move in closer around us and squat to watch our process, not one word spoken among them. A distant explosion has us startled and leaping for weapons; the Vietnamese boys do not so much as flinch.

We return to work, stopping at ten bags to tie strings and load the sandbags into the back of Newsom's and Talmadge's CTT1 truck. An hour later, the two are on their way back to Dog Patch to unload the heavy cargo.

I jump on the tailgate of our truck to rest. Whitman attempts to squat as the boys have. He soon finds the position uncomfortable and difficult to recover from. The boys grin at his awkward attempt to stand and break out in laughter as his butt hits the sand.

"Whitman," I call to him, "give me a cigarette."

"You don't smoke," he shouts back, dusting off the back of his trousers.

"Will you just give me a damn cigarette?"

He pulls out a fresh pack and offers it to me. "I always carry a couple of extra packs. Take it," he says.

"Only need one cigarette," I tell him.

He gives me the smoke and scratches his little head as I make my way to the boys. I teasingly hold out the cigarette. I point to it and then to an empty sandbag and perform a poor gesture of shoveling sand into a bag.

The boys comprehend my imitation and instantly take on the job with enthusiasm and organization. The littlest of the children separate the bags and open the necks before handing them to a seven- or eight-year-old who holds the bags open while the older boys take turns filling them. It is an assembly line that would have impressed Henry Ford and has me now wondering how many other G.I.s have engaged these river urchins to fill sand bags, and whether I should have negotiated a better price.

"At two hundred cigarettes per carton," Whitman thinks out loud, "we are going to need three cartons to pay off these steam shovels before this day ends."

Talmadge takes a seat at the cribbage table outside to challenge Seagram, the unit's reigning champ. "You boys have a nice, quiet day?" he inquires of his opponent. The rest of the unit moves in to watch the game, beers in hand, as we generally do after supper.

"Yes, it was a most pleasant and delightful day," Seagram sarcastically replies. "Very nice of you to ask."

"Then the blisters on your small, sissy hands had a chance to heal?" Talmadge continues.

"Let me spare you further humiliation, Cherry," Seagram leans forward and looks seriously at Talmadge. "Your Cherry pal, Baby Face, told us about your little helpers at the beach. He walked out with three cartons, and absconding with that many smokes from our stash requires explanation."

Nieman exits the crapper and approaches our gathering in the evening shade behind our hooch. He makes no effort to break into the circle of observers or to speak; he just stands outside our gathering, waiting or perhaps hoping, to be invited to join.

Talmadge is dispatched in little time. Cardona jumps into the challenger's chair, ahead of others waiting to take on Seagram. No one objects, as Cardona is the only player to have a degree of success against the champ.

"Sergeant Nieman," Talmadge calls out, spotting him lurking behind the others. "Told you we would get more done using both trucks."

Nieman smiles at the acknowledgment, which quickly fades as no one else bothers to so much as look back at him. "The lieutenant was surprised and pleased with today's effort. He estimates we need forty-five hundred bags to finish that job. He has ordered more bags to complete the task."

"We have a pallet load of bags remaining," Cardona snaps, at Nieman. "More bags can only mean future projects. We don't want any more."

Whitman has been occupying himself making mental calculations. "We'll need twenty-three cartons," he says, looking perturbed. "To finish this project, we need twenty-three cartons of cigarettes. We only have seven or eight left, and the next ration is weeks away and far too few."

"Not a problem," Tillman casually states. "If we stretch out the work over the next three months, we'll have the smokes covered."

"The lieutenant doesn't see it that way," Nieman interrupts. "He wants the work completed in seven days or less."

"Then he'll need to talk to our union rep about that," Thompkins says to laughter from all but Nieman. "We are trackers, not engineers."

"Newsom," Nieman bellows, annoyed by the current discussion. "Your team is on sandbags and Team 2 is on standby again tomorrow."

We stay on sandbag duty the next three days. Though we despise being ordered to do so, I sense the others joy in the assignment as I do. We look forward to our sightseeing trips to the river, in spite of the manual labor under the scorching heat and heavy humidity of this tropical country.

I find myself recovering from the constant trepidations of the past two missions. That constant tightness in my chest seems less conspicuous and only detectable when I take mental stock of my physical well-being. The black eyes that have been my constant companion since the firefight, now stay hidden, venturing forth to haunt me only late at night. My now distracted mind spends less time being sorry for my current lot in life or worrying over what might occur the next forty-four weeks.

Those treks, back and forth from the river and the sights and sounds of a community in an exotic region of the world, have also eased my soul. They anesthetize dark, festering memories far longer than the late-night beer drinking and passing of joints at the other side of the kennels. I have started to reconcile and accept the new me, as the old selfish narcissist that I once was slowly fades from mind.

The two sad waifs of the first day welcome our arrival on the second day, still donning those smiles from a day earlier. Three other young girls, one holding tight to a male toddler with no pants or shirt are with them, hoping to be entertained by the tall, freckle-faced American.

Talmadge does not disappoint. He makes his way across the sand to them, halts, arms akimbo, and squints, peering down, long and hard at each of them. Then, like a zany, madcap magician, he pulls out candy bars from behind ears and collars, under chins and from noses of astounded waifs. They smile in amazement at his performance, while checking behind ears and under noses, searching for other delectable treats, somehow managing to lurk undetected there. They are especially awed at his generosity of a sweet reward.

Talmadge then turns his attention to the naked little boy. He reaches out to the child's torso and exhibits a candy bar magically removed from under an armpit. The child retreats behind his sister, stomping his feet and crying loudly at such a thing having been found and taken from there. He raises his arms and checks both armpits to laughter from the girls, but goes on to apprehensively accept the treat that a strange, smiling giant, holds out to him.

The sight of Talmadge's interaction with the children, once again tugs at my heart. I close my eyes and struggle to hold back tears at the loss of who we once were, and at what we all may become.

Newsom renegotiates a price with the labor crew, four cigarettes for every five bags. A debate erupts among the boys. None of us comprehend any of their discussion, much less the issue, although we assumed that it is over the lower payment.

"May have a problem if they reject our offer," Newsom whispers to Whitman and I, as if the kids understood English. "We'll have to do our own bagging, until they hopefully cave."

The great sing-song debate finally ends. One of the older boy sprints along the river for a piece of long drift wood. The rest move to the bags and shovels, and get to work. The assembly line is soon at peak efficiency. The boy with the stick watches us load bags into the truck, regularly drawing a short line in the sand with the stick.

It's unclear if the boy uses the stick to mark the number of cigarettes due, but it is evident that the kid's discussion was on how to keep tabs with the more complicated payment system. Their willingness to work for lower compensation leaves me to wonder if indeed I overpaid yesterday, and whether these little river pirates are now taking advantage of Newsom.

The work proceeds well the three days. The course of sand bags lining the berm around the kennels grows higher each day. Members of Combat Tracker Team 2 lend hands, but only after four in the afternoon. Sunlight begins to fade at six and disappears all together by seven, rendering our ability to find tracks futile, and the chance of a mission call after four, unlikely. They help by stacking bags, although of greater importance, they broke into the

Scout Dogs stash of cigarettes and pilfered ten cartons, the exact amount needed to complete the job.

Both trucks return to our piece of LZ English at three o'clock on the third day, fully loaded. The heat, bearing down from a tropical sun, is insufferable, scorching everything its rays come in contact with. It will continue so for two to three hours. There is no escaping those rays at Dog Patch. The engineers bulldozed the ground clear of all trees before erecting the compound. Only the inside of the hooch offers protection, but we have yet to unload and stack bags.

Newsom and Whitman back the trucks as close to the kennels as possible. We grudgingly start to unload, throwing the bags into a pile, cursing the sun and heat as we do so. Talmadge's back is the color of a pomegranate and all are drained by the unrelenting radiation and sauna-like condition.

Hanson and Cooper exit the hooch with cans of cold beer in hand. We gratefully accept the offerings and guzzle them down as if water. "The others got called out, two hours ago," Cooper offers, while we drain cans.

"A LOH went down in the mountains," Hanson adds with his typical mumbling. "The two-man crew of the small observation chopper have not been spotted from the air. They went to find them."

Our dog handler has of late taken to verbalizing with greater frequency. My feelings on the matter are conflicted. I sense that his mumbling may be a handicap, resulting from a physical impediment, or perhaps mental, from something in his childhood. Whatever the case, I am pleased to see him open up, but yet, there is the matter of that necklace.

I stare at Hanson as he strips his jacket to help. The necklace of human body parts is still around that neck. His trophies have turned a dark caramel, almost chocolate in color. Wrinkles of loose skin on the lobes demonstrate further decomposition.

Hanson catches me staring at his unfashionable accessory. "L J, want them?" He asks me, though by his expression, the mumble appears to be more a plea than a query.

"Hell no," I reply.

He cast a glance at the others, and finds only distasteful looks, with no one desiring to accept the gruesome offering.

I continue to watch the man. He saunters to the berm, a sandbag on each shoulder, unaware of my gaze. He drops the bags at his feet and unties the strings on one. I watch as he removes his trophy, and bury it deep into the sand.

We regularly gather at the rear of the hooch after supper. Most stand, the others sit on the steps of the hooch or the two lone chairs at the game table. No one plays at cribbage this night. Newsom is explaining to Team 2's members, how to deal with the river urchins. "Four cigarettes for every five bags," he explains displaying four fingers on one hand and all five on the other. "Coke girls will come by with cold drinks. We buy a drink for the boys during lunch, but don't be surprised when three share one can and take the other drinks home. I wouldn't put it past them to give the drinks to their older sisters to resell back to us the next day, but they are great kids. As for the coke girls, don't mess with them. They are not Boom Boom girls, just kids."

Newsom is the most pragmatic of us. I suspect that he may have put aside an ideologic past against the war to survive the conflict. He drinks, but while the rest of us guzzle our fourth or fifth beer, he still nurses his first. He joins us behind the kennel berm when we smoke a joint, but he never takes a drag. Survival, is his principal effort whether in the field or back at Dog Patch, although he tends to find refuge among the unit's members amity.

"We shouldn't have any problems with the kids," Thompkins speaks up. "We only need eight hundred more bags, and we have smokes for over a thousand."

"The extra pallet of damn bags that Fearless Leader ordered arrived today. For what purpose, I have no idea," Cooper bellows. "We best get the full thousand and save the extra bags for whatever else that Bozo has in store for us."

"By the way, how did y'all's mission work out," I ask of no one in particular.

"A Light Observation Helicopter went down due to mechanical failure," Thompkins explains. "It was running a Big Brother/Little Brother operation in the mountains. The LOH was flying tree-top, searching and inviting the bastards to take pot shots at them so they could call in their big brother, a gunship. They developed engine failure in the process. The crew managed to land the little chopper in a tight opening, but big brother, their gunship back-up, had no place to land. Our heroes claimed they heard noises and took off into the boonies to hide rather than stick around and wait on help. They said they got temporarily disoriented, which is Latin for fucking lost."

"We rappelled down for nothing," Seagram abruptly interrupts. "Let me tell you, it's the second time that I have had to rappel on a mission. I do not like dangling in the air, offering Charlie a chance to get lucky."

"Oh, stop your bellyaching," Thompkins dryly intervenes. "It was a short drop, and I thought it was fun."

Seagram empties his beer and lets out a monster burp at Thompkins. "The crew heard all the commotion around the LOH," he continues to explain. "They found their way back in time to reboard as little brother was air lifted up and out by a Sky Crane chopper. We had to hump three kilometers to a clearing to get picked up."

"No one in this army ever thinks that we may have a need for gloves in this climate," Cardona butts in. "Rappelling raw, down a rope, with all our gear and blistered hands, I would not wish on anyone, not even our very own Fearless Leader."

"Speaking of the man," Tillman points to Nieman's approach. For some unexplained reason, all suddenly cast eyes in the direction of Nieman. The eyes halt the man and cause his upper torso to jerk back, away from the group. He looks fearfully at us from the corner of an eye, before speaking.

"Team 1 goes on standby tomorrow," he cautiously speaks, but in such a low, fearful voice, some have to ask what was said. "Team 2 is on sandbag duty," he now speaks with his normal tone.

Cardona returns to gripe, "Nieman earned his pay today. Having to hump through the jungle is a lot harder than flipping a coin as to which team goes on standby," he adds to laughter. Nieman leers on with angry disdain at those words and takes a bold step forward. "Yes siree, our boy earned his pay today," Cardona continues.

I sense that at this very moment, Nieman has concluded he will never be invited to join our inner circle. Worse, I sense that he questions why he ever wanted to be accepted. He is now free to finish transcending to an authoritarian position over both teams, not just over the new guys like myself, but the older members as well.

"Newsom!" he snaps, before anything else can be said. "The lieutenant wants to see you," he bellows. "He wants to ask you about cigarettes missing from his supply room."

"And he wants to ask me?" Newsom points to himself, glaring hard at Nieman. My team leader appears incredulous at the man's implication. "Anytime something goes wrong or missing around here, he wants to talk to me about it."

"You are the only team leader here," Whitman offers a plausible explanation, naively as it sounded, which cause snickers from the older members, and a suspicious look from Talmadge.

"Let me educate you in the way of life, my son" Cardona speaks, pointing a finger at Whitman. "You are from the state of Washington and may have no experience in many of the social facets of life outside your little secluded commune. Our Grand Wizard is from Mississippi. He has a hierarchy of people to suspect in the event of any dubious acts committed within his realm. Newsom, as a black man, is far at the top of that list. Tillman, a New Jersey Jew, is second after Newsom. I, as a brown man, am third on that list."

"I think I warned you about using derogatory names for the lieutenant, or insulting him" Nieman steps forward fully enraged. "One more insubordinate word, and I'll report you."

"C-a-r-d-o-n-a," he spells out his name, "soon to be spelled C-i-v-i-l-i-a-n. Wouldn't want you to misspell my name. Oh, tell the Lil Bastard, it was the brown man that took his fucking cigarettes."

"Let's go, Newsom!" Nieman shouts and storms off to the headquarter hooch with Newsom lagging behind.

Tillman approaches a fuming Cardona, who watches the pair walk away. "Why did you tell Nieman you took the cigarettes. Seagram and I were the ones who snuck into their supply room and took them."

"Oh, I tend to get carried away," he smiles and winks at the dog handler.

CHAPTER 6

Though the morning is early, the oppressive heat and humidity has descended upon us like the weight of the world on Atlas' shoulders. Not a cloud hangs in the sky to block the sun, and all indications point to yet another, hot, muggy, miserable day in hell's paradise. I pray that no mission call comes in, not out of fear for what that entails, but because of climatic conditions.

Thompkins enters the back of the hooch. He wears a clean, starched uniform, and his puritanical look. Wet hair and a powerful odor of aftershave indicate he is up to something out of the ordinary. His look and scent gather the curiosity of those inside.

"You going on a date?" Seagram begs to know.

"Going to chaplain service," he replies, throwing a hard frown at the source of the sarcasm aimed against him.

"Is it Sunday?" I ask, as all days here are alike.

Newsom enters the hooch, equally clean but without the aftershave. "It's Easter Sunday," he announces, flopping his palms up and down to get everyone on their feet to go.

"I'm Baptist," Talmadge states.

"The service is non-denominational," Thompkins advises. "Even Tillman is going."

"I'm atheist," Whitman proudly announces, and lays back on his bunk. "Don't believe in a supreme being other than Ann-Margaret. And Thompkins," he goes on, raising his upper torso on elbows, "Don't you see the irony of this very day. The followers of Jesus, that found his Church, centered their religion at the heart of the hometown of those who killed him, Rome. After having murdered him, those Romans then call for the celebration of his having risen. Don't you see this bizarre irony to your belief?"

Talmadge hurries to Whitman's bunk while Baby Face continues talking. He jerks him up by the arm, virtually dragging him off the bunk. "Get your ass up!" he hollers. "Don't want no God damn atheist with me while on track, so get your ass up. You're going to Easter service."

Seagram moves in closer to Thompkins, invading the man's personal space. He gives the cover man a close examination and a whiff. A frown of disgust quickly follows. "What if a call comes in?" he asks, continuing to sniff at that staunch face.

Thompkins moves his head back away from the sniffer, "Nieman knows where we'll be," he answers.

"Nah," Seagram squinches his face once again, "You smell like a Boom Boom girl," he explains. "If we get a mission, you'll get us all killed. Charlie will smell that cheap, offensive aftershave a mile away."

"It washes off," Thompkins snaps back at him.

"I wouldn't worry about it," I offer. "Five minutes in this infernal heat and Charlie will have something more horrid to smell."

We head out the door into the sweltering conditions, with Talmadge towing a reluctant Whitman.

Today marks the one thousand, nine hundred, thirty-sixth year of celebrating Jesus's rise from the dead. Christians throughout the planet are celebrating that event with worship services, family gatherings, food, and outdoor egg hunts. We all head to a religious service, though nothing else will be forthcoming to mark the special day.

Grunts in the field have no idea that today is Sunday, much less, Easter Sunday. Some, in a desperate struggle for their lives, just pray they survive this day.

Weeks have passed since my team's last mission, but yet, one team must always be prepared for a call. Army life in Vietnam is one of long periods of pure tedium that at the drop of a hat can transform into a chaos of terrifying events. That terror commences whenever Nieman enters our hooch with clipboard in hand. For now, he stays away, and we are left to pass the hours away.

I woke before dawn, dressed and rechecked my gear in the event of a call. After an early breakfast, I return to my bunk to sit, bored, and anxious at yet another long, monotonous day of sitting and waiting, perchance on a call to another deadly chase.

Whitman is on his bunk, reading a past issue of his hometown newspaper. Talmadge, the only other person in the hooch, is also at his bunk; his sling shot rests across his chest.

I watch Talmadge, as he moves his arms to seize the weapon, all in slow motion. Ever so gradually, he pulls at the projectile pouch with one hand and pushes the Y-shaped wooden handle forward with the other. He takes aim at a large, black rat, brazenly staring down at us from the rafters. A loud "clang" sounds as the ball bearing strikes the underside of the galvanized metal roofing.

Whitman leaps from his bunk, alarmed and looking about for danger. "Damn you, Talmadge!" He screams once he recognizes what transpired. "A warning would be nice, you inbred hillbilly!"

"What, and scare off your cousin?" Talmadge guffaws.

"Hey, look! Our visitor is still up there," I point out to Carl. "Must not think much of you or your aim."

"Well, I'll be." Talmadge takes aim at the hideous creature for yet another attempt. "Warning, Whitman, warning," he chuckles. He lets loose the bearing, and the darn, metal projectile hits the ugly beast square on the head, bowling it over the side. The rat hits the floor, screeching and squealing something awful, unable to stand, much less run away.

We all grab entrenching tools and pounce on the injured vermin. Once we are certain the vile thing is dead, we halt. We stare down at the ugly creature, with a sense of overwhelming remorse, at yet another life taken.

Whitman and I head back to our bunks with our heads low. Talmadge turns, surprised by our walking off, "Hey, you guys going to help me clean this shit up, or what?"

"It's your toy, your kill, your mess," Whitman declares and plops back down on his bunk. "You clean it up."

Nieman enters the back door of the hooch carrying the box with the monthly rations. He also carries mail and a package from home. This is the one occasion we joy at having him visit, and he appears to relish in the effect on us at his playing postal carrier. The rest of the unit trails behind. Like the Pied Piper of Hamlin, Nieman waltzes in leading a parade of delighted followers.

A dripping wet Seagram with a towel draped around him and Thompkins sporting shaving cream, bring up the rear. Nieman drops the ration box, less cigarettes at the door of the break room and continues onward; his sudden devotees still in tow. He goes bunk to bunk, stops to cast off sealed envelopes addressed to the bunk's owner, before proceeding to the next bunk. At each stop, a member of his parade peels off to get at the prized deposits. He drops the package and two letters on my bunk. He waves the final three letters in front of his nose and deposits them on Tillman's bunk.

"Talmadge, get that dead shit on the floor cleaned up," he shouts, before stepping out the front door.

"Got a letter from my folks," Newsom proudly announces. He sits on his footlocker and starts to read. "Hey, my dad is making plans to open a second hardware store when I get home. Wants me to run one," he proudly announces.

One of my letters is from home, the other letter is from an old high school buddy. It's posted in-country, which tugs at my curiosity. His assignment is in Saigon, in an air-conditioned bunker, he writes. A girl we both know from high school gave him my unit and APO address, although, I personally have not gotten any letters from her. He goes on to say that his stepfather died in an accident. His mother, who fears for his life in Vietnam, has wrangled a way to get him discharged. After less than three weeks in the city regarded as the Paris of Southeast Asia, he is being sent home for his personal safety. He ends by writing that he will have a cold one waiting for me when I get home.

"Talmadge, how many babies have you killed?" Whitman asks, drawing everyone's attention at such a strange query. Whitman's baby face dons a grin at all the bewildered faces. "It's my girlfriend," he explains. "She claims that her sociology professor said soldiers in Vietnam are nothing more than baby killers. Says that she can't respect a man serving here and is breaking-up with me. Does this qualify as a Dear John Letter?"

Newsom is first to offer a reply to Baby Face, "There is a lot of angry protesting going on at the World right now: civil rights protests, women's rights protests, voting rights protest, antiwar protests, and a whole lot of free love when they are not protesting. No one there is innocent of any one of all these things being protested, not even your ex-girlfriend. Somehow, we here in Nam get a hell of a lot more than our share of the blame for all the shit going on at home. I bet that ass of a sociology professor never served a day," Newsom insists. "They never do, but seem to think they know what we do here."

"You are better off without her," Tillman injects. "She sounds wacko."

"Probably getting humped by her sociology professor," Cardona casually injects. "I wouldn't worry though, she'll come back to you once she's pregnant."

"She's on the pill," Whitman insists. "And thank you all for the moral support during my time of severe emotional crisis," he adds with a chuckle.

"If she is on the pill, then you have nothing to concern yourself with," Seagram offers. "She's just getting the crap humped out of her."

"Cardona, you should visit Whitman's girl when you get home," Cooper joins the frenzy. "She lives a state over from you, and she sounds like the right girl to relieve you of a lot of things," he sternly offers before breaking into laughter.

"Et Tu, Coop," Whitman admonishes the man he thought was a good friend.

Tillman approaches Whitman. "They're just yanking your chain," he apologizes. "Don't let them bring you down."

Whitman snickers at the man. "I know. I dumped her months prior to my enlistment," he softly proclaims. "Wouldn't surprise me if this is her way of trying to get back at me."

"L J," Talmadge whispers, as if we are hot on track. "How many girl friends did you have in high school?" he asks, and waits patiently for my reply with a troubling, but earnest look.

That serious expression on Talmadge's face indicates that the answer he seeks is not intended to demonstrate anything about me, but rather, it has to do about himself. I avoid engaging in conversations of the romances in my life, because of guilt and of anyone discovering that to be the reason for my having enlisted. But I see in that face a need for me to offer up something. "There were some," I finally offer a vague answer.

"Yeah, I knew you would. You got that boyish look that girls like," he continues. "Guess you had no problems getting them to step out with you, huh?"

"Wait," I reply, surprised by his remark. "Are you suggesting that I look like Baby Face?"

"No, no," he insists, sounding apologetic. "Whitman has a toddler's face that only a mother could love. You've got looks that makes girls comfortable to be around, and want to be around. So how much is some, two, three, or more?"

"I played the field," I offered the ambiguous explanations, hoping to satisfy his thirst for an answer to settle what demons torment him. "Why the interest in my love life?"

"There was a pretty girl in my school named Ethel Hackman that I dearly wanted to ask out, but I was just too scared," he says. "Hell, I was far more scared of walking up to her at school, just to talk than of getting caught up in a firefight here. Never got the chance to build up the nerve to talk to her. I quit school, and what girl wants to date a high school drop out with no future?"

There are a lot of things that I can say to alleviate the man's trepidation. They swirl about in my mind, waiting on me to pluck the most appropriate one. I finally settled on speaking of something along the lines of the noble act of his sacrifice at coming to the aid of his family, and that any girl of merit would appreciate such devotion, but the words fail to escape my lips.

"I'm thinking of becoming a prof," Cardona loudly announces, catching Talmadge's attention. "Those civilians are treated as gods, isolated from all the ugliness of the world around them. Everyone thinks them special and provides them with a fabulous work environment and all the young chicks a man could want. They teach one to two classes a day, but only when school is in session, and they have the rest of the day to lounge at the faculty club or to hump Whitman's girlfriend."

"If you plan on being a professor, you'll have to get your GED first," Seagram chuckles.

"Hey, I'll have you know that I already have twenty-four hours towards a degree in marine biology," Cardona snaps back at him. "My dad added a third boat to our fishing fleet and asked me to drop out for a semester to help out. That's when your nasty ass "friends and neighbors" nailed my butt and sent me here to be a... what was that, a baby killer."

"My wife wrote and said the country feels the same way as Whitman's girlfriend," Tillman chimes in. "Ever since Walter Cronkite put in his two cents on the war, the country has turned on us. She said that her cousin, a marine, was spit on at the Denver airport, and they ended up arresting him for the ensuing scuffle."

"I'm going to get a roll of quarters as soon as I land, in case anyone wishes to spit on me," Cardona adds to smiles. "Wouldn't want to break a knuckle busting a jaw."

Nieman enters through the front door soon after playing at mailman. He carries his clipboard and wears his mission assignment demeanor.

We are in the air shortly after eight-thirty. Below us, the coastal plain of white sand, rice paddies and small villages gives way to lush, uninhabited mountains. A smooth sea of dark green now lies below us, belying steep heights and deep gorges of the Central Highlands. It looks a sea of tranquility that contradicts the truth of what lurks underneath. For over twenty minutes, we fly high above that dense canopy of trees, dreading our destination and of having to once again go forth to search and engage with that truth.

No one speaks, and there is little aboard the chopper to occupy an anxious mind. My mind tries to go numb. It fixates on the hypnotic greenery to escape thoughts of the upcoming perilous labor and a lengthy period at high vigilance, but to no avail.

A sense of forlorn creeps over me. It shakes me loose from a temporary coma-like state. Though I am confined in the space of a Huey's cargo filled with friends, an indescribable sense of utter loneliness engulfs me. At this very moment, no one exists, not family, not friends, or even the enemy to share life's joys or sorrows. I am alone, orphaned by an uncaring world that shows no interest at what happens to me. It is a cold-hearted world to which I am but one of many in olive drab, to be cast at death's feet for someone's sense of righteousness. A thick, black bag with a long zipper is all that I am assured by my merciless overseers.

The depth of this aloneness dredges up an unfathomable sense of despair that has me melancholy. Breathing becomes difficult and my limbs now feel numb. I now find myself fantasizing, sky diving into that vast sea of green, but without a parachute.

It suddenly strikes me that I am not alone; fear is my companion. It has been with me since the beginning of that first mission. Though I continue to dread death, I am not seized or filled with the level of terror it had over me on that beach. It is with me now, skulking about my mind, waiting on the proper moment to fully reveal itself. There is little purpose to allow it to overwhelm me just yet. I sense that for now, it serves only as a reminder of what looms ahead and to caution me to stay alert. What occurs in the hours to come will be, no matter what I do now. Harping on what may happen is nothing more than an exhausting mental exercise, a cerebral effort that I must try to push aside.

Below, the passing jungle continues to offer nothing to engage a mind, fleeting with bizarre thoughts. I stare out the open door once again, at the lackluster image of greenery.

The Huey transport suddenly dives, catching me off guard. It swoops into a narrow winding valley, like a bird of prey in pursuit of a meal. The ship soon levels, feet off the ground; it now chases a stream.

These tactics aim to limit exposure to enemy fire and to diminish the distance the propellers wash sounds, noise which alerts the enemy to our approach. Though no landing site is visible, the low-level flight signals we are closing on our destination.

We all start to nervously shift in place, as we mentally prepare ourselves for what lies ahead.

The pilot and his co-pilot appear to enjoy themselves on this part of the flight. They snake their way around sharp bends of the stream, banking the ship hard to the right and left, while we are left in ignorance to wonder, where they take us and if we will arrive alive. The pilot finally slows the ship. He points ahead to a cloud of red smoke. He slows further near the only open area, a small sand bar in the middle of the stream that will serve as a landing zone.

Nine seconds later, the Huey is out of sight.

A squad from an air rifle platoon is there to cover our landing. After routine acknowledgments, they lead us to the rest of their unit, high atop a mountain ridge.

It is a vertical climb through thick vegetation to the crest of a long, narrow mountain, one of the countless thousands in these highlands. The walls of the steep elevation at times rise at sharp angles. Grunts grasp at saplings and struggle to pull themselves up, causing the tops of the small trees to flap like flags, exposing our location and direction of movement to curious eyes. I and the rest of the team rely on half-buried rocks and clumps of dirt and grass to creep upward. At the steepest angles, Hanson has to tow up Prince by the leash, while Newsom pushes the canine from behind.

We finally attain the top, exhausted. The weary squad then guides us on a trail along the ridgetop. Empty, earthen bunkers, covering the footpath, soon show at either side of the trail. Two Grunts behind an M-60 machine gun cover our approach at that point. Beyond, dozens of bamboo structures with thatch roofs are scattered about, most without walls. Soldiers, some smoking, stand loitering, waiting on orders. A tall, thin major, a few years my senior, but appearing far more mature, waves us to him. He is on a radio, speaking into the transmitter, without looking at us, yet inviting us to join him.

The major gives the hand set to the radio operator and faces us. "Sorry to get you out here for nothing," he apologizes. "This base camp has been abandoned for some time. We thought there might be a need for you guys, but there's nothing here. We are going to torch the place and head out to our extraction point. Your chopper has been notified to pick you up there."

CTT1 takes us from our transport's landing pad at LZ English, back to Dog Patch. It is the hottest part of the day. The sun's heat, and the humidity are unbearable. Sweat beads up on our faces without exertion, and everything is hot to the touch. But, like a bunch of truant kids, we wear smiles at not having chased after armed men, smiles which sooner, rather than later fade to routine, petty squabbling.

We missed lunch at the mess hall, and the six-hour mountain excursion left us ravenous. Large amounts of calories were expended on that trek, calories that need replacing. There is talk about consuming a horse, and of having only picked through C-rations to eat at the hooch. Whitman then curses at Talmadge for having given away all the candy bars to the waifs at the river.

"Don't recall you complaining at the time," Talmadge snaps back at Baby face. "Besides, they were the candy bars no one liked or wanted."

"Well, I hope you find that horse you keep talking about, because my stomach is growling and we've got nothing to eat at the hooch," Whitman scolds the lanky Tennessean.

"Wait, didn't Nieman bring in a new rations box this morning?" Talmadge wonders out loud.

"Yeah, but the others have by now picked over the best stuff," Whitman whines.

"Hey, I forgot to open my package before we left," I interrupt their bickering. "Only had time to see who it was from. It was from a neighbor, Mrs. Pierson. She's French, a war bride, and a fantastic cook. We may be in luck. There's likely to be munchies inside."

Loud clanging noise of heavy equipment ends further discussions of candy bars, munchies, and hunger. We stand to look over the cab of the small truck to check on the source of the noise at our compound. It's a backhoe.

The operator is digging out a second twenty-foot trench behind the hooches. This one, is between our hooch and the next, while a completed trench lies further up. The operator dumps the scooped red clay into a pile alongside the trench.

"Oh, crap," it was Whitman, sitting back down.

Our hooch is soon perfumed by the odor of a Caribbean spirit, rum. It spreads throughout our quarters, faster than the juiciest of gossip. Team 1, less Hanson, surrounds my bunk, woofing down the delectable contents of my package from Mrs. Pierson. In short time, Cardona and Seagram approach, curiously hunting the source of the aroma. "It's rum balls," I explain, extending the box out for them to partake of the goodies.

"Uhm! These remind me of the whisky balls my mom makes on the holidays," Seagram reminiscences with his mouth full. "Heck, I think they're better."

Cardona pops another ball into his mouth. He turns to the rest of his team at the back door, watching the digging outside. "Get your asses here," he shouts. "This shit's great!"

A festive mode evolves. Perhaps it's the aroma in the air or perhaps happy bellies, but a party atmosphere is underway. A cassette player blasts out *In-a-Godda-Da-Vita*. Heads bob to the beat, and a sated Whitman takes the floor, beer in hand to show off his dancing ability. His moves draw the others attention as they woof down the liquor-soaked cake balls. Near one hundred rum balls are quickly disappearing. I place five on Hanson's pillow, lest they all get consumed, before he shows.

Newsom digs into the box and takes one of the few remaining balls. "Baby Face has some serious dance moves, for a white boy," he chuckles.

"My mom's brother, Uncle Frank, used to cut a mean rug," I reply, watching Whitman as well. "When I was a kid, I used to marvel at his jitterbug moves. That man could move body parts in a dozen or more directions, all at one time. He was a dance machine, much like our boy, Whitman. Days prior to my being shipped here, the folks threw a going away party for me. Uncle Frank could still dance, but he looked stiff. He could only move four to five body parts at any one time. It was as if time had fused his joints. A sad sight to see, although, I suspect that he may not realize that he has lost any of his moves."

Nieman surprises us by encroaching into our festivities, he enters the hooch with clipboard in hand and heads straight to Newsom.

"Oh, crap!" it was Talmadge this time.

"Get your team ready," he orders Newsom. "Prepare for up to five days in the field. There is a company of grunts to the north that patrols between farm villages and the highlands. Every few days, a sniper takes shots at one of their platoons and then disappears into one of the many nearby villages. They want that sniper found. He is due to strike one of those units any day now."

"What the hell, Nieman!" Newsom protests. "You know damn well we just got back from hiking up and down mountains. We've been here only fifteen minutes. We are beat, and we are hungry. Now you come and tell us we have to go back out! You must be out of your mind."

"Not my decision," Nieman fires back while taking a safe step back. "You got a problem with these instructions, take it up with the lieutenant. At least your team will be spared having to fill sand bags for two bunkers."

CHAPTER 7

It was the second night, and the following night, the third time that I slept under a blanket of stars in Southeast Asia. No incandescent or florescent glow mars nature's night time beauty in this region of the impoverished nation. The two clear nights, offer up more stars than I have ever seen at any one time, the second night, seeming far more spectacular than the first.

I am awed by the nightly spectacle taken for granted by others. Grunts, grounded by what may be lurking in the nearby darkness have no idea of the majestic display over their heads. But I do find a glorious night sky, in such a hostile place, to be as incomprehensible as the beauty of this murderous land.

A poncho liner for a blanket and a back pack for a pillow serve as my bedding. On both nights, I lay on my improvised head rest, gazing upward, until sleep overtakes me.

The northern region of Binh Dinh Province is under a Pacification Program, a concept dreamed up by politicians back home. Peasants from the mountain interior have been herded against their will into the coastal plain. The theory is to deny the enemy the resources of small mountain villages by relocating whole communities from the interior to the coast, leaving behind, an unpopulated, free fire zone.

Local militia are expected, in time, to provide the necessary security in the densely populated region, freeing the South Vietnamese Army to pursue and engage the enemy in the mountains, and us to eventually depart. For now, Grunts venture deep into vacated lands, searching for the enemy during the day and provide security along the coastal settlements by night.

Booby traps, snipers, and small unit ambushes inflicted on ground troops are the enemy's answers to the politician's solution. Viet Cong and NVA forces marshal larger bodies of men and devote their meager resources to the southern part of the province from where American forces have been withdrawn to deal with this political catastrophe.

Frustration is high among the Grunts in this sector. Snipers and booby traps have taken their toll. Suspicion abounds concerning the local militia, made up predominantly of resettled refugees from the interior. Most American troops doubt their loyalty to Saigon, and many openly accuse them of being communist partisans, posing as militia during the day and layering the countryside with booby traps to kill Americans by night. Stories of brutal interrogations of captured enemy are rampant in this part of the province. Higher-ups do nothing to stop the brutality, fearing drawing attention to the program's poor results, and angering the very politicians that created the program and which hold their military careers in hand.

Once a week to ten days, a sniper encroaches a campsite of Bravo Company. Cloaked by darkness and guided by the light of stars in the night sky, he creeps in close to one of four platoon's night perimeter and takes shots at the men as they stir from sleep. Three to five rounds expended, the sniper disappears into the murky light of early dawn.

Another such attack is expected, and soon. The four platoons of Bravo Company have a plan of action to box him. We are then to locate the precise location of their culprit in a nine square mile trap; a task we fear will have us exposed, to a sharpshooter's gunsight.

Newsom wakes me on the second night. The luminous hands of my watch show two till six, and the sun has yet to appear. A light fog, envelops the area, obscuring most stars. "Movement," he mouths, pointing outside the perimeter. "Prince alerted Hanson. Keep down, and radio Lieutenant McMurdo to initiate the trap," he softly whispers.

Grunts are nudged from slumber and quietly crawl on bellies to defensive positions. They peer into the predawn gloom, fearful of well-placed rifle fire about to be unleashed at them.

A chunk of plastic explosive is lit by match inside our perimeter. It is set ablaze in an empty C-ration can with holes poked along the bottom to feed air to the burning, plastic explosive. The can serves as someone's makeshift stove to heat water for instant coffee or hot chocolate, but on this early morning, it serves to lure a sniper, into a trap.

I watch from the ground as the can is slowly maneuvered into the open with the aid of a long stick. A hot, blue flame glows in the can, exposed for an assassin to see, all as pre-arranged. Ten to twelve seconds later, the early morning quiet is shattered by rifle fire. Three rounds from a semiautomatic rifle strike near the can at where a soldier attending his stove should be. An uproar of gunfire and grenade launcher explosions retort. Red tracers converge in the darkness in the direction of the sniper's rifle sound. It goes on for an interminable fifteen to twenty seconds before the cease fire shouts take effect. It is quickly followed by that god-awful silence.

The snooty-looking platoon leader from Massachusetts, McMurdo, approaches Newsom shortly after the firing ceases. He has all the hallmarks of an Ivy League School, fresh from the land where appearance and arrogant behavior outshine competence and performance. He smirks at us, as we yet cringe to the ground. "You boys ready to do your part, or shall I send out a patrol to see if we got lucky?"

"Not enough light to find tracks," Whitman answers for Newsom as we all rise and dust ourselves off.

"And, if you send out a patrol, they will likely destroy signs left behind," Newsom adds. "An hour or forty-five minutes should do. We'll have coffee and then we'll find that bastard for you."

McMurdo appears dissatisfied at a delay, "You best do just that," he firmly states pointing his finger at Newsom, before walking off.

The sun rises. The light-yellow sphere glows through a light fog. It soon rests atop thatch roofs to our far left. A welcome sight, it burns at the morning shroud, enhancing visibility. Minutes from now, its task of burning away the fog will be complete. Then the evaporated moisture will combine with the oppressive heat, to make life insufferable.

We are on track, chasing over lightly nicked, dry soil, across a barren rice paddy. It is one of many acre-size growing fields in this over populated farm belt region, where paddies butt up to one another. From the air, the entire region looked like a giant, beige patchwork quilt, as each plot is walled in by berms of dirt from the others. During the wet season, the three-foot dikes of clay serve to retain water for planting and growing rice, as well as dry paths for farmers to reach their flooded fields. For now, lightly grazed clumps of parched soil inside the paddy reveal a trail left by a fleeing shooter. An occasional splatter of blood on bleached earth indicates the sniper was struck during the fray of return gunfire.

The trail crosses over several paddies, but maintains a straight course south. We hurry from berm to berm, fearful of being caught in the open by a wounded sniper. At the middle of the eighth paddy, the sniper's trail takes a sharp turn due east. It heads over a berm and across another paddy to a tree line at the other end. A cluster of thatch roofs is visible the far side of those trees. We take a knee and shelter behind the berm to discuss a course of action to take.

Lieutenant McMurdo with two squads has been following a short distance behind. He approaches, alone, and in a hurry to investigate the holdup. "What's with this delay?" he inquires, looking down angrily at us. "I want to get that son-of-a-bitch, before he gets away, so move your asses."

Newsom starts to rise to answer the insolent man, but then decides to minimize his exposure, by staying low. "We've got problems. First, your sniper is not a man, it's a woman. You can tell by the length of the stride," he explains, pointing at the trail leading toward the tree line, a clearly visible track that this lieutenant is not likely to see.

"So! Let's get the bitch then," the impatient lieutenant replies, refocusing his attention back to Newsom.

"She is wounded, and she crossed the berm to the adjoining paddy, here, at this very spot," Newsom continues. "You see why?"

McMurdo looks to the berm, but soon turns back frustrated and angrier. "What are you trying to show me?" he snaps.

Newsom points to a wire, coated with dry earth, sprouting near the top of the dike wall. A clump of wilted grass covers the top near where the cable emanates. The wire hangs, running eight feet forward, at points disappearing into the berm wall, before finally vanishing altogether into the soil. The partial bottom of an unexploded artillery shell, peeks out the side of the berm near the wire's end.

"She crossed here," Newsom explains. "We think she hopes to lure someone to step on that dry clump of grass while climbing over. No doubt there's a detonator under that clump of grass, ready to blow the artillery shell when stepped on. She plans to take out a bunch of guys with it."

"Alright, once we get her, I will send men with C4 explosives to deal with this damn thing," McMurdo angrily vows. "So, can we please continue?" he mockingly pretends to beg.

Lieutenant McMurdo fails to comprehend the extent of our concerns. He is blinded by a desire to get the sniper that has for months plagued not only his platoon, but the other three of his company. No doubt, commendations will be extended to the officer who succeeds in getting the sniper, and I am beginning to fear he desires those commendations for himself, no matter the human cost, especially to that of our team's.

"Her crossing at this point shows she is aware that we are tracking her," I bluntly inject. "She's in that tree line, lying there, waiting on us."

McMurdo takes a knee and looks to the tree line across the rice paddy. It's a long stare as he finally comprehends the problem and attempts to work out a feasible solution with a mind more accustomed to formulating dramatic and glitzy solutions to enhance his personal standing. His lengthy deliberation sends a chill throughout my body.

"I am going to take my men across to the tree line," McMurdo suddenly speaks, pointing to a line of trees to the left of where his men await his return. "From there we will sweep down along that tree line. Once we start, take your group across the paddy, from here to the tree line. We'll have her in a crossfire."

I look to Newsom, horrified by the narcissist's plan. The others do so as well.

"Sir, I am not going to endanger this unit," Newsom protests. "Going across this open ground will leave us exposed to sniper fire the entire way. Our job is to locate the enemy and to specifically avoid engaging them afterwards. We have strict orders about deliberately exposing ourselves to enemy fire."

"I have given you a direct order," McMurdo admonishes Newsom. He stares hard at our team leader before casting an angry face to the rest of us. "I expect you and your people to carry out my order," he says, pointing a finger at us all. "That bitch is mine, and I don't have time for whining from a bunch of frightened, rear echelons."

We watch the lieutenant scoot back to his men. We stare at him for several long, angry minutes.

"What a cocksucker," it's Whitman, wearing his angry cherub face that finally breaks us from our spell of anger and grave concern.

Newsom has a look of his own. He wears a look of confusion, mingled with worry. He turns and we lock eyes. I sense his confusion.

Being a team leader has no reward other than a slightly higher paycheck. There is no officer that we can radio to correct or counter a field lieutenant's dangerous orders. We have a platoon leader at Dog Patch with little aptitude or interest with trackers, and an engineer captain that dislikes all the specialized combat units assigned to his construction company. All burdens of the field are laid on the shoulders of a young man, including those that involve life and death decisions affecting teammates. While income levels are meaningless to a high velocity metal projectile, the cruelest thing, is the likelihood of having made that god-awful, wrong decision.

I live with Asiatic eyes descending upon me in my sleep, but I cannot phantom what a wrong decision may conjure. Sorrow for the weight burdening on Newsom's shoulders sweeps me.

"I don't want to spend my next three years in Long Bien Jail for insubordination under fire, and I don't like being dangled as bait for some Hot Shot's glory," I squeak out, trying to initiate a group discussion to search for a reasonable solution to this dilemma. "How about once McMurdo starts his sweep, we just climb over the berm, hit the ground and stay put. The sniper may decide to fire at them or didi mau the area," I suggest.

"If she's badly injured, she may not run," Talmadge cautions. "She may just stay put and go out in a blaze of gun fire."

Whitman scoots closer to enter our discourse. "We are talking about a sniper waiting to waste us," he fretfully adds, pointing at the tree line where we suspect she hides, "and she's just two hundred feet away. I am scared at the notion of crossing open ground while she takes aim at us," he continues. "I don't mind telling you that I do not have the iron nerves that L J has. Let's just stay put, behind this berm. I don't want to end up in a body bag."

"How you feel about ending up at LBJ prison?" Talmadge asks Whitman.

"That prick lieutenant isn't going to do squat, if we stay put," he snaps back.

"What iron nerves are you talking about?" I suddenly bark at Whitman. There is an angry undertone in those words that surprises me, an unexpected belated reaction to an incorrect assumption. "I just want to go home. I want to wake up each morning with a soft, warm, beautiful girl next to me like all the other guys here. I don't know what the hell you're talking about."

"If one of his men gets hit while we stay put, hiding behind this berm, that asshole is going to be pissed," Talmadge cautions, bringing the discussion back to our immediate quandary. "He's going to want someone's butt if that happens, and we will be his obvious choice for a scapegoat."

"Yeah," Whitman sighs. "That bastard did make it clear that it was a direct order," he reluctantly acknowledges.

"They've made the trees," Hanson points to Grunts running and disappearing into the thicket of trees along the edge of a paddy.

"Hanson, you and L J climb over at this point," Newsom lays out his decision for us. "Whitman,

Talmadge, and I will go over the top, sixty feet further up. We will all hit the ground once on the other side. When McMurdo gets to within sixty feet of the trees to our front, we will scoot forward in relay fashion, but once and only once, dropping and staying safely down twenty-five feet up. Keep an eye out for muzzle flash and unload on her ass if she fires. My group will climb over first, and we will also scoot first."

Hanson and I watch Newsom and his group move to their position. We wait on them to reach their designated area and climb over the dirt wall.

A taste of fear strikes my mouth. My tongue suddenly feels far too thick for my parched mouth, and a bit of acidic bile has spewed up. That tap-tapping heel from a shaky leg has also returned, all courtesy of my companion's warning to stay alert and vigilant of the enemy sniper.

I close my eyes and let out air, once again, inadvertently held far too long, all the while cursing my life's decisions that have led me to this point. Young men at home are deliberately injuring themselves to obtain deferments from the draft, just to avoid being sent here and placed in similar predicaments. Mrs. Pierson's son, a member of my high school track team, was medically rejected due to a highly irregular heartbeat. Mrs. Pierson, a registered nurse, works in a doctor's office where many drugs are readily available, some capable of inducing a temporary, but dangerous heartbeat in a healthy young man. Frank Ranzino, whom I met and befriended at a party near campus, broke his left arm, days prior to his induction. He had someone slam a car door against the appendage, just to buy him a few months.

It suddenly occurs to me that three years at LBJ may be a far better consequence than having a high velocity round rip through flesh and bone or having to be carted off in a body bag. Prudence calls that I not climb over the low wall, but logic does not exist, once your "friends and neighbors" send you out to kill.

"Come on, Prince!" I hear Hanson angrily call out.

I open my eyes. They flash wide, horrified at the sight before me. Hanson is attempting to climb the berm at the very spot of the concealed detonator. A reluctant canine pulling back on the leash is the only reason we have not been scattered over several paddies. "Hanson!" I scream loudly. "The damn booby trap."

He freezes. He is a second away from reaching and depressing a trigger, detonating a 105mm, high explosive, artillery shell. Now cognizant of the near catastrophic blunder, he steps back, shudders, and gives me a stupid looking smile.

"Prince has more damn sense than you," I castigate the careless man.

We move a short distance back down the paddy berm. Hanson and Prince climb over with me on their tail. We hit the ground on the opposite side, weapons trained forward, searching the trees and shrubs for the slightest movement or muzzle flash.

McMurdo and his two squads are visible, leap-frogging tree to tree. Terrified young men, take their time, before committing to dash from one tree to another. They expose themselves to sniper fire briefly while hurrying tree to tree, no doubt hoping they not be the one in her crosshairs. In the meantime, we are left exposed on a dry paddy, while they take their sweet time sweeping forward.

Newsom, Talmadge, and Whitman suddenly leap up and race forward. They drop to the ground after a short distance and train their weapons forward.

"Let's go," Hanson calls out.

Tightly coiled muscles launch me up. I sprint forward as if the demons of hell are at my heels. A spot of ground, some feet to my front, is my objective. Once there, I dive to the ground and land far too hard. The radio pack slams hard against my lower back inflicting severe pain, and the antenna whips loose near my face, kicking up dirt. Regardless, my attention fixes to the tree line, while I pray that I am not in her crosshairs.

A rifle shot sounds. I see the yellow flash of the weapon's fire from deep in the shrubs. Three quick bursts from my weapon add to that of Newsom's group's fire, all aimed at the source of the firing in the tree line. A second flash, and I empty the remainder of my magazine. I release the empty clip and reach to a pouch for a full one. It is then that I realize that Hanson is not alongside and that Prince is whimpering from behind.

I look back, fearing our dog has been hit. Instead, I see Hanson, holding his left knee with both hands, rolling side to side, grimacing and crying out with pain. A loud uproar of weapons fire jerks my attention back to my front. McMurdo's men are charging the sniper's location, firing as they move.

"L J!" Hanson cries out. "I'm hit."

Why is he calling for me? Why not Whitman or Talmadge, or our team leader? Why me? Anger overtakes all fear of the sniper. Hanson's cry out to me has me livid. I was careful to avoid booby traps and prolong exposure to sniper fire to the point of injuring my back; he was not. Now that he has been struck by a bullet, he expects me to rush to deal with his torn flesh. I did nothing to warrant or encourage such a plea.

It suddenly occurs to me that I have deliberately avoided getting too tight with the guys. The reason jumps to mind just as quick. It's clear that I have built a wall around myself. Since that day along the beach, when Whitman ran to me, begging that I look to see if his face had been blown off, I have tried to avoid establishing deep attachments to the others out of fear of something happening to them. I do not want to fear for or care at what happens to anyone else but me. There is enough on my plate just seeing to it that I leave this damn place in one piece, but they just keep dragging me into their band of kinship.

Hanson's call out to me is proof of that and of their failure to comply with my unspoken desires. They have no idea of the zone that I have crafted around me and venture in and out, violating that sanctity as if they were immediate family. With overwhelming reluctance, I hurry to Hanson, angry at having to abandon the safety of my cocoon and dreading what I might find.

"It hurts!" Hanson cries. "Oh God, L J, it hurts bad," he blubbers as I kneel next to him.

I have no desire whatsoever to see mangled flesh. Such sights can only add to the recurring memories that I will certainly take to my grave. I pray to dear God, for my sake, as well as that of Hanson that it's not a grotesque wound.

The tip of his left jungle boot is tattered and bloody. Hanson continues to twist and rock side to side as I try to establish the extent of his injury. I grab his leg to immobilize it, and Prince moves in and licks at his face.

"It's probably a million-dollar wound," I advise to calm him, as well as myself. "You'll likely beat Cardona home."

Newsom arrives. He stares down at Hanson and then the boot. The man looks to be as equally distressed as our dog handler.

"Hanson, I am going to untie and remove the lace from your boot," I warn, but just as quickly question myself as to what I am doing.

"No, no!" he screams out, fearing my inflicting greater pain.

Something tells me that removing the boot is the correct thing to do. Something else tells me that someone other than I should be the one to examine that wound. "I will do it slowly and carefully, so that it doesn't hurt," I offer. "But we need to take off your boot to see how bad the wound is."

"It's okay," Newsom tells him, while kneeling opposite me. "We will do it gently."

The lace is eventually removed. A leg, shivering with fear and pain, make a simple removal awfully difficult. Newsom then grabs the back of the heel, and I trap the knee in my arm pit. The boot comes off, but not without screaming and further pleading from Hanson.

Prince lets out a low growl at the height of Hanson's screams. "It's okay boy," I speak to settle the canine.

"L J, we need a Dust Off to get Hanson to a field hospital," Newsom advises. He hands me his map to give our location.

I stand and walk away to radio for the medical helicopter, relieved at averting my eyes from a closer view of the wound.

McMurdo stands near the tree line observing us. He wears a solemn expression, perhaps wondering if any repercussion due to Hanson's wound will affect his chance at a Distinguish Service Cross or perhaps a Silver Star for his brave leadership this day.

I flip the bird at the bastard.

From my rear, I hear Newsom call to Talmadge. "Hold his leg. Keep it up and still. Got to take the sock off."

"No, don't, please don't," Hanson pleads and starts to scream.

CHAPTER 8

The stock and barrel of my weapon rest across my lap. Other pieces are scattered about my bunk, clean and as always, smelling of gun oil. Once again, I find myself steep in graphic memories, this time, of disgraceful behavior from earlier this morning.

I realize that I am traipsing through dangerous, uncharted ground, both physical and mental. My body is fit and trained to handle the rigors demanded of it by this war. But, no one, not even I, thought to prepare the mind for what it had to undergo. Maybe that is an impossible task, an inconceivable part of war that no military trainee can possibly fathom, and so, deliberately neglected by trainers. Perhaps it is also neglected because there is no means to avoid the randomness of death and injury in battle, although my mind struggles against that notion. I just cannot allow fate to dictate my existence or my physical condition when I eventually leave this place. I must have input to skew those random odds to my favor.

Although the sniper's fire called forth my new companion, it did not exact that level of immobilizing terror it had weeks earlier or that out-of-body experience while the body scaled that protrusion of earth. Returning fire seems to alleviate a great part of the terror, or perhaps, it may be that I am learning to adapt and to better function under the acute stress of a firefight.

The new "me" had cloaked itself in fear as a mental shield to navigate through the horrors of war for the remaining months. That mantle of fear was meant to keep me alert to danger and to stay clear of ugly, gruesome sights. The latter part failed, not of my volition but that of others. I tried staying afar and clear of deep ties with fellow teammates to avoid suffering at their misfortunes, but everyone is far too reliant on each other for that to succeed, and who will I call out for aid, should I stop a bullet?

This morning's act of shameful behavior was from other than fear of the sniper's fire. It emanated from my reluctance to examine and care for body damage inflicted by a high velocity, metal projectile.

Images of chest and abdomen torn open, limbs shorn from bodies, and obliterated facial features of the dead from that beach firefight are forever etched in my memory. They are ugly, vivid memories that venture forth late at night, but which I fear will eventually come to also haunt me during daylight hours. Hanson's cries for help at his wound were far more terrifying, than having to face that sniper's crosshairs. The sight of a dead enemy is ghastly; but having to inspect and deal with the mutilated flesh and bones of a brother tracker, is far more appalling. The fear that I had cloaked myself to avoid such sights is useless.

Also, I am shamed at the shabby treatment that I had extended Hanson. The man had taken a liking to me, and I had not reciprocated. In fact, I went out of my way to shun him. His devotion to Prince and his limited time left to spend with others kept him at the far end of our unit's sphere of comradeship. It was therefore easy for me to keep him afar, just as others had, especially after that matter of the ear necklace.

Hanson was either not aware or did not care what I thought of him. He made the effort to get close to me, more so than he had to the others. Whether at Dog Patch, the beach, or today, he demonstrated a desire for close friendship. It was my opinion of his mangled foot that he elicited, and it was my words that afterward soothed his fears. I was also the one that he entrusted with the care of his canine, now safely in his kennel, a bowl with food and another of cool water are with him, just as he begged of me. However, I suspect that it will be the bloody flesh and the exposed bone of where Hanson's toes had been that will stay with me, rather than my cruel treatment of him.

The guys on Team 2 are loudly discussing a curious matter. It distracts me from my self-pity.

"He uses his pay to buy prisoners," Seagram continues recanting a curiosity. "He then methodically slips on a pair of white gloves; the kind head waiters wear at a fancy restaurant, one finger at a time, as if relishing the moment, before he leads his prisoners into the bush. There, he chokes them dead."

"I'm not buying that," Cooper challenges the story. "Someone would have reported it."

"Heard it myself," Thompkins chimes in. "Also heard that he is a cook."

Cooper moves toward the door, "Why would anyone waste his paycheck doing that?"

"Haven't you seen the movie, Psycho?" Thompkins asks.

Nieman's sudden entrance into the hooch breaks up the discussion. He enters and commences interrogating Talmadge over the events of the morning's mission. The lanky Tennessean refuses to comply with the questioning and shoos him away. "Leave me alone," is all he says.

Nieman then proceeds to sit at the foot of Whitman's bunk to pose those same questions to him. His inquiries catch my attention and draws in the others. His questions deeply concern us as to their purpose. He has already asked some of those very questions of me, while I fed and watered Prince. I did not understand the reason of his inquiry then, but those questions angered me, and I halted Nieman's interrogation with questions of my own. No good can come of such questions, I suspected at the time, as I do again.

Those questions are now posed to Whitman. Nieman's third query, "did you think that the sniper would be lying-in wait?" stirs Whitman's ire. Baby Face then takes exception to the fourth question. He rises from his bunk, angry resentment on his cherub face, "Why the hell you asking such stupid questions?"

"It doesn't take a genius to understand that we now have two inoperable teams," Neiman shouts, exposing his hand. "We hoped to have two full teams in four to six days, but thanks to Newsom, that won't happen. Hanson lost two toes and will not be returning. It may be weeks or months before we get a new dog handler, and then, he has to train and familiarize himself to Prince."

"Why are you dumping this shit on Newsom?" an indignant Baby Face interrupts.

Talmadge leaps in, to challenge Nieman's assumption that our team leader is responsible for Hanson being wounded. "That prick lieutenant is the one to blame. He gave us an order to charge the sniper and made it clear that it was a direct order. Call that bastard and chew his ass out, but leave us all the hell alone."

"Already told him about McMurdo," I force myself into the discussion, while stepping up to the gun rack. "That prick is probably getting pinned with a silver star as we speak." Hanson's Carb 15 is at the gun rack with a magazine still in the well of the rifle. Whoever placed it there, did so without having first cleared the weapon. "But why blame an officer when a draftee, buck sergeant is available, or is it because he's a negro?"

Nieman snaps to face me, "Stay out of this, Lejeune. This doesn't involve you."

"What the hell you talking about?" I bark at the man, forcing him to stand and step back. "I was there! My hands were covered with Hanson's blood. Don't tell me this shit doesn't involve me."

Silence hits the hooch. All eyes train on me to see what I might do or say next. I slam my weapon down hard to its place in the rack, shattering that brief silence. A second or two later, I snatch up the Carb 15, remove the clip from the magazine's well and in an angry, yet dramatic fashion, eject a round from the weapon's chamber. The bullet flies out, strikes the floor and rolls next to Nieman's left foot.

"Newsom was warned not to expose his team again, and no less than two weeks ago," Nieman argues back. "Trackers do not grow on trees, and Brigade is not pleased to hear we don't have a team ready to go."

"Then contact Brigade and explain to them how Lieutenant McMurdo cost them their precious team," I yell out, forcing Nieman's head to jerk back. The notion of sticking Newsom with the loss of Hanson is ludicrous, and Nieman's failure to accept the absurdity of his effort infuriates me.

Bert Thompkins moves next to Nieman and picks up the round from the floor. He takes time to examine the bullet before speaking, "Is all this about your disappointing Brigade?" he asks, but no sooner dons a fake smile and holds out the bullet for Nieman. "Our team is ready, whenever you are."

Newsom enters our hooch. For the first time since my joining the unit, the team leader appears relaxed, almost relieved. We had all expected that he would be distraught after reporting to Crachet or Rachet or whatever that lieutenant's name might be. Nieman is equally surprised as the rest of the unit, by an almost jovial look on the Kissimmee, Florida native's face.

"You guys interested in some lunch?" he asks. "We haven't eaten since last night, and then, we ate C-rations. If we hurry, we can make the mess hall for some hot chow before they stop serving."

I had forgotten how long it had been since I last ate. With all that transpired this morning, I had not had time to think of eating. Now, and only after being reminded, my stomach starts to growl like a hungry bear after hibernation. Talmadge and Whitman must also be ravenous, for they lead the way to the door.

We make the half mile walk to the engineer company's mess hall in short time. The overhead sun is unbearable, and not a cloud is available to offer relief from the rays, but hunger, nevertheless, propels limbs there in little to no time.

Spaghetti with meat sauce, Texas toast, wilted lettuce salad, apple pie, and ice tea without ice are on the menu, the perfect meal for a blistering hot mid-day.

"I ship out tomorrow," Newsom drops the bombshell. "Going to an artillery unit to finish my final two months. They cleared out the top of a mountain peak and set up shop two weeks ago. It seems they need manpower to help with security."

No one speaks. No one even shovels food into their mouths. We are just too stunned by the revelation. The son of a fifth-grade school teacher, and an owner of a hardware store, appears calm, almost pleased at leaving, adding to our bewilderment. He looks up at us, surprised by our silence. "Look, I am sorry to leave you guys behind. It's not my choice, and abandoning the team is the only regret I take with me."

"Is this about Hanson getting hit?" I ask.

"Nah," Newsom shakes his head. "This is about the past hundred years. Hanson being wounded is merely an opportunity for people stuck in the past to get rid of me."

"Thompkins' uncle is now the Brigade's Inspector General," the Tennessean injects. "I think Bert will be willing to speak to his uncle if we ask him."

"No, no," Newsom responds. "Not because of me. I am happy at the notion of finishing my tour atop a mountain, with three hot meals a day and 105s and 155s to do my shooting for me."

Newsom departs the following day. We all ride to the chopper pad to wait with him for the supply ship to his new post. He looks to have lost some of his keenness to go. A frown and downturn eyes say it all. The disappointment on our faces likely do not help. We wait, and we watch till his helicopter lifts off and disappears over the nearby mountain range.

There is little time for us to lament Newsom's departure. The unit is tasked with finishing the construction of the two protective bomb shelters at the back of the hooches. It is our punishment for diminishing the chance at promotion for a Scout Dog lieutenant. In four to five days of laboring at the shelters, Newsom will be forgotten and perhaps, never spoken of again.

We toil nine hours each day filling and stacking sand bags. We stack them around and on top of long planks of perforated steel over the two lengthy slip trenches to create hardened shelters. Thousands of sand bags are required in the construction of each refuge, and each must be built to a specification of withstanding a direct mortar or rocket strike. Long, hot, miserable days are spent filling bags with the clay left behind by the excavators. Backs are soon blistered by the sun and hands from shoveling clay. Hatred of the Scout Dog leader and his cohort prevails to a point where Nieman acknowledges our hostility and stays clear of us.

A new pallet of sand bags arrives on the third day of laboring to complete the first shelter, infuriating us to no end. Morale hits bottom. Angry speculation abounds, and muffled threats against certain people teem with each passing hour. That lively enthusiastic comradeship disappears without anyone realizing that it has. Silence and despair pervade the unit. No chattering gatherings take place after supper. Nighttime drinking is done alone or in pairs. Our hatred for Nieman and the Scout Dog platoon leader reaches a boiling point.

Tillman fears the slightest provocation may act as a catalyst to set Dog Patch aflame. He tries to bring the teams' gathering back, by trying to restart cribbage play, to no avail. On the evening of the third day, the pallet of new sand bags catches fire. Suspicion from the front office abounds, but we offer and stick to a plausible explanation that a carelessly discarded cigarette is the likely culprit.

Shortly after lunch on the fourth day of back breaking work, Bert Thompkins is ordered to the headquarter hooch. No explanation is offered. Tensions peak, as all theorize a dark purpose to his being summoned. We follow him to the very door of the HQ hooch in support.

Thompkins exits less than ten minutes later, grinning, ear to ear. We hurry and gather around him to find out why he was called.

"The little bastard's name is Prattchet," he happily announces to the gathering.

"Oh, that's such wonderful news, great to know, but who gives a shit?" Seagram sarcastically states. "So, what the hell did he want with you?" he demands to know.

"Fearless Leader is desperate to put together a team," Thompkins chuckles. "Brigade is kicking his ass to put together at least one from the remnants of the two. He offered me a team leader spot," he continues. "I politely told him, no, but hell no," he says, breaking into full laughter. "Prattchet even offered me sergeant stripes. You should have seen the shock on Nieman's face when he made that offer. It was priceless."

"Wonder why he didn't ask me?" an indignant Cardona speculates out loud. "I'd love to go home with stripes."

"Maybe, because you told him that you broke into his stash of smokes," Tillman suggests. "But more likely, because your ass is out of here in six days and a wake-up," he says and smiles.

"Just the same, it would have been nice of him to have asked," Cardona replies.

"Let's get back to working on this last shelter," Seagram suggests. "Maybe we can finish this shit before Cardona goes back to the World."

"Why?" Talmadge loudly demands. "We just got a replacement pallet of bags. Nieman is only going to tell us to fill them for some new project. Why rush? Screw him!"

The following day, we return from lunch, another heavy meal weighing everyone down. We all head for our bunks tired and stuffed.

"Am going to take me a little snooze before getting back into that hot sun," Whitman groans, stretching out on his bed. "Don't disturb me. I'll wait for Nieman to scream his head off at me."

"Not a good idea," Tillman cautions. "Napping will only make it worse when you do go back into that hot sun."

"Hey, look it there!" Talmadge shouts. "There's a duffle bag and guitar on Hanson's bunk."

Everyone perks up, eyes strain at the bag and instrument.

"Guess we got us a new Cherry," Seagram advises.

"Yeah, but where's he at?" Tillman wants to know.

"Maybe he's in the crapper or meeting with Ratchet," Cardona suggests.

"It's Prattchet, and he never meets with Cherries, or anyone else," Thompkins offers.

"Yeah, you're right," Cardona agrees. "He never does, but if you don't mind, I prefer to call that Lil Bastard, Ratchet."

Talmadge and I make our way to Hanson's bunk through all the speculations and mindless commentary. Talmadge rolls the bag over to read the name stenciled on the Olive Drab canvas bag. He looks at it for some time before attempting to pronounce the owner's name. "It belongs to a T. Puteoli," he states, butchering the ancient, historical name.

"Tony?" Cardona blurts out. He rushes to confirm the name stenciled on the bag.

"What the hell is he doing back here?" Seagram demands to know. He brushes Talmadge and Cardona aside to see the lettering on the bag for himself.

"Y'all know this Puteoli fellow?" Talmadge asks in his finest southern drawl, bungling the name once again. "Guess he must be I...talian, huh?"

Tillman approaches the gathering to also inspect the stenciling. He offers an answer. "Tony caught one in the shoulder three months ago. He held your position as cover man until that happened, and he was the best there was at it," he explains to Talmadge. "With under three months left in his tour of duty when he got hit, none of us expected to see him return."

The idea of the best cover man catching a round in the shoulder piques my curiosity. Zeus' handler is a genuine, great guy and well-liked by all the new arrivals. He was the first of the older members to make us new guys feel at home in the unit, and the only one to offer tips like: what and how much to carry to the field and where and how to pack each item for quick retrieval and to not rattle. Tillman is also the one guy that may be willing to open up and tell us what happened to the older members we replaced. "How did he get hit," I casually inquire.

"The VC group they were tracking, for some reason decided to double back in a hurry," he offers up without hesitation. "They ran smack into each other. Wadley lost part of his left hand in the firefight. He was the visual tracker, and their team leader, Nichols, was killed." He continues while sadly recalling the event, "Newsom, who had your position as RTO for the team, and Hanson were the only ones to make it out unscathed."

Nieman enters through the back door. The sound of two pairs of boots on a wooden floor draws everyone's attention. Behind him is a young man. Black, wavy hair and a moustache that trails down past the corners of his mouth to a distinct jaw bone offer a smart, fashionable appearance on the returning tracker. He grins ear to ear as he pushes past Nieman.

"Tony!" Thompkins shouts and moves to intercept.

A pandemonium of shouting, handshakes and slaps on the back take place at the back of the hooch. Nieman is shoved further aside as the older members move in to hail the returning member. When the greetings cease, a myriad of questions are put to the new arrival; each new question asked before the last can be answered.

Cooper, Talmadge, Whitman and I, watch the ongoing celebration from the other side of the hooch. We feel like outsiders, but we are not alone. Nieman has been pushed further and further aside by the celebrants. He looks to be trying to get in a word, with frustrating results. For some five minutes, the four of us watch Nieman's exasperating effort to get the group's attention. When he raises a hand and waves it over his head, the comical spectacle causes us to break out in laughter, infuriating him to no end.

"Pay attention!" Nieman suddenly screams. He pushes through the throng of greeters, with no concern to guard against being assailed. "Pay attention," he angrily repeats. "Tony Puteoli is taking over as leader of Team two. The lieutenant has granted him four days to get his team ready. For the next four days, Cardona, Whitman and Talmadge will go out after breakfast and lay a two-mile track outside the LZ for Team 2 to train on.

Cooper, you are replacing Cardona as RTO. After lunch, everyone will return to working on the shelters through the remainder of that day.

It dawns on me that I have been overlooked. No mention has been made of what I am to do. The logical thing is for me to be assigned to lay track with the rest of my team and the soon-to-depart Cardona. I decide that it is not important or necessary to inquire, and will just go with the track layers in the morning.

"Team 1 will have to be reinforced before they can be made operational," Nieman continues. "We placed a request to Saigon for replacements days ago. We asked for one with experience to serve as a team leader. Lejeune, you will train as Prince's handler. In the mornings you will go out with Team 2. Tillman will teach you all that he can."

"Whoa, hold on! Wait. I don't want to be a dog handler," I blurt out with little forethought of the consequence of those words. I know that I do not want to go on a track tethered to the end of a leash, with my vision fixed on the dog rather than what may lay concealed nearby. Hanson devoted as much of his attention watching for alert signs from Prince as opposed to what may be lurking around the next bend. I plan to rely on my own eyes and not on Prince or Talmadge, our cover man. There is also a selfish angle; Prince requires care, and that is time spent away from socializing with the others at Dog Patch.

Nieman steps toward me, scowling. "Didn't ask you what you wanted," he snarls.

"Perhaps you should've!" I blow up, holding hard to my ground. "Dog handler jobs are not on-the-job training positions. They spend six to seven weeks training under experienced instructors at the Jungle Warfare School in Malaysia or at Fort Gordon, Georgia. I have no interest in going out there, untrained, and getting my ass shot off, all because you want to hurry and field a second team to impress Brigade. Screw you! Maybe you should have also thought of that before you shipped Newsom off."

"Don't much care what you think or if you or your team gets wasted, but I'll pass on your words to the lieutenant," Nieman sneers. "If I was you, I'd start packing." That said, he storms out the door, no doubt to report on my refusal.

CHAPTER 9

CT 1 returns from dropping off Cardona and what remains of my old team. The others are outside, loading their equipment into the small truck. In minutes, they will leave to chase after a two mile track that Cardona's group have laid down for them to follow. For now, they just stand about, speaking softly at the back of the truck.

Goodbyes were said at breakfast. I will miss this small troop of guys. Though I have made an effort to avoid getting too personal with them, who cannot help but liking them. They are a conglomeration of happy-go-lucky fellows, all from different parts of the country. The sharing, of their home life, the interactions with local children and young women, the afterhours games and excessive drinking, and all the friendly banter will be sorely missed. We have opened up and shared our thoughts, other than our deepmost fears and what plagues us late at night.

They have become like brothers to me, their future absence will be felt. But then, departing now, will spare me the pain of having to suffer through a tragic incident to befall them, an event, which seems so inevitable for these naive boys.

My foot locker lid stands open and a small, donated canvas satchel is on the bed, waiting on me to transfer items from one to the other. There are but a few personal things inside the locker. Packing will be a breeze. Once I know the unit I am to be assigned, I will pare down what to take. Socks, insect repellant, and maybe a bar of soap and tooth brush will go with me, if I am ordered to a Grunt unit. All of my few personal things will go, if I am assigned to a unit with a fixed location, like Newsom was.

It suddenly strikes me that I will also miss the living accommodations. Having a bunk to sleep on and a roof over me at nights is a luxury for an infantryman. Hot chow, only a half mile away, is also a great blessing. Perhaps, these are among the reasons why Newsom, at the very end, appeared reluctant to leave.

Boots enter the hooch through the back. They stop, just inside the threshold. I look back, expecting Nieman with transfer papers. Instead, I see the new guy, Tony Puteoli.

"LJ!" he calls and waves for me to come. "You're with me."

"Thanks, but no thanks," I cry back. "I haven't changed my mind about being an OJT dog handler. I'm waiting on Nieman and my orders."

Puteoli enters and crosses the hooch; his shiny dark eyes gleaming as he approaches. "The guys are correct about you," he states, all smiles. "They all said you were stubborn as a mule, but sharp. They also said that you had experience and can handle yourself in action."

"They are a great bunch of guys," I reply, without correcting him. "Take good care of them."

"Look, I spoke to Prattchet about keeping you on as my RTO," he explains. "No need to train a new radio man."

"You can train a monkey to lug around a radio," I sorely state, but then realize that I sound like the mule the others think that I am.

"Yeah, but monkeys are far too intelligent to go chasing death," he responds, once again smiling, his eyes gleaming like it was Christmas morning at home. "Nieman objected to your staying, but the platoon leader is keen to get my team operational. Cooper will train as Prince's handler. So, what do you say?"

There is little that I know of this new guy. This is only his second day back with the unit, and most of yesterday was spent by him catching up on events with the older guys. I have no idea how he will take my refusal, or whether he will understand my reasoning. "My staying as your RTO will only put my old team at risk," I respond. "Prince on a leash, tethered to a handler with no training can only lead to a catastrophe. I can't have that keeping me up nights. Too many other things already do."

"I hear you," he says. "But that team will not be ready to go for four to six weeks. They need an RTO and a leader. Bert Thompkins is the only experienced member of our unit that can be spared to take over that team, and he has already said no. By the time they find a new leader, a properly trained dog handler will have likely shown up, and Cooper can then serve as their trained monkey. So, you coming with us?"

There is little else to say. My concerns, or most, are alleviated by the man's reasoning. Puteoli has gone through a great effort to retain me, no doubt at the request of the others. He is an experienced tracker, and his having suffered a wound, may make him a very cautious leader. Nevertheless, I take the time to weigh other matters, before replying to the proposal.

I do like it here. I do not like the deadly hazards associated with what we do, but I like being a part of this little troupe. Then, there is the matter of Nieman's opposition to my staying. That seals my decision.

"Give me a minute to grab my gear," I answer.

The next three days flash by. Mornings are spent tracking down Cardona, Whitman and Talmadge on a trail they set outside LZ English's perimeter. They throw every trick known to cast us off track, and they wait, laying in mock ambush at the end of each day's track. Zeus and Prince warn of their pending attack on each occasion. Tillman patiently points out for Cooper, Prince's sign alerting to the ambushers each and every time. Afterwards, we sit under the shade of a tree and talk, till it is time to head back for lunch.

Team 2 demonstrates the agility to move fast and undetected, acting as one, singular body. There is far better coordination and stealth of movement with this team than my old one. But then, Whitman, Talmadge and I were wet behind the ears when we started, and the guys on this team have months of experience and the best of training by New Zealander and Gurkha instructors in Malaysia or the Fort Gordon school in Georgia.

Afternoons, the slowest part of the day, are spent under the sweltering rays of a hot, tropical sun. We sweat and labor hard those afternoons, filling and stacking bags for dug-out shelters behind the hooches. The clay mound of earth, from when the trenches were dug, finally peters out. Puteoli, who appears to have juice with a desperate Scout Dog platoon leader, goes over

Nieman's head and obtains permission to take both trucks to the river to fill more bags. Nieman fumes as we depart, which only adds to our joy at sightseeing through Bong Son, and engaging once again with the little steam shovels and watching Talmadge perform his magic for a swarm of little waifs.

On the evening of day four, the second shelter is completed. We celebrate, sprawled atop sand bags covering the trench. With cans of cold beer in hand, we laugh heartily and speculate at what new project Prattchet has in store for us, and whether another carelessly discarded cigarette may be due.

Morale has crept back. Sometime after the arrival of Tony Puteoli, our afterhours socializing, drinking, bantering and cribbage playing returned. A sense of optimism, once again prevails, in spite that one of the more lighthearted characters of our small band is to depart for home in two days.

Nieman drifts into our celebration atop the completed shelter. Like an unwanted guest, he cautiously approaches our assembly, holding papers behind his back with one hand and a bottle of Drambuie in the other. "Here," he says, extending papers out to Cardona. "Your plane for Cam Rahn Bay departs at 08:30 tomorrow. Have a safe trip." That said, he turns back to the HQ hooch.

Cardona studies the papers closely. "I'll be damn!" He jumps to his feet, shouting. "Holy crap!" he yells out and looks up at the gathering that has converged around him. "I'm out of here tomorrow!"

Cardona erred on his DEROS, date of expected return from overseas. His departure is a day earlier than he calculated. He now rejoices with an impromptu attempt at an Irish jig.

It is Seagram, who first comes out of shock at what should not have been such a surprise. "We need to put together a goodbye party," he says with a wicked looking grin. "We can't let this wild man go without a serious adios tonight. Thompkins, you and L J go pick up four cases of cold beer. The rest of us will get cleaned up before supper. Afterward, we'll party like there's no tomorrow."

"Whoa, Kemosabe." I speak in opposition to his instructions. "You guys haven't coughed-up your share from the last run that Whitman and I made," I remind them, open palm out and fingers flapping. "Give me some military scrip and none of that worthless Shirley Temple or W.C. Fields Hollywood shit you guys got stuck holding. I want some of that new scrip with outer space stuff on the face of the paper."

"Boy, I was just starting to like you," Seagram whines, but digs out his waterproof wallet. "You're getting to be too much like that tight-wad, Tillman."

That night, we party like it was Mardi Gras on the streets of the French Quarter in New Orleans. The music is loud and our drunken singing is deplorable, but who cares? It is a ruckus farewell celebration that goes late into the night, and only ends when a sleepy Nieman, in his army issued briefs, screams angrily at us to cease and go to bed.

The following night, just before my new team goes operational, Whitman wakes me, freeing me from nightly visitations by an inquiring pair of black, Asiatic eyes. "They're hitting the chopper pads with...," his last words are drowned out by a loud "whump" that shakes the dust free from the rafters and me from the bunk.

A mortar shell explodes, a quarter mile away. The flash from the explosion lights up the hilltop across the wide ravine at where helicopters and their fuel tanks are kept. Mortar shells are dropping and exploding every six to ten seconds. By the third explosion, Baby Face and I, with weapons and full gear, dive into the newly completed shelter.

"Get off me," Thompkins screams to either Whitman or I, for in our haste, we both manage to land atop someone sitting in the dark.

"Looks like we are all here," Puteoli chuckles in the dark as explosions continue. "I sure hope we did a good job in building this thing. It would be damn humiliating if it was to cave-in and bury us alive."

"You guys realize that we are located between two of the three prime targets for enemy rockets and mortars," I say as it suddenly occurs to me. "The chopper pad is to our northwest and the supply dump with all their ammo to our northeast. We are dab next to both."

"Those zappers are inaccurate with their firing," Thompkins speaks out in the dark. "Wouldn't be surprised if some shells miss their targets and land on us."

"Well then, good thing we thought to build this here bunker," Cooper offers up to resounding laughter in the dark.

"Hey!" Someone cries out in panic. "Something just crawled over my legs."

"It's rats," Seagram informs. "The shelling is scaring them."

"Talmadge," I call out. "Did you bring your sling shot with you?"

"Sure hope he didn't," Whitman intervenes. "You know what a bad shot he is with that damn thing. He's worse than those zappers; he's more likely to hit one of us in the dark than a rat."

"It's not me popping you with a ball bearing that you need to worry about," Talmadge laughs. "Rats on the ground invite predators. Y'all need to worry bout them Two-Steppers."

Dawn finds us parking CTT2 near the chopper pad. We are soon walking to the concertina wire at the far side of the pad, looking at the damage from the night's shelling. The mortar shells appear to have inflicted no damage on any helicopter or nearby fuel tanks. Most of the shells fell on the barbed wire protecting that sector of LZ English's perimeter and on a corner of a nearby hooch housing chopper crews.

Men from the engineer company are busy unloading strands of new concertina wire to repair the damage to the perimeter. Restoring the perimeter wire should take three to four hours; repairs to the hooch, perhaps a day or two.

A door gunner that we recognized, painstakingly examines us from the damaged hooch; an angry look that he wears draws our curiosity. As we move toward the rows of razor-sharp defensive wire, he yells to us, holding up three pieces of a broken guitar for us to see. "You find those animals that broke my "Sweet Emma," and don't take no prisoners, you hear," he hollers at us.

An elongated, finger of a large valley lies between the wire and a mountain range the other side to the west. The tip of the flat ground terminates at a marsh near the foot of another mountain. Rice paddies cover the bottom of the valley, including the finger extension, up to, but short of the marsh; though today, all paddies are bone dry. At the far side, scraggy mountains, devoid of significant vegetation, rise sharply, towering not only over the paddies, but the hilltops of LZ English as well. A small village of hovels with mud walls and thatch roofs at the north end of the valley's extension is our destination. It lies at the base of a mountain, a short distance from the marsh.

Brigade determined that the mortar shells were launched from just north of that farming community. We are to search for tracks used by the enemy to withdraw after their attack. Finding the mortar tubes used to launch the shells is paramount to Brigade. A platoon of Republic of Vietnam troops, RVNs, is to rendezvous with us in that vicinity at 0830.

Concern at having to rely on South Vietnamese troops as our infantry support prevails through the team. We have heard stories of their breaking and running at the slightest of contact with the enemy.

Past the wire, we proceed northwest to our destination, comforted by the knowledge of the tremendous nearby firepower available to us. Walking diagonally across the slope of the hill to avoid offering silhouettes against a rising sun, slows us, and the rendezvous time is quickly approaching. We pick up the pace without compromising vigilance; we do not wish to appear unprofessional to the RVNs by showing up late.

Two hundred meters from our intended destination, we spot a lone soldier approaching from the village. We take a knee until we can get a better sense of who he is, and why he is out here, alone. What is readily visible of the man, is that he is dressed in camouflage fatigues and matching boonie hat. A rifle, with a very elongated barrel resting in the crook of an arm, adds to our confusion.

"Ranger?" Seagram ventures.

"Rangers work in teams," Thompkins answers. "This guy is alone."

Tony Puteoli rises and waves at the strange soldier. The man waves back, and we head for one another.

The strange weapon the American soldier carries turns out to be an M-14 rifle with a thick, foot long extension, possibly to muffle gunfire. The older infantry weapon was replaced by the M-16. It is far heavier and longer, but continues to be considered far more accurate at longer distances and fires a larger caliber round with a greater knockdown punch.

"You lost or just out for an early morning stroll?" Seagram inquires of the unusual fellow, who appears to be of the age of Nieman and just as warm and fuzzy.

The man attempts at a smile, "Neither."

"Were you out here last night, by yourself?" I ask puzzled by his lack of candor.

"It's how I do, what I do," he says, forcing a grin.

"Doing what?" I continue to quiz the man.

The forced grin disappears. He looks to be annoyed by all the questions. "I'm not at liberty to say," he answers and frowns.

Tony takes a step closer to the soldier. "You hear mortar fire last night?" he asks.

A quick turn of the head, the soldier points in the direction where we were headed before the impromptu gathering. "Sounded like two heavy tubes firing. They were too far from me to be certain," he adds, turning back to us and giving us a close going over. "What you guys about?" he asks, with eyes settling on Zeus.

"We are not at liberty to say," Seagram sarcastically answers. That said, we continue on our way to our rendezvous with the RVNs. We double time, all smiles, at having left the fellow as puzzled as he left us.

Indentations, set deep in the soft soil, identify the location where the two mortar tubes were fired from. Eleven to twelve men appear to make up the enemy mortar crew. Heavy tracks lead to and from the marshy watershed of thick underbrush and reeds. A lighter set of tracks leads back up the mountain side from where someone, possibly the same group of people, earlier came down.

"We've got a clear set of prints going up," Seagram states. "Want me to start tracking them?" he asks of our team leader.

"Not just yet," Tony answers. He has a pair of binoculars to his eyes, studying the side of the barren mountain. "Those heavy mortar tubes are our principal objective, and I bet they are hidden somewhere in that marsh."

"Zeus can find them and any surprises they may have left behind," Tillman advises.

"They may have left one or two guys to keep an eye on the weapons till they return to recover them," Tony warns. "We'll wait for our support to arrive, before we go in there to look for them."

I glance at my watch, it's 8:56. "They're late," I laugh, recalling our hurrying to avoid appearing unprofessional.

Seagram and Thompkins follow the tracks a short distance up the mountain. Puteoli, Tillman and Zeus venture into the marsh to look beyond an immediate clump of reeds obstructing our view, all staying within easy shouting distance. I am left alone to keep a lookout for our support.

A large group of RVNs finally arrive, an hour and twenty-three minutes late. They lollygag toward were we sit, waiting on them. No rucksacks with supplies or even web gear to hold extra ammunition are carried by our support. Weapons are not at the ready; they are held by the barrel, with the stock resting casually on shoulders. Tight fatigue pants on bony legs give them a childlike appearance, to match their level of professionalism, and a few with bow legs, look outright comical. A short, heavy-set captain who does not speak English, and a boyish looking lieutenant, with working knowledge of our language, lead the amateurish crew.

"My old Boy Scout Troop back home look tougher than these guys," Tillman whispers.

"Hell, my little sisters Blue Birds look far more formidable than this bunch," Seagram one-ups Tillman.

Thompkins takes to his feet, a towering giant compared to the new arrivals. "Who is going to support who?" He wonders out loud.

It takes me a minute or two to recognize why these RVNs do not possess that intimidating appearance exhibited by their counter parts, Viet Cong and NVA, that I had come across. This group of Vietnamese are all scrawny compared to the enemy. I vividly recall the live and dead enemy seeming bulkier. They also looked far more mature, and staunch to purpose. This carefree bunch appear more annoyed than staunch.

Zeus locates the tubes in the watershed in little time. The RVNs struggle far longer to haul them out of the wet, thicket. Once on dry ground, they all have to closely examine and touch each of the tubes. When they finished playing with the darn things, our Vietnamese support group proceeds to return from the direction in which they initially came, hauling the tubes with them.

Puteoli chases after the head of their column. "Where are you going?" he asks the lieutenant. "We still have to climb that mountain to find and kill the guys that brought those things."

Sing song words are exchanged between Vietnamese officers. The lieutenant points towards the top of the mountain during the discourse and the captain ends the discussion with a stern shake of the head.

"My captain, he found weapons," the lieutenant explains as his unit continues heading back to their compound at the far side of LZ English. "We not go mountain. Bye, bye now."

CHAPTER 10

Five long, monotonous days pass without a mission. Brigade's Operations Unit, S-3, which insists on having a team ready to track, has nothing for us to do. The province is quiet, but Brigade Intelligence, S-2, expects something serious to happen, and sooner rather than later.

Restlessness strikes hard at the unit's members. Young men, bored by inaction, struggle through those long, monotonous days. Our minds tend to gravitate to dark thoughts that lie festering within, when left unengaged.

We lay on bunks, read, write letters, and pace the floor like caged animals, trying to keep ugly memories at bay. In time, we pray for a mission to beat the doldrums of inaction, the very source of the consternation that now gnaws at us.

Prattchet, on the other hand, is not waiting on anything. Through Nieman, he has Cooper, Whitman and Talmadge toiling at new projects. He has them back at filling and stacking sandbags.

I watch Talmadge and Baby Face drive off in CTT1 to the river each of those mornings, envious at their break of tedium from daily life at Dog Patch. They have the wonders of the market place of downtown Bong Son and the kids at the river to divert their attention.

We offer them financial assistance to purchase the smokes to pay the river urchins. We also provide them with physical assistance, which is limited to late afternoons, when the chance of a mission is unlikely.

The new task assigned to Whitman, Talmadge, and Cooper calls for erecting a four-foot wall of bags around each hooch. Of course, the chore commences with our hooch, with a deliberate and conspiratorial effort to save the HQ hooch for last. It is the little things as such, that keeps up morale.

Mail arrives. There is nothing for me. Seagram gets a letter from his mother, while Tillman receives a small stack, mostly pinkish, perfumed, Hallmark-style envelopes from his wife.

A standard envelope in the stack catches Tillman's curiosity. He opens it ahead of the others and reads the enclosed message. He rises from his bunk and walks to the front door looking solemn, almost sad, the letter hangs at his side. After some deliberation, he turns and catches me watching.

"It's from Cardona," Tillman explains, holding up a single page. "Says he is stationed at Fort Lewis, a couple of hours drive from his home. He misses us, and says he is having trouble being home."

The rest of the guys approach to hear what else Cardona wrote.

Tillman hands the letter to Seagram to read and to pass around. "Cardona added that he got busted down for getting into a barroom brawl at a joint outside the main gate. Claims he slugged some civilian who snuck up behind him. The poor fellow only wanted to borrow a match."

Nieman returns. He calls Puteoli and Tillman outside behind the hooch. Shouts ensue. They draw my and

Thompkins's attention outside. Nieman is in a shouting match with Tillman. Tony is there, but he just stands, eyes closed, shaking his head. To my surprise, mild mannered Tillman is shouting the loudest. He is vehemently arguing against some sort of new mandate, which Nieman appears to have proposed and insists on being carried out.

"I'm not going along with such a stupid idea!" Tillman angrily insists. "Court-martial me, or kick me off the unit, but I refuse." That said, he storms past us into the hooch.

My curiosity gets the better of me. It is not my being nosey that has me interested; it is my survival that is at stake. Nieman's judgement of late has been dangerous. He has attempted to push poorly thought-out assignments that could endanger lives, all in hopes of appeasing Prattchet's needs to have two teams operable. The notion of his having riled Tillman with some new initiative, as to create such great opposition from the dog handler, has me seeking the reason.

"Tillman," I call out to halt him.

He stops and turns, but before I can pose a question to him, he unburdens himself on those in ear shot. "Do you know what that mad man wants to do?" he asks, his face in a snarl. He doesn't wait and quickly blurts out, "That buffoon is insisting that Cooper and Prince go out with us on the next three to four missions. Nieman expects me to train Cooper while we track. He says the British and Malaysians use two dogs on a team. They do, but they employ two trained handlers and two dogs. The second set serves as a back-up, not as trainee. And just how do you instruct someone while on a track without speaking, with cue cards?"

Tony enters and joins us. "I just got these sergeant stripes," he says, smiling, glossy eyes adding warmth to that smile. "Never thought that I would lose them so quickly." He moves further into the hooch to draw Seagram and Cooper into the discussion. "Nieman and I just had a mano un mano talk," he says, surrendering his smile. "Team 2 may be looking for a new leader and dog handler in the near future."

"What's this here buffoon, Tillman talks about?" Talmadge curiously begs of Baby Face.

"You don't know what a buffoon is?" an incredulous Whitman fires back.

"A buffoon is a creature of low intelligence that clowns around all the time," I leap in to answer the fellow that dropped out of school to support a family.

"Oh, you mean like Baby Face, here," he grins, as Brandon Whitman is taken aback.

"Ha!" Thompkins lets out a howl.

Nieman enters our hooch on the morning of the sixth day of inaction. He wears an ugly scowl, but carries a clipboard. "Got a mission," he snarls at no one in particular. "A mine sweeping crew took fire from two Viet Cong less than twenty minutes ago. The location of the attack is three kilometers north of LZ Uplift. CTT2 is fueled up; people are waiting on you at the site. Talmadge, you and Whitman get busy finishing with those damn sandbags." A brief pause, and he softly adds, "Cooper, you go with Talmadge and Whitman."

A rush to gather gear and head out the door takes place. Nieman, who stands near the back door, is intentionally jostled by the stampeders. He continues with his scowl, as all smile, happy at a diversion and at keeping the team's configuration intact.

Landing Zone Uplift is a base camp, a short drive south of Bong Son along Highway 1, the principal north/south road for South Vietnam. That coastal plain highway crosses a mountainous region some twenty miles south of LZ English. Uplift is located at that area, securing that highland crossing from the enemy.

Several military vehicles, including two deuce-and-a-half trucks with 50 caliber machine guns mounted on top of their cab, await us at the location of the attack. Attentive gunners behind the heavy caliber machine guns have their weapons pointed east, presumably in the direction of the enemy's withdrawal. A helicopter gunship circles overhead, searching the grounds for the illusive attackers.

Petite Vietnamese Military Police in their tight-fitting uniforms, direct a backup of local traffic through the site. They halt the oncoming traffic, and signal frantically for us to approach through the temporary vacated lane. An engineer captain on the side of the road is speaking on a radio mounted at the rear of a Jeep. He sees us, and waves frantically for us to join him. Tony guns the engine up the mountain.

"They went in that direction," he shouts, pointing east of the road to a sloping field of low grass. Dozens and dozens of mysterious, dirt mounds are scattered about that field. Most mounds are covered with heavy brush, providing perfect hiding places. "There are two of them somewhere out there. The gunship hasn't been able to spot them from the air. I hope you men can."

"Thank you, Sir," Tony thanks the officer for the information, although we had already discerned all that he provided. "Can you direct us to the very spot from where they fired at your road clearing crew? We will also require back-up to engage them once they are located."

Puteoli has a diplomatic way of dealing with officers. He cajoles them in the manner they expect to be addressed without patronizing, as if he was near, or equal in rank to them. I hope that this new leader's manner results in more cooperative spirit from field officers in the future.

"Sergeant Logan," the captain calls to a group smoking at the side of the road. A soldier breaks free of the cluster and runs toward us. "Sergeant, take these men to where the VC fired at you, afterwards, you and your men will follow them." He then adds for our information, "The gunship will stay and supply all the heavy support you need."

Seagram soon points out signs left behind by two men fleeing the area. From there, Tony assigns Sergeant Logan and his handful of men to follow, on line, to our right rear. He expects the VC to break for the safety of higher ground to the right, and posts Logan and his men where they can engage them without shooting us in the back.

We commence to track in a diamond formation, a tracking form of movement that resembles more an arrowhead than a diamond. That shape is suited for open terrain such as we now trek through. It allows us greater visual coverage to the front and for quick deployment of limited fire power to any side of the formation.

Tillman and Zeus take point. A stern-face Thompkins, follows behind the handler, his eyes scanning the area to their front.

There are many overgrown mounds in this vast, downward sloping field. The engineer captain ventured that they may be ancient, family, burial plots. We anticipate flushing out the two-armed VC from one of those mounds, but we have no idea which of the dozens of mounds to our front will be the one, or whether they are prepared to stand and fight.

I am at the left flank of our five-man formation, feeling perilously exposed on that side of the field. The mine sweepers are stretched out to the far right of the team, but no one is between me and the vast open area to my left. That lonely, abandoned feeling returns. That combination of anxiety, self-pity, and terror strikes me once again. The chest, again, feels ready to implode, and that heavy pounding emanating from there, spreads to my temples. But, as I follow Tillman's and Zeus' lead deeper into the field, and while examining every mound to my front and left, I start to realize that we are all out in the open, dreading that anticipated sound of gun fire.

Two men bolt from behind a large mound less than two hundred feet to my front. They run diagonally away, to my left. My upper torso snaps back, shocked at their sight, and my stomach feels to sink to my groin. Though I expected something to occur, their sudden action, nevertheless, surprises me. "There!" I quickly recovered and scream like some helpless wench, fearing the mound and shrubs may have obscured the view of the others to my right. I fire a full magazine at them, though Tillman fires a split second ahead of me.

The pair goes down to my and Tillman's rifle fire. The gunship hurries over the to two VC, and the door gunner makes sure they stay down.

I would later discover that Zeus had alerted Tillman to the pair, prior to their abandoning their concealment.

Black Asian eyes encroach my sleep. Once again, I find myself, atop that mountainous protrusion at the beach, gawking with horror at those Asiatic eyes. I stare in disbelief as the husky man proceeds into a pirouette, lifting the barrel of his weapon as he does, hurrying to kill me. I also rush to raise my rifle, but this time, to no avail. The weapon is far too heavy, and I lack the strength to lift it. Kak kak kak kak sounds.

A cry in the dark wakes me. My chest heaves, as I gasp air. A quick look about assures me of my safe whereabouts. The others are asleep on their bunks; no one stirs. So, was I the source of that cry, or was it just a part of that strange nightmare?

I sit on the edge of the bunk and hold my head in my hands. My head is about to split wide open; no doubt from excessive drinking, late into the night. Though the night air is mild and a light breeze blows through the mesh screen wall around the hooch, my head is soaked with perspiration, an issue likely unrelated to the alcohol consumption.

The vividness of the nightmare has me once again focusing on the issue whether it is in fact something other than a bad dream. In past experiences, nightmares, and dreams in general, always have a whimsical sense about them. It is about a brain at work as the body sleeps, taking disjointed memories temporarily stored in a holding area and trying to find a suitable permanent place to file away that information. These nighttime sequences do not fit that pattern. There is little disjointed about this thing I question a nightmare. Other than my inability to raise the barrel of my weapon, the event is exactly as I recall it having occurred, down to the trees, rocks and heat. But then, perhaps this is about alcohol yet coursing through my arteries from earlier this night. A bloated bladder in need of emptying is the more pressing matter at the moment.

Outside is as quiet as the inside of the hooch. Landing Zone English has taken on its nighttime mantle. Nothing moves to draw attention or to make noise. Silhouettes of structures resting on hilltops stand out against the backdrop of a starry night sky. Four soft, orange glows of street lights are visible illuminating road junctions in the crevices between hills. That hard military appearance of an active, security enclave has given way to a quiet, peaceful ambience, not unlike the late-night serenity of suburbs back home. But unlike those neighborhoods, an alert, lethal perimeter keeps a watchful eye, ready to react against any provocation or perceived threat.

A voice suddenly sounds from the dark. I drop, startled and tensed by the unexpected voice.

"That you screaming in your sleep?" Nieman repeats, lightly slurring his words. He approaches, staggering as he moves, a bottle of Drambuie is in his right hand and a dark object in the other. He lifts the bottle to his lips and holds it there for three long seconds. The left hand rises to wipe spillage off his chin. What looks like the pistol he confiscated from me weeks earlier, is in that hand. "Get your ass back to bed, may get a mission call tomorrow," he drunkenly snarls.

I rise, staring hard at the pistol, fearful of its purpose this night. "I came out to take a leak," I softly explain. "What are you doing up this late?" I ask, thinking to open up a dialogue to discover his intentions.

"Clearing my head," he answers, scratching his forehead with the pistol. He closes his eyes and tilts his head back slowly. The movement causes him to lose balance. He staggers backward until his left side strikes sandbags protecting the hooch.

"I have no leadership skills," the man then relates. "Do you know that I lack leadership qualities?"

It is a statement which I fully agree with, but one that I have to heed how I reply; if I do so at all.

"Prattchet told me so," Nieman continues, now smiling and chuckling to himself as he speaks. "Says I cannot control my unit. Because of that, I show a lack of leadership, and am being passed over for promotion because of it."

Nieman attempts to straighten, but instead, stumbles backward. He holds the bottle high to protect the contents from spilling, but releases the pistol from his grasp, as he reaches out to brace himself against the bags.

A quick step forward, I plant my right foot on the weapon. "That lieutenant has made a lot of mistakes," I offer to distract the drunk from my actions.

"You, young warrior, are correct," he slurs. "Prattchet is the one lacking at everything," he adds with a smile and wide-open arms to emphasize everything. Once again, he closes his eyes and tilts his head and staggers back. I seize the opportunity to retrieve the weapon from the ground.

Nieman then proceeds into a long discourse in a foreign language. He fails to consider that I do not understand. I just stand there, trying to catch a recognizable word or two to make sense of what else disturbs him.

"Go on. Take care of your business and get back to bed," a drunken Nieman now orders. With that said, he turns and staggers back toward the HQ hooch. Suddenly, he stops and looks back over his left shoulder. "Newsom is dead."

The sun finally rises, a start to a new day. The pistol that I had left on top of my footlocker is gone. I start to wonder if all of last night was just a bad dream, then I recall Nieman's last words.

We soon head outside into the early morning swelter. We wait on Puteoli before heading to breakfast. He has gone to the headquarter hooch in search of details of Newsom's death. We wait, consoling one another over our old teammate's loss, without seeming to do so, lest we appear unmanly.

Death in a place where killing is actively pursued and far too common, presents the same level of grief and sorrow as it does in noncombatant areas. As at home, the level and duration of the suffering is based on the age of the bereaved and on the extent of one's knowledge and relation to the deceased. The only evident difference between here and at home, lies with the savagery and the violence associated with death in this paradise.

We talk of the unfair treatment that Newsom received at the hands of Prattchet and Nieman, but fail to mention our culpability at having said little. Whitman is exceedingly distraught by Newsom's death, by far, more so than the rest of us. He vents of dropping fragmentation grenades under the HQ hooch and of other deadly means of retaliation against Prattchet, a man he has never laid eyes on.

"Shut the hell up!" Thompkins finally yells at Baby Face. "We do not want to hear about what you're not going to do."

Puteoli returns, looking sickly. He and Newsom had served on the same team prior to having been wounded.

We quickly gather around him to hear what he found out. He looks to the ground, as if gathering his thoughts, before speaking.

"Newsom's fire base near the Loatian border got hit at dusk with a mass attack, two days ago. It sounds as if it may have been a human wave attack. Our guys blew all their foo gas barrels, but there were hundreds of NVAs. They went past exploding claymore mines, broke through the wire, and into the firing trenches, where they went at it hand to hand. Our guys prevailed and drove them back. Seventeen dead, including Newsom, and dozens wounded. Boo coo dead NVA inside and outside the wire, some burnt to a crisp by the foo gas. Grunts went in early the following morning to secure the area. They did not call us, because Brigade suspected the surviving NVA had already retreated back across the Laotian border."

"How did Newsom die?" Talmadge begs to know, although the rest of us cringe at his request for details.

"They don't know. All they know is that he died from wounds in a field hospital at An Khe," Tony replies.

"If that Bastard hadn't kicked Newsom off the unit, he'd still be alive," Whitman injects those words with such venom as to draw instant concern for Prattchet and those of the headquarter hooch. Baby Face storms into our hooch, abandoning a group, highly fretful of his purpose for going inside, but none willing to follow to investigate.

I know that this calls for me or someone to take immediate action, to go in there and check on the brash guy. After all, it was our inaction that indirectly helped contribute to Newsom's death. But then, there are too many mixed emotions, broiling in my head for me to take any decisive action. One, a vengeful thought, rejoices in the fantasy of Whitman carrying through his threat.

"So, what is foo gas?" Cooper unexpectedly asks.

His question draws eyes away from the rear door to our hooch. It is a welcome change from the issue of whether or not to check on Baby Face. I had heard the Grunts of McMurdo's platoon speak of foo gas, but only of the horrid effects.

Seagram accepts the challenge to the question, "Foo gas is a mixture of jet fuel with chemical additives to thicken it," he explains to Cooper. "Fifty-five-gallon barrels of that shit are buried at an angle in the direction the enemy may approach. An explosive device placed underneath, sprays the burning mixture dozens of feet out."

Thompkins looks down at Seagram. "Wrong, again," he condescendingly states. "It's kerosine mixed with diesel fuel, and saw dust added to thicken it."

"Who died and left you a chemist?" Seagram snaps back at him.

Talmadge joins the verbal brawl, "You guys are both wrong. It's the same stuff they use in flame throwers."

"What the hell you know?" Seagram now barks at Talmadge. "Just yesterday, you were a Cherry."

It took time, but eventually, boisterous laughter fills the air. Talmadge laughs the loudest at the complimentary insult. A lone German Shepherd from the kennels joins in by baying loudly. Our laughter is spurred on by a subconscious need and desire to ease tension over Newsom's death; the wolf-like cry adds and prolongs that roaring.

Tony breaks away as the laughter subsides. He moves to the door and sticks his head in, "Get your ass out here Whitman. We're going for breakfast."

No reply, not so much as a sound to signify compliance or refusal. The team leader steps through the threshold and cries out, "Whitman!"

A sinking feeling overwhelms my gut. It soon tightens into a knot, not unlike that when on a track.

"Oh crap," someone lets loose a prayer. We all turn our attention toward the HQ hooch.

I look, expecting to see splintered wood and shards of galvanized roofing suddenly flung high into the air. Instead, I see Nieman, shoving and pushing Whitman in our direction.

CHAPTER 11

We are once again on the road south of Bong Son. This time, praying to reach LZ Uplift. We steer down Highway 1 in the dark, hoping to arrive safely at the military enclave by sunrise. It is an extremely dangerous time to travel by roadway. Prattchet and Nieman refused to disturb Brigade Operations, S-3, to arrange for a predawn flight for us.

It is a slow, harrowing trip. No other vehicles are on the road, and we drive expecting enemy fire to erupt from behind every dark shadow or black shape. The Viet Cong and the NVA rely on the cover of darkness to slip about our secured areas, to prey on soft targets, such as a lone vehicle.

Downtown Bong Son is dead. We course our way through the dimly lit town with trepidation. The stillness in driving past this generally bustling commerce center, is eerie. Nothing moves or sounds along the shops and homes, other than CTT 2 and the pounding in my chest. Of more alarming nature, are the five, road crossings over creeks and streams, guarded by local militia. We keep skeptical eyes on those crossing guards and our weapons' selector switch on automatic fire as we approach each bridge, until safely out of range of the militia's World War II era, M1 carbines.

The sun's rays are breaking out to the east as we approach the gate at Uplift. A large sign, spanning the entry welcomes those arriving with the bold words, "***Our job is killing, and business has been good.***" Military Police manning the entrance expect us. They direct us to the chopper pad, where we are also expected.

A major is ready to conduct a briefing for a group, all armed and prepared to head into action, save one. The meeting is held next to the landing pad. Two small Light Observation Helicopters, three Cobra gunships, and a half dozen Huey transports are sitting and waiting on the tarmac. The officer is that same tall, gaunt major that called us out once before, then to an abandoned basecamp, deep in the interior. He invites us over to his briefing, recalling my face, but not the others. It took me some time to remember that I was with a different team on that earlier occasion.

The briefing concerns the purpose of the day's mission. The major dives directly into the matter.

"Enemy contact is on the increase in this area. Friendly forces between LZ English to our north and Phu Cat to our south are thinly stretched," he speaks with a booming voice against an early morning breeze off the nearby coast. "The enemy is fully aware of the shift in manpower to protect the so-called pacified northern sectors of this province, and is looking to take advantage of that change. This is likely to be a repeat of Tet from last year that left the cities vulnerable to attack by the NVA and VC. They have tested our perimeter here on several nights, as they have the road to our immediate north and south. Brigade is convinced that a major push is to occur in the southern sector of the province, although uncertain as to where or when. I agree with their inference from recently gathered intelligence, but I am convinced that the push will be directed at this facility, and will occur in a day or two. This facility sits on a critical spot for a principal highway. Closure of the road, for a day or any length of time will be considered a major propaganda victory."

"Yesterday afternoon, a supply ship, twenty kilometers to the northwest of Uplift, reported sighting a large body of men moving east. The precise size of that force is unknown. We can expect those visitors tonight or tomorrow night at the latest, assuming, of course, we do nothing, but that is not how we walk it here!"

He suddenly speaks with greater bravado, causing people to shift where they stand. "We are going to perform a combat air assault into an open area two kilometers to our northwest. We will land between them and their intended destination, engage and destroy them." Then, like a seasoned orator, he quickly reverts to his earlier articulation pitch. "Our one glitch is with the size of the only available insertion zone into that heavy canopy region. It will only accommodate three transports at any one time. We will need to approach the area and land in two waves of three transports. The first two squads of the air mobile platoon and command will go with the first wave, the rest of the platoon, and a combat team out of Bong Son, along with a journalist from *Sky Soldier* magazine will go in with the second. Gun ships will cover the flanks of the zone during the landing."

We are, once again, called to a maybe tracking mission by this officer. Although, I am concerned that we may encounter that "unknown" size force, a term which is nothing more than a euphemism for a god-awful, large number of enemy soldiers, possibly numbering in the hundreds. I am, nevertheless, comforted by the heavy fire power wielded by this small, aerial assault force. I also find the publicity nature of the forthcoming event, somewhat amusing. The major is obviously an ambitious officer, skilled in the art of self-promotion, and the reporter is here to bring attention to his upcoming exploits.

The briefing ended, the major raises his right index finger high in the air and twirls it and the hand aggressively. Helicopter engines whine. NCOs break from our gathering and hurry to the tarmac, yelling instructions and directing their squads to particular transports. Lines of well-trained infantry rush to board.

"That last slick is yours," the gaunt officer hollers to Puteoli over the engine and propeller wash noise. "You'll have seconds to disembark when we get there, so place your people in accordingly." He shifts his attention to the reporter, before resting his stone-cold grey eyes on me. A smile quickly warms them, "Hope this time we can dig up some excitement for you guys. It won't do, disappointing you twice."

Minutes later, we are sitting on the floor of a transport's cargo hold, heading to a small clearing in the jungle. The coastline, with its inviting white, sandy beach and a grey sea beyond are visible to the right. Lush mountains are to our near left, and to the front, slightly skewed below and to the left, a flock of heavily armed air ships precede us over heavy canopy.

The reporter has occupied himself, eyeing us, especially Zeus. There is nothing warm about this fellow. He is tall, demonstrates excellent posture, and is stylish in his army attire. He models a well-tailored, hard starched uniform with the rank insignia of a specialist fourth class proudly displayed on the collar. The jungle boots appear brand new, as does the camouflage cloth covering his helmet. Since boarding, he has donned a look of arrogant superiority on an elongated face that must certainly limit his sphere of friends. He sits to my right, and he fidgets, toying with a camera hanging around his neck. "Guys, ok if I take a few shots of you and of your dog?" he finally ventures to ask over the propeller noise. His request, as might be expected of someone with a snooty attitude, comes out sounding more like an advance directive than a request.

Seagram to my left firmly retorts for us over the Huey's noise, "No can do. It's against regulation to leak what we do, or how we do it, punishable by up to thirty years at LBJ. Hush hush stuff, old boy," he adds with a fake English accent, "James Bond shit."

We all try to hide our smirk from the reporter, not that it matters; he now occupies himself, gawking outside, to the first wave, as they commence their descent. We all glance to where his vision lies, but return to watch him, as he curiously removes the steel pot off his head, lifts his butt off the aluminum floor, and maneuvers the head gear under his ass.

"What the hell you doing?" I bluntly ask.

He gives me a condescending look, and runs fingers through, well-manicured, blond hair before providing a snobbish reply. "I am protecting myself in the event a bullet penetrates the undercarriage of this transport."

"So, you value your ass more than your skull," Seagram chuckles. "If we hit a hot LZ, the rounds will be flying in from the sides, not the bottom."

"The infantry guys with the air unit assured me that this was the correct, precautionary measure during a combat assault," he argues, undeterred by Seagram's logic, while we all break into laughter.

"They were pulling your leg," I offer while yet smirking.

The pilot interrupts our comedy relief with an announcement. "Stand by. First wave going in," he hollers over the helicopter noise. "We'll swoop right in behind them. You'll have five seconds to hop out."

Laughter ceases. All heads in the cargo hold of the transport turn to watch the first two squads' ground approach.

Combat air assaults are never laughing matters. They never take place on safe, secured terrain. Disembarking troops have to be prepared to leap from cargo holds, directly into a firefight for their very lives. The high occurrence of landing directly into hostile fire has coined the term "hot LZ", and allows combat ground troops to earn the Army's Air Medal, just as helicopter pilots and crews.

The two small LOHs break away from the lead ships and proceed to tree top hopping between the landing area and the adjacent mountains, scouring the ground under the canopy for signs of the enemy. Three Cobra Gunships move forward of the first wave to protect their landing. They fly and hover in a V formation, covering the small, light green, elliptical opening within a dense canopy of dark green.

Lines of green tracers suddenly burst upward. Tension strikes; all crane necks downward for full comprehension of what is occurring.

Tracers by the hundreds shoot up from around the clearing. A massive display of enemy rifle and machine gun fire streams out, crisscrossing the sky toward our ships.

A metallic ping sound reaches ears. Green tracers fly past the left side of the open hatch. Seagram attempts to climb over me, seeking safety in the center of the cargo hold.

Communication traffic explodes from the cockpit's radio. Loud, erratic voices come through air waves, demonstrating high levels of stress, all which adds to the level of tension in our cargo hold.

Retaliatory explosions of rocket and cannon fire join the fray. Flatulent-like sounds of mini guns spraying the ambush site reach our ears. The light green field and the immediate surrounding canopy disappear under black plumes with hellish colors of red and yellow flames erupting within those ominous clouds of smoke and debris. Smoke and debris drift higher and higher into the air over what is to be our landing zone.

"Oh crap," the door gunner cries out. The sound of the bolt chambering a round into his machine gun comes through his repeated, "Oh crap, oh crap." He now engages in dispensing his own share of killing.

A well-placed ambush awaits us. Our transports are about to deliver us directly into a kill zone.

Our slick takes a hard dive toward what could well pass as hell on earth. That old friend, fear, once again emerges, prepping my body for the horror it is about to engage. Muscles tense. The heart pumps a hard, fast beat, in anticipation of compensating muscles soon to be oxygen deprived. My stomach once again tries to escape through a gaping mouth. Dante Alighieris' written words, "Abandon all hope, ye who enter here." resonates in my flighty mind.

A pain at my right shoulder comes to my attention. I snap around to check on the root of that pain, fearing the worst. Instead, I find a distraught journalist, squeezing that shoulder with such a degree of pressure that can only derive through sheer terror.

I feel for the noncombatant soldier, but I shake free of his grip, wanting nothing to restrain me when I jump clear of the cargo hold.

"Oh God, oh God," the man squeals, pointing with that now free hand toward the inferno of the hot LZ. The man has lost a safety line, physical contact with another person, and now seeks other means of assurance, speech, to calm his terror. "We're not… we're not going there, are we?" he asks. "Please, please no," he now begs, as if I or the others can prevent it.

"When we land, follow me, stay close behind, and do as I do," I tell the terrified noncombatant to calm him, though it strikes me as strange that I should be offering advice. Afterall, someone needs to calm me, and instruct me on what to do once we land and engage in the butchery.

Zeus, laying between me and Tillman, is the only creature in the cargo hold seeming relaxed. He lays there, looking at us, as if sensing our anxiety. His handler, with eyes gazing down at nothing, is mouthing a prayer. Thompkins, to his right, has eyes closed and rocks his torso forward and back.

I take another look at the disturbing hell hole we are about to be dumped into. As I do, a most bizarre thought occurs to me. It dawns on me that the level of fear and stress that I and the others currently suffer, and further, on what else is about to transpire, cannot be fathomed by anyone back home. Nothing in their life's experience can possibly have them relate to what is happening to us this moment, much less the violence that we are about to engage in. Anger and resentment with those safely back home, going about their daily lives, just as quickly encroach a jealous mind. All such thoughts, though, just as quickly migrate to wondering what my buddies at home are doing at this very moment. Are they sleeping, lining up dates for the weekend, drinking and carousing, or at work, or in class? The possibilities to those notions, juxtaposed to what I am undergoing, brings on a nervous chuckle, followed by a second, longer chuckle.

Thompkins ceases his rocking and cocks an eye on that dour face at me. His look, brings on a third chuckle, until I realize that he may be measuring me for a straightjacket.

Garbled radio communication from the cockpit suddenly peaks. The chatter is louder and far more stressed than earlier. I recognize the major's voice among the voices. A second later, our chopper engages a hard bank to the right that takes my breath away. It quickly starts to climb, away from the raging inferno below. Relieved, but yet curious at the sudden change in course, I look down to what had been the opening in the jungle. The entire area is shrouded in black. Three Huey transports emerge through the clouds of smoke. The gun ships are also moving, continuing to fire and laying to waste everything before them as they go. All now seek the safety of higher altitude to the right.

Minutes pass between our aborted combat assault and shaky boots touching ground back at Uplift. As we step off the tarmac, a pair of F-100s out of Phu Cat screech past us, a mere hundred feet above the canopy. Their reflective, aluminum fuselage contrasts sharply against the backdrop of green mountains. They zoom past, loaded with napalm canisters, to avenge a well-placed ambush.

The grunts with the air unit jump and cheer with arms raised high. Seconds later, the aftermath of incendiaries dropped on the enemy sound. Loud booms of detonations reach us, followed by pitch-black, willowy puffs that rise high and higher. A minute later, a second set of explosions resonate, raising the plumage further into the air. The two F-100 soon reappear, this time, flying directly overhead. They tilt wings as they head home.

"Why are we just hanging around in this damn heat?" Seagram gripes. He wipes at sweat on his forehead with his boonie hat. He has been wiping at sweat for the past forty minutes. The current inaction has him deeply frustrated, though it takes little to frustrate the little fellow. "Are we finished here? Can we head back to Dog Patch?" He throws out the questions for anyone to entertain his frustration.

"Don't know, but the major ordered us to stay put," Puteoli replies sounding a bit aggravated with the visual tracker's ongoing grumbling.

"A cold beer while we wait would be nice," Thompkins adds.

"Yeah, it sure would," Seagram agrees, satisfied he is not alone in his exasperation. "That is the first intelligent thing I've heard you say since you joined the unit," he suddenly snaps at Thompkins.

I glance at my watch. "You guys realize it's just ten in the morning."

Both Seagram and Thompkins turn to me with squishy, irritable faces. "So?" They ask in unison.

"Well, even for you, Seagram," I snap back at the pair, "ten in the morning is mighty early."

"Not after that ride we just took," the visual tracker argues. "I plan to drink a case of that stuff once we get back to Dog Patch."

"Assuming that little shit, Whitman, hasn't drunk all our cold beer," Thompkins joins in.

Tillman now speaks out, appearing perturbed as well, "Seagram, you still owe me a dollar from the last beer run. Cough it up."

"Anyone have an idea why we are hanging out here?" Seagram asks, hoping to distract and avert payment.

"Now!" Tillman demands.

"What, out here, with all these thieving Grunts around to watch scrip being passed?" He asks, looking concerned with the demand at such an inopportune time and location.

The *Sky Soldier* reporter has been shifting nervously, within ear shot of us. Fear from earlier, clearly continues to plague him. He moves closer to engage in our bellyaching. "The major said we would return in about an hour," he squawks, as if he expects us to miraculously terminate the man's plan. "The hour is almost over. Do you think he was serious?"

We had already guessed that we would go back. Our ongoing griping is about having to return to that carnage, fueled by anxiety and the endless prolongation of that stress. No one has the heart to tell the reporter that we are, but perhaps, his words are just his means of lessening anxiety.

The engines of the two small LOHs' start to whine. That horrid knot in the pit of my gut returns, and the noncombatant snaps his attention toward the tarmac, as if death has suddenly come knocking at his door.

The pair of small ships take to the air, soaring away like a pair of hungry Peregrine falcons in search of prey. We watch them head to the north, but soon angle west, toward the higher ground. A single Cobra gunship follows. The LOHs will return to tree top hopping, eager for a sight of the fleeing enemy or to draw their fire. The Cobra will be close by, ready to pounce on any sightings or ground fire.

The maintenance crews that had been inspecting, re-arming, and refueling the helicopters withdraw from the tarmac. Minutes later, we are in the air on the way back to that small, green field. Everyone is as tense and anxious as the reporter, the memory of that earlier attempt fresh on everyone's mind.

All six transports soon descend upon a broad, swath of scorched earth, yet burning and smoldering from the ordinances that struck it. The patch of green that had initially been our objective is gone. The entire area is now unrecognizable, and the new opening in the canopy is far wider, capable of accommodating dozens of helicopters at any one time.

Our slick descends with the others and hovers a foot or two off the ground. We leap clear and spread out further into the aftermath of what had been Hell on Earth.

The place reeks of heavy refined petroleum. Glowing embers of what had been massive tree trunks, still burn red at the stumps, adding to the egregious, choking odor. I feel the heat of the blackened earth through the protective soles of my boots. It is highly uncomfortable and has me moving to minimize the effect on my feet. How could anything, much less anyone, have survived such destructive firepower?

I watch Tillman bend and lift Zeus over his shoulders. The poor dog has no protection against the heat searing at the pads of his feet. But Zeus is a large, heavy Labrador. The rest of the team will have to take turns, carrying him, until we clear of the hot, scorched earth.

The reporter is occupied, snapping pictures of the devastation. Grunts not on security, scour the charred ground, presumably searching for evidence of human remains or their military equipment. The burnt area is vast, and a thorough inspection will likely take several hours.

A waste of time, I conclude. All the trees and shrubs that once grew here have been obliterated. Why would flesh and bones have survived such vaporization?

Puteoli goes to speak to the major, who is busy directing the search and checking on perimeter security. The major listens and points toward the line of surviving trees, a hundred yards to the northwest. The base of steep foothills commences there. Our team leader waves for us to follow him to where trees still stand.

CHAPTER 12

Soldiers come and go, to and from this war. With combat tours set at twelve months, this war zone has turnstiles that stay in perpetual motion, turning with departing troops and fresh replacements.

We all agree on the foolishness committed by those in charge of the execution of the war. Whether it's allowing the enemy sanctuaries to operate out of Cambodia and Laos, to not bombing North Vietnam to its knees, or to a limited tour of duty, we trackers have strong opinions, especially on the latter.

This is the enemy's home turf. He has nowhere to go, and he has demonstrated a will to devote his life, as a jungle warrior. Some fought as far back as the French colonial period, decades before our arrival.

Our soldiers are shipped home shortly after they develop sound combat experience. It takes upward of seven to nine months for Grunts to reach the bottom rungs of seasoned status in the art of killing and with surviving in the process. Those honed killers are sent back to the U.S. to finish the final five to six months of their two-year conscripted service, soon after they acquire the fundamentals to do the job, and do it well. They are ordered to some military installation that has no need of them or their newly acquired skills, to languish there in boredom, while they waste time till discharged. They are replaced in the rice paddies and jungles by fresh, young meat, until they too, develop combat skills and are shipped back.

Yet, in spite of all our expert analysis on this matter, none, other than Tony, and Nieman, have voluntarily extended their tours, or expressed interest with doing so. Nieman hates communist, whom he claims chased him and his family out of his eastern European homeland, and is motivated by that hatred against all of such ideology. Puteoli, well, he appears to suffer from paternal instincts. He has asked for an extension to protect friends and teammates. I, for one, plan to exit this hellish paradise after my remaining thirty-four weeks are up.

A new arrival has joined our unit. Talmadge has christened the Cherry with the nickname, Red, due to a light complexion and ruddy color of his hair. That name sticks, and by a lack of protest and acceptance, we assume that our Cherry, Ronald McAllister, has borne that handle, long before his arrival.

Red is of average height, but of robust build. His booming voice does not suit the rest of us. Thompkins is of the opinion we should have tagged him with the nickname, Ethel Merman. We also find his thuggish bearing and Neanderthal-like movement unsuitable. Wide shoulders and a stocky frame give him the appearance of a linebacker wearing shoulder pads. He is also a gregarious person to the point of being annoying.

Conversation is a healthy form of distracting a mind looking to dwell into vile memories. We constantly engage in friendly bickering to circumvent drifting into dark reflections. But our Cherry is constantly harping about topics like the boonie, the enemy, and of those that preceded him, all such discussions that we avoid. Tillman is the only one of us willing to offer the new guy time. But then, Red is also a dog handler, fresh from Fort Gordon and has a form of professional kinship to Tillman. Red's arrival also leaves us one person short of making Team 1 fully operational again.

Cooper, who has yet to go on a mission, is reassigned back to an RTO position. He does not take well to the constant change in assignment. Worse, he does not withhold that displeasure from Nieman. We all try to calm him whenever he shows signs of physically taking after Nieman, lest he end up on the same shit list with Whitman.

Cooper now joins Tillman and I, as we discuss the new guy who bumped him from his last position.

Tillman is convinced that Red is a good guy who will settle down and blend in once he gets to know and trust us. "You guys were not much different when you first arrived. L J, you were observant, a listener, always thinking about things, but just as nosey. Talmadge and you, Cooper, weren't much different from Red when you first arrived, and even Whitman has managed to settle down."

"You had me going till you said Whitman has settled down," I offer to boisterous laughter.

The very devil rushes through the back door eager for all our attention. Baby Face is shirtless and reeks of sweat. Nieman has the poor fellow on every nasty detail in lieu of an Article Fifteen, since storming into Prattchet's lair and verbally assailing the officer. In spite of all the punishment duty, he still manages to maintain a jovial attitude.

"Hey, Nieman just arrived with a fat ass E6," he announces. "The sergeant looks old, probably a lifer, and he is lugging a suitcase. They went into the headquarter hooch."

Thompkins moves to the rear door and sticks a hard-faced head to peer around the corner. "Must be a new platoon sergeant for the 39th Scout Dogs," he speculates.

"Platoon sergeants are E7s, dumbass," Seagram rudely replies. He pushes Thompkins aside and peers out the door himself. "I am not sure their Table of Organization calls for a platoon sergeant. Hadn't seen one since I've been here."

Thompkins jerks the smaller Seagram back inside by the back of the collar. "What do you know," he shouts in protest. "You've never even seen Prattchet. Besides, I've seen many E6s serve as platoon sergeants till orders come through."

"See, there you go again, showing your ignorance," Seagram replies. "I saw Prattchet stick his head out his door when Nieman led Whitman out by the ear."

"What! He didn't have me by the ear," Whitman protests the implication. "I'd kicked his ass if he had."

Tony steps to the rear threshold and glances out to the right, bringing sanity to the discussion. "Our Table of Organization calls for a noncommissioned officer of higher rank than a team leader. That may be our new boss. Perhaps he'll bring some sense to that front office. But if he is our new boss, Nieman will have to revert back to being a team leader."

"Oh, crap!" it was Whitman, Talmadge, and Cooper in unison.

As speculation rages at the back door, Nieman pops through the front door. "Listen up!" he shouts, as he crosses toward the gathering at the rear. "Get to lunch.

We have a unit meeting in here afterwards, so don't dally around at the mess hall."

The man does not appear happy, although that habit of turning his face aside as he issues instructions is still with him. The rest of us share in his unhappy look at the announcement of a unit meeting.

"Whitman, after our meeting, I want that crapper cleaned out and the shit in the cans burned. See to it that the shithouse is clean enough to eat from."

Whitman steps forward, a perplexed look on his cherub face as he looks right and then left. He has all of us curious, and causes Nieman to tilt his head further back. "That's a hell of a strange place to eat. Wouldn't you find it more appealing to eat at the mess hall like the rest of us?" he offers to snickers, even from our Cherry.

"Move!" Nieman hollers.

We have a new NCOIC. His name is Claude Hooper. Three bold, yellow stripes and the rocker of a staff sergeant are on his sleeve, a grade higher than Nieman and Puteoli, though he appears far older. A 9th Infantry Division unit emblem above the stripes on the right sleeve identify him as having served earlier with that division.

Sergeant Hooper welcomes himself to the unit most heartedly. He dons a grin, on a mustached face, so broad as to seem bogus. All the while, he individually shakes each member's hand aggressively, as if, he, is welcoming us to his unit. He asks our name, team number and position within the team in a pandering manner while pumping our arms. It is all a failed attempt to ingratiate himself with each of us.

That syrupy mannerism, whether contrived or not, has me uneasy. I hope that this is not what we have to look forward to in the future. Also, I sense that things will not improve with his arrival and may actually get worse. From the look on everyone's else's face, I sense that they all share in my first impression of the man.

"My last duty station was at Fort Gordon," he speaks, after all the awkward formalities have been completed. "I was an instructor at the Visual Tracker School and helped to establish it, so I am well versed with what you guys do here. I also attended the first class for Americans at the British Jungle Warfare School, and learned the tricks of the trade from the best at that school," he continues talking, but commences to pace the aisle between bunks, with arms firmly clasped behind him as if a Sergeant Major with a Scottish Highlander battalion. "Unfortunately, an injury requiring hospitalization stateside, prevented me from finishing my training there. Fortunately, I now have the opportunity to lead this unit. I have a number of innovative ideas that I am eager to exploit."

We all look at one another with that same wide-eyed, gaped mouth look. Innovative ideas to experiment on do not sit well with any of us, especially here, where lives are at stake should they fail.

"I am optimistic that great things are in store for us as a result of the forth coming new changes," he continues to a distinct, heavy groan from a disheartened Seagram. Sergeant Hooper immediately halts his pacing, and snaps about to face the source of the disparaging sound. "You got a problem, boy?"

"Depends on what you mean by new changes to try, and great things," Seagram answers in his typical sarcastic manner. "My DEROS is in two weeks. Tillman departs a week later. Great things to us means leaving here, unscathed, on our due date, and we old dogs don't need to learn new tricks. As you say, we also learned from the best at the British Jungle Warfare School or VT School. Why change anything, and why experiment here rather than at a safe rear area, such as the VT School?"

"We will employ my new techniques at tracking," the man angrily insists. "Cowards and shirkers will find themselves out of this unit so fast, their heads will spin."

"Like I said," Seagram continues, "Tillman and I leave here in days. Is that what you mean by heads spinning?"

Hooper steps closer to Seagram. He looks into his face for several seconds. That mustached face soon squinches and eyes squint at the visual tracker. "I remember you from VT School at Fort Gordon. Didn't much care for that mouth on you then. I suspect you and I are going to be seeing a lot of one another in the future," that and nothing else said, Hooper storms out the front door.

"I think that went well," Thompkins speaks out to no one, but which makes several of us grin.

I begin to wonder whether retribution will be forthcoming, and if so, in what manner, not that it really matters. Seagram and Tillman are short timers with just weeks remaining on their tour. They have little to worry about, especially considering Whitman reaps all the nasty assignments around Dog Patch.

"Nice going, Seagram," Nieman breaks his silence. "Real nice," he repeats, before chasing after Hooper.

Our next two days are spent on stand down. No one knows why or how long this will last. No one even cares to go inquire a reason from the front office. If our new NCOIC, Sergeant Hooper, views inaction as a form of retaliation, let it be. As Tillman puts it, "It is a brief, but welcome interlude from the war." But of greater importance is what Seagram added, "Two days closer to DEROS." To add to our delight, we are charged with running track to help Red acquaint himself with Prince, the perfect excuse for exiting Dog Patch and going outside the LZ perimeter.

Whitman, Cooper, Talmadge and Tillman lay a three to four mile track each morning. Red and Prince, along with the rest of my team track them till lunch. CTT 1, along with Hooper, mysteriously vanish on each of those mornings. We find ourselves relying on our lone remaining vehicle and the Scout Dog truck to get us outside the perimeter to run the test tracks. We are fine with that as well. We are left free during the heat of the afternoons to do as we wish, as is Whitman.

Three days later, we learn that Nieman will continue to perform his earlier duties. Shortly after lunch, he enters through the front door, his clipboard in hand, as if still the acting NCOIC. "Got a mission," he shouts, which surprises us, considering we thought we were still on stand down.

"A roving Vietnamese military police checkpoint, not far from our front gate got into gunfire with a Xe Lam carrying three men. The RVN MPs suffered casualties; that number is unimportant. What is of importance is that two of the three men in the Xe Lam are dead, but the third ran off. He disappeared near a cluster of homes and buildings. Brigade wants him found and taken alive for interrogation."

"What the hell is a Xe Lam?" Red wants to know.

I for one have no idea what a Xe Lam is. Of more importance to me, is Brigade's insistence that the VC be taken alive. How are we to accomplish that? Every means that comes to mind for taking the VC captive comes up with grave consequences. Besides, why tell us? We are classified 11F, not 11Bravo. That responsibility needs to be addressed to our Grunt support.

Tillman comes to Red's rescue concerning Xe Lams, "It's that three-wheel scooter bus you see the locals using to haul people or goods in the back."

"I once rode in the back of one used as a taxi, noisy and bumpy as hell," Thompkins adds.

"Cut the chatter and grab your things," Puteoli orders our team.

We all head to the gun rack. "Not you Seagram and Tillman," Nieman barks out. "Red and Whitman are going instead."

"What now, Nieman?" an angry Tillman demands.

The man smiles, a sinister smile that can only be derived from savoring sweet vengeance. "Seagram said it himself, you and he are soon to depart our company. Sergeant Hooper wants Red and Whitman on Team 2. The man wants nothing but professional trackers, not Sad Sacks in his unit." He gives off a guffaw which is difficult to interpret, perhaps as something akin to a chuckle or maybe, a most contemptuous scoff. "And you, young hunters thought that I was your problem."

"This is pure bullshit," Tillman replies as he heads for the door. "I'm going to talk to Hooper myself. I'll have a few words with that buffoon."

Tony Puteoli stops him before he reaches the door. "Let it go. This is a gift horse handed to you and Seagram. Don't blow it."

"Sergeant Hooper is not here anyway," Nieman scoffs loudly. "He is sky tracking," he adds and breaks into full laughter, "Yeah, that's right, sky tracking; the new and modern way to track," he laughs and exits the hooch.

It is early afternoon and hot as blazes when we exit LZ English. The sun is so bright, we are left to squint to avoid the harshness of the glare. Whitman, Thompkins and I sit on wooden bench seats in the back of the vehicle. We make every effort to avoid all contact with metal heated by the sun, although the occasional curve or bump on the road brings on a curse that attest to a failure. Thank God, we have just a short drive of under a mile to travel.

A dozen MPs are waiting on us at the check point. Unfortunately, they are all petite, Vietnamese military police in their tight-fitting olive drab uniforms, trying hard to look like tough authoritarians. Three other armed Vietnamese nationalists, appearing far older than the MPs and attired in tiger camouflage fatigues, squat at the side of the road. The trio silently observe all the activity taking place at the checkpoint; dark, somber eyes on brooding faces scan everything and everyone as if their very lives depended on finding something.

"You notice how little these Lilliputians sweat?" Whitman asks. He wipes away the flow of sweat at his forehead before it reaches an eye.

"We sweat enough for everyone," Thompkins injects, his face looking just as dour as that of the three squatters.

I make a radio call to our rear as we park. No American troops are present to back us up, so I call for further instructions. I inform the rest of the guys of the dangerous reply to my concern.

"Those bastards are going to get someone killed," Baby Face screeches.

"At least the guy we're to track is supposedly unarmed," Thompkins offers.

"Supposedly," I remark.

An ambulance departs as we climb off CCT 2. A faded, light blue colored Xe Lam lies on its side in a dry paddy at the edge of the road, riddled with bullet holes. Three RVN MPs are busy, carefully unloading weapons and munitions strewn in the back of the three-wheel vehicle. Four other MPs carry the bodies of two men to the back of a waiting truck.

One of the MPs approaches. Tony snaps a smart salute to the officer as the rest of us curiously watch. The officer snaps back an equally smart salute to our team leader, looking pleased by the American's acknowledgement to his rank. "These men, go you, arrest VC," he speaks, pointing at the squatting trio. "They Nationalist Police."

"Any of those men speak English?" Tony asks the officer.

The officer looks back to the three, before politely shaking his head.

"Then I must ask that you join us to translate," Tony insists in such a manner as to dissuade a refusal. "Of course, we will start, when you are ready."

The officer barks out gruff sounding instructions in his sing-song language to a pair of MPs. "We go now," he tells Tony.

Prince takes little time in picking up a scent. By the length of the stride left behind, we establish the person was running from the checkpoint. We all agree it is the trail left by the person we seek and hurry to track.

Red, with Prince on a long leash lead the way. The rest of us follow in our standard diamond formation, weapons ready to react to danger.

The scent left behind by the VC takes us past paddies to a grove of trees, mainly banana and mango trees. At the far side of the grove, a cluster of colorful, plaster wall buildings with red tile roofs loom. Those are the homes of far more affluent citizens than their agrarian counterparts with their simple thatched roofs and mud-like walls. We cautiously, but swiftly, proceed through the grove, checking each tree from trunk to lower branches for a sign of someone hiding.

We were told by those safely at LZ English that the man we seek was unarmed. "Take him alive," were the orders given to us. Their words mean nothing to us at this point. Anxiety and level of fear will dictate how we will deal with the man once we locate him. It is our lives that are at stake, and we intend to treat the VC as armed and highly dangerous.

Our Cherry dog handler, Red, routinely turns to look back. He keeps checking on the rest of us as we hurry to cross the grove. His action is both distracting and alarming. He needs to concentrate his attention on Prince and to his front rather than on what the rest of the team is doing. Thompkins finally puts an end to the Cherry's irresponsible behavior. He angrily jabs a hard finger forward, during one of Red's look back.

The MP officer and two of his men follow directly behind us. One speaks out in the grove, prompting Tony to turn and signal them all to shush. The older, three National Policemen bring up the rear. Their stealth, cautious movement demonstrate experience in the field.

It suddenly occurs to me that I have neither experience nor training at tracking through a community, such as the dozen or more buildings we are approaching. The closest that I have come at tracking anywhere near homes, was the day Hanson was shot and lost his two toes. Even then, the VC sniper was hundreds of feet outside the closest dwelling. Prince is now leading us directly into the cluster of residences, and I wonder what I am to do, should Prince walk into one of those homes.

My companion suddenly returns. My body tenses tight in anticipation of possible action. Breathing is once again arduous, and I find myself having to think about exhaling; an automated, bodily function that is subconsciously performed and not forced.

Our fearless canine, Prince, hurries into a wide, open plaza between homes. My eyes scan windows, doors and corners of each building to my front and left. I have little idea what to look for, much less how to react, other than shoot first.

The three National Policemen move to the right of our formation. They advance along the walls of homes on that side, peeking into windows and through open doors as they move. The three MPs continue to follow close behind the team.

Something to my left moves. I see the movement from the corner of an eye. My right thumb flips the weapon's selector switch to automatic fire as the barrel swings hard toward the direction of the movement. A trigger finger is less than a split second from spewing eighteen murderous rounds at what stirs, waiting on instructions from a mind stricken with terror.

It is a child. A little girl, drawn by unusual activity outside. She exits her home to investigate, having no idea of the sudden danger involved.

Shivers run up and down my body. I close my eyes and force myself to breathe. I finally sense my shoulders relax and droop as I shudder in relief at not killing the poor thing. That leg shaking, heel tapping returns. I glance down at the nervous system-like tic, that once again plagues me. As I resume scanning the area, I catch Whitman staring down at my leg and foot.

An MP shouts and flaps a hand to the child to go back inside. A young woman pops up at the home's door. She hurries outside and retrieves the child by the arm. One of the MPs leaves our group to chase after the young woman.

A glance back reveals the woman shaking her head aggressively at the MP. She hurries back inside with the child without offering a word.

Civilians do not cooperate with authorities. They may be communist partisans, but more likely, innocent citizens who live their lives in fear of their communist neighbors' retribution.

Prince continues moving fast on track. He has led us over four miles and now leads us clear of the group of homes. He hurries along a path that bisects a dense bamboo thicket. We follow him into the thicket in single file.

I warily study the stalks of bamboo at either side. My eyes search for anything out of place or any movement within the thicket, though only birds flapping wings are evident. I particularly keep an eye out for chartreuse balls that may be wrapped around stems along the trail. As we clear the thicket, the grounds open up and we fan out.

A man squats in the shade of a nearby avocado tree to our front. He rests there, smoking a cigarette. His eyes open wide once he sees us. He begins shifting anxiously in his position, as if contemplating whether to rise. Soon, he eyes our fast approach with trepidation, eyes wide and mouth open. A husky man with a muscular frame, he just keeps watching, as Prince closes the distance. He finally rises as Prince takes a seat twenty feet from him.

Tony waves to the trio of National Police. They move forward and grasp the smoker, roughly, bordering on cruelty. Not one word is spoken between them as they take him. Though the man shows painful discomfort at the treatment that he is harshly dealt, he accepts his treatment without protest. They bind the detainee's arms behind him, high above the elbows with a thin wire.

The man finally attempts to say something. He is rewarded with a harsh, resounding slap across the face that takes him to the ground.

CHAPTER 13

Grey clouds appear with greater frequency. They move past LZ English at a higher rate of occurrence, hurrying toward the northwest, on their way to the mountainous interior. With them comes, a milder temperature, but no rain, least not just yet, I am told.

I joy at standing at the front entrance, watching those clouds sweep across the sky. There is a comfort of sorts that their arrival brings. Perhaps they strike a chord with my memory of rain clouds in Louisiana. Or perhaps, it is a revival of my interest with more mundane things; currently, the illusion those clouds present of making the nearby mountain range appear so much more distinct and somehow much closer than before. With those water-bearing clouds also comes a sense of hope, maybe only an optimistic desire on my part, that they wash away all the killing, and allow this land to revert once again to being just a paradise.

Five days have passed since the last mission and nine since Prince leads us to the smoker arrested by the Nationalist Police. The last mission was a complete waste of time. An overnight shower, deep in the interior, erased all traces left behind by fleeing Viet Cong.

We are on stand down. No explanation has been provided as to why our team has been designated as so. This has been the case since our last mission. Nieman, who spends more and more time, quietly sulking in our hooch, offers no insight as to a reason and no one, as of yet, appears inclined to ask him.

Sergeant Claude Hooper drives off each morning in CTT1. He returns to Dog Patch in the evenings. He has had no contact with us since that initial group meeting weeks earlier and speculation as to his daily disappearances run rampant.

Seagram is set to depart in the morning. A sense of melancholy pervades. No party is planned and no one appears willing to break free of the current mood to contemplate such a thing. Besides, Tillman returns home to his wife the following week. The loss of two brothers so close together is no cause to celebrate.

"Warning, Whitman," it's Talmadge, calling out in a mocking tone. The tease is instantly followed by thunderous metallic clang of a ball bearing striking galvanized roofing.

Whitman leaps from his bunk startled by the sound. "Screw you, Talmadge, screw you and the horse that brought you. I've told you a thousand times that I wanted prior warning, not after you let loose the damn shit."

"What, and scare your pet away?" Talmadge laughs.

Inactivity brings forth a number of human endeavors. Some use the occasion to sharpen the mind through reading or even writing letters home. Cooper uses such occasions to clean and re-clean a weapon never fired in fear. Others use such opportunities to strengthen bonds of friendship, while others tend to test those bonds. But those measures are meant to distract thoughts, except for Cooper, who longs to fire his rifle at another human.

Thompkins approaches Nieman, who sits bored on a footlocker listening to Whitman and Talmadge squabble. The man leans his torso back, shying away from the approaching figure as he typically does. "Where does our sergeant in charge disappear to each morning?" Thompkins bluntly asks. "We use to think he was spending his time with boom boom girls or at the NCO club boozing it up, but he should have been flat broke, long before now. So, what is he up to?"

Nieman takes to his feet. "Sergeant Hooper has a friend at Brigade Intelligence. He has been promoting his innovative tracking ideas there, to anyone that will listen to him," he states, keeping a safe distance from Bert. "He seems to have had some luck. Operations, by way of S-2, has authorized his use of a LOH to do sky tracking," he adds with a chuckle.

Seagram steps forward to box in Nieman. "Well, that's good," he pronounces over the explanation. "He can only get himself wasted looking for tracks from up high, and he stays out of our hair while doing so."

Nieman breaks free of the box and starts for the front door. "You're right for now," he tells Seagram. "But the monsoon season is almost here. Choppers will be grounded, and what you young warriors fail to understand is that Hooper thinks trackers are supposed to be hardcore John Wayne, and therefore, as your leader, he, a heroic figure. He wants to maintain that image through the wet season, so he'll come up with something to continue doing just that," he adds and departs.

Red saunters over to Seagram and Thompkins. He is reading the front of an envelope. "I found this letter stuck behind my footlocker. You guys know who this fellow Newsom is?"

A gut-wrenching silence erupts. It is just as quickly followed by a state of silent anguish. Bert Thompkins and Seagram return to their bunks without replying.

Red recognizes he has dredged up something meant to stay buried. He turns, looking for help in understanding this sudden malady. Not even Tillman is up to the task of offering an explanation to the bewildered guy.

"Give it here," I tell him.

Red hands the envelope over to me. He appears eager to rid himself of his toxic finding.

"L J," Whitman calls out from his bunk. "What are you going to do with that letter?"

"It's from his parents," I explain, while studying the writing on the face of the envelope. "Am not sure. Maybe I'll read it, and then write to them of our sorrow over their son's death."

"Yeah, good idea," Baby Face solemnly adds. "A letter of sympathy from his buddies will console them."

"L J," it is Talmadge as he approaches. "Do you mind if some of us add our John Hancock to your letter?"

Black, ominous clouds slither between mountain tops and a dark grey sky. They shift and roll with exaggerated movement, melding with one another, but just as quickly breaking apart and reforming, all the while moving closer and closer.

Bolts of lightning, illuminate inside the water-laden spectacles, making them look like flickering fluorescent bulbs. Earsplitting, thunderous crashes sound after each of those flares. Their sounds reverberate, rumbling across mountains and down gorges, crashing hard against earth in a seeming attempt to crumble those very heights. Waves of the thunderous sound slam into us; they feel like concussion from explosives, pounding against eardrums and rattling at internal organs.

Those oncoming waves of cloud after cloud, with their abundant electrical discharges and booming thunder, depict an apocalyptic wrath about to descend upon us. Yet, I stand before a massive precipice, in awe of another of nature's great creations. It is a mesmerizing wonder that I gaze at, a gorge not unlike the Grand Canyon. It is one of those sights that by its mere natural grandeur, smothers a person's narcissism and makes us realize, what insignificant creatures, we truly are.

A caramel ribbon of water soars through the gorge. It lies hundreds of feet below where I stand. The fast-moving current, fed by rain storms, is littered with green branches and brown dead trunks. Water and rubbish smash against massive granite boulders along the edges of the river. I watch, fixated by the white water and the wood crashing into those boulders.

The helicopter that brought the team, less Prince and Red, has departed for LZ English ahead of the next cloud burst. Four of us have been deposited near a platoon-size compound, atop a mountain, God only knows where. The camp, a distance to our rear, is protected by massive bunkers, strings of concertina wire and deep ditches that surround the small basecamp. Each perimeter ditch is planted with punji sticks. Thousands of these sharpened bamboo spikes poke out from either side of the walls of each ditch. They look like quills on the back of a porcupine and serve as another line of defense.

ROKs, Republic of Korea troops, man the camp. They sport the South Korean flag high above one of the bunkers. The VC and NVA fear these Asian soldiers. They steer clear of engaging with them.

Our team has been sent here to support a Mike Strike Force, a unit of American Green Berets, working with local, indigenous people. They are hunting for Viet Cong tax collectors, reportedly hiding in the area. We are waiting on an element of that strike force to arrive and lead us to the rest of their unit.

Earsplitting thunder, followed immediately by a nearby electrical strike, startles me. I find myself on the ground, terrified and desperately searching for an explanation. A tree lies split feet from us and what remains standing, consumed in flames. In my attentiveness to the gorge and the fast-flowing river below, I failed to keep tabs on the approaching tempest. It is now directly overhead, causing havoc and mayhem all around me. A second bolt of lightning hits a boulder the opposite side of the gorge. A blue glow ensues where it struck, and lingers there for several seconds. Other electrical discharges follow, one after the other, lighting up the sky and striking around me like an artillery barrage from heaven. I am left to debate whether to rise and risk life, or stay on the wet ground till the worst of God's wrath passes.

Tony Puteoli and Bert Thompkins have taken a knee. They alternate watching between the strobe light effects of the fast-moving clouds and where the bolts of lightning hit. Whitman lies next to me, also prone. We eye one another, but quickly rise to take a knee, not wanting to appear frightened of a passing thunder storm.

A lightning bolt smashes into the slope to my right. I spot a group of men moving diagonally across just beyond where the bolt struck. It is hard to distinguish who they are in the grey distance, but it is clear that they are moving up toward us.

"Down there!" I point and bring that groups attention to the others.

Tony rises and braves the lightning. He trains his binoculars on the group. "Two Americans and nine Montagnard, likely our contacts," he advises and waves an arm to gather the groups attention. He continues to study the group as the rest of us take to our feet. "One of the Americans is signaling. Think he wants for us to head straight down to intersect with them." That said, he acknowledges with another wave, and we proceed down the steep incline.

It is a wet, slippery slope that has us struggling to maintain our feet as we head down. The ground is saturated with water, and there is little to grasp hold of to keep from slipping. We zig-zag our way down, stepping on the rear of tufts of grass to mitigate the dangerous angle of descent. Whitman soon manages to land on his ass. Tony comes back to help, but ends falling on his face.

Twenty minutes into our descent, the tail end of the thunderous tempest unleashes its heavy load. A downpour, unlike anything that I have ever experienced, commences. Our uniforms are instantly soaked, and our rate of descent virtually ceases. Visibility in the deluge is instantly limited to a meager foot or two, and presents a far more perilous trip down.

Suddenly, a half-naked man appears at my right. I nearly lose my balance, while hurrying to train my weapon on him. With the constant struggle at staying upright, I had forgotten the new arrivals. The man makes his way, nimbly alongside of me, barefoot, confident of footing, and grinning at my awkwardness at retaining balance.

The mountain tribesman wears only a black loin cloth. A black frontal flap with red and yellow lines along the edges covers his groin; otherwise, he is naked, totally exposed to the elements. His face shows age, but his physique is of rock-hard muscle.

Another Montagnard comes to view. Though not as old as the first, this one is as muscular as his elder, but wears what looks like checkered, boxer briefs and a faded tan shirt with half the buttons missing. Both are armed with M1 carbines that seem but extensions of upper limbs.

The rest of their group soon pop into view. There is only one American among them, a staff sergeant. A tall Asian with a serious demure, in camouflage and jungle boots, was mistaken by Tony as an American.

We take a seat, on the wet, muddy slope, as the downpour worsens. I feel flowing water, splashing and pushing against the radio at my rear. It is not a soaked ass that I now worry about; I start to wonder how long this torrential rain will go on and whether my radio will work afterward. If not, how am I and the team to get back to LZ English?

The elder tribesman takes a seat next to me, almost on top of me. I refuse to look toward him for fear of seeming to offer any sort of social interaction that may encourage the man, as to his purpose.

I am a provincial person with no backwoods, *National Geographic Magazine* experience until of late. It is not just his proximity to me that has me apprehensive, it is also the fact that he is practically naked.

I deflect my attention in Whitman's direction, who sits on the opposite side of me. Baby Face chuckles at my predicament. "Looks like you have a new boyfriend," he teases and breaks into hearty laughter through the ongoing downpour.

Facing Whitman turns into a greater challenge than dealing with the half-naked man next to me. Thompkins often refers to Baby Face as "That little Shit," and a reason is evident. It is time to put my embarrassment behind me and find the old man's purpose for having taken a seat next to me.

The tribesman's eyes widen once I face him, lighting up a warm smile, complete with gingivitis and severe tooth decay. When certain that he has my attention, he puts two fingers to his lips and nods to indicate he wants a cigarette.

"Whitman," I shout through rain noise. "Give me a cigarette."

"Do I look like, a cigarette dispensing machine?" he yells back. "Besides, this is not the time to take up smoking."

"Just give me the damn thing," I insist.

Baby Face fishes in a breast pocket and takes out a half empty pack. He hands it to me.

I, in turn, give the pack to the tribesman, wondering how he intends to smoke, much less light, a cigarette in this rainstorm. By the happy, yet puzzled look on the old fellow's face, I realize he is deliberating that very issue. A tap to his shoulder gets his attention. I grasp the front brim of my cloth boonie hat and lower my chin. I mime a smoking gesture under the shelter of the front of the brim. He understands and snatches my hat.

"Whitman, your Zippo," I demand.

Baby Face turns annoyed by yet another request, but then spots the tribesman sporting my hat and plants a grin on that cherub face of his. He shakes his head, chuckling as he does, but passes the cigarette lighter.

Halfway through the tribesman smoke, the rain slackens. I have no idea where the Montagnard has stowed the rest of Whitman's pack, but I suspect that Baby Face will not be wanting them back. Tony and the sergeant in charge of the motley crew stand, and we all continue with the descent. The old man is no longer in sight, and neither is my hat.

The Montagnard demonstrate no difficulty with negotiating their way down the muddy slope. They move down and across as sure-footed as mountain goats. Thompkins, to my far-left slips and takes Whitman down with him, who in turn takes down the staff sergeant to his front. The tribesmen find great humor with our inability to stay upright. They stop long enough to observe and laugh at the entertainment before continuing down.

Two hundred feet from the base of the abyss, the rain ceases altogether, although rain water continues to cascade down the slope. A haze lingers, congregating at the bottom of the gorge. From that misty haze, I spy a dozen heads emerge along the bank of the river, running to the left. Seconds later, I spy a larger party giving chase, and a split second later, a firefight is underway. Suddenly, a loud commotion erupts around me. It sounds like Apache war cries and adds to the sudden chaos of the firefight below. Montagnard hop and jump past me, eager to join their brethren. In that confusion, I managed to do what I have succeeded avoiding until now. I lose my footing. To my horror, both legs suddenly fly upward. A sense of free fall overtakes me. All I see is dark sky. I start to wonder how far down the slope this aerial flight will take me and what shape I will be in after striking ground.

My back is first to make contact with the soft ground, forcing the radio hard against the spine. There is no time to suffer the pain; the sounds of battle are all around, and yet, I suddenly find myself outpacing the others on the way down the slope. I am sliding on what feels like a water chute, hydroplaning straight toward the VC, all while on my back. My vision is restricted by the angle of descent. I cannot see what awaits me below, although I hear that loud kak, kak, kak, kak of the VCs' weapons. I kick and kick at unseen ground in search of traction, but fail to find a foothold in the liquid soil. It is a matter of seconds before a burst from enemy rifles rip into me. I pray that the bullets not strike my groin or my face.

Something jerks hard at the right strap of the radio pack. I am suddenly upright, and my hat flashes by to my right.

A woman to my front, carrying an SKS, tries to escape the murderous crossfire by climbing a formation of massive boulders at the edge of the river. She collapses and disappears among those rocks. To my right, an Asian male abruptly turns to face our group. His chest jerks forward, while his shoulders pop back. An expression of horrid shock on his face, he drops his rifle and collapses face first into the bank of the river.

It is over. Just as fast as it started, it ends without me having fired a shot. That silence that generally succeeds each of my previous firefights, does not occur on this singular occasion. Montagnard are busy, calmly chattering to one another while gathering weapons and equipment from the dead. They rummage through pockets and even check oral cavities of the dead, all while conversing as if nothing occurred. Two teen boys, in loin cloths and matching vests, stand on one of the large boulders discussing something between rocks. One breaks away and hurries up the river bank. He has a machete strapped to his back that he withdraws as he runs. The other is now lying flat on the boulder, reaching down into the gap between stones. Just when I suspect that gravity will take its toll on the boy, he crawfishes his way back out, holding an SKS.

I join Whitman, who sits nearby, watching things unfold. We both watch the returning teen, rejoin his partner atop the boulder. He brings with him a ten-foot bamboo pole. He cuts several long slits on one end of the thick pole. Together, the two teens lower the cut section of bamboo between the rocks and start to rotate the pole round and around. Satisfied at their purpose, they proceed to pull up on the bamboo, weighted down by a load at the other end.

A curious Baby Face rises to climb the boulder. He halts once he sees long, black hair tightly entangled around the pole's bottom. A head soon emerges. One of the youths grabs the hair and pulls up a woman's body. Something, light, pasty grey in color, slips out from her skull. Whitman vomits at the sight and runs back to retake his seat.

I rise and walk a short distance. Behind me, Baby Face continues to empty his gut.

Are we to end up desensitized to such sights as these young boys are? I walk further off as Whitman continues to vomit.

Something shiny silver in a bush catches my attention. The body of a dead, male Vietnamese with pockets turned inside out lies nearby. I approach the object carefully, fearing it may be a booby trap. It is a camera, a near new Nikon 35mm camera.

CHAPTER 14

We were sent to perform a mission deep into the interior with no conceivable means of extraction other than air or days of difficult hiking through enemy patrolled territory. Continuous rainfall prevents our being picked up by a helicopter, and my radio has stopped working. Rain water may have penetrated the electronics inside the casing, or perhaps, the slide down the gorge damaged the darn thing, but we have lost all contact to our rear lifeline. The only way out and back to safety is to hike back.

It took five, miserable days to work our way back to LZ English, with no one in the rear having any clue of where we might be found, should they perchance come searching for us. A cold, wet, sleepless night, just the four of us, was spent along the bank of the swollen river with dead tax collectors lying but yards away. A day long struggle to climb back up the mushy slope of the gorge followed. Finally, four days and three sleepless nights of fearing for our lives, as we trekked through enemy controlled terrain to Kon Tum. There we caught an equally harrowing helicopter flight to LZ English.

We arrive at just past noon on the fifth day, more tired than angry at the predicament that we were abandoned to endure. CTT2 that we left parked near the chopper pad is gone. Someone from Dog Patch must have come and got it, caring little as to how we should get back. An angry Puteoli takes this as yet another sign of mistreatment and desertion of his team. Whatever the case, we are left to hump our exhausted carcasses back to Dog Patch. At least the sun is not visible. A low ceiling obscures sight beyond an altitude of a few hundred feet, sparing us the heat.

A Brigade jeep, with an officer on the front passenger seat, passes. We offer a salute, as we trudge onward, much too tired to pay particular attention to the officer. The vehicle halts and backs up, which instantly garners paranoid attention. No doubt, the others, as I am, are wondering if one of us failed to salute, and who that guilty party may be. Thompkins shoves Whitman in the back, who instantly denies any wrong doing.

No less than a brigadier general, exits the vehicle. The short, thin officer wears a gruff expression as he nears, and he walks straight at me. Anxiety overwhelms me. I know that I presented a salute, so what does he want with me?

"Where is your headgear, soldier?" he barks at me.

His question stuns me. I had forgotten until just now that the Montagnard had taken off with my hat. With the constant overcast skies, there has been little need of the protection it offered from overhead, but now, back to a military regime that requires head cover when outdoors, I recognize the seriousness of the infraction. "Sir, I last saw it during a firefight up in the highlands. That was several days back. We just returned, and I have not had a chance to replace it."

The General examines all of us closely before engaging in further communication. His expression appears to soften. I begin to sense that I may survive this encounter. "What unit are you with?" He now asks.

"Sir, we are Combat Trackers with the 75th Combat Tracker Detachment," Tony joins in. "We just got off a chopper from a mission deep in the interior and are heading to our compound."

Tony's explanation stuns me. There is a sense of esteem in his voice when relating the unit that he serves in. Never once have I felt the slightest bit of pride in serving with the 75th Combat Tracker unit. I have been too scared with what we do or too angry at the leadership to take pride in the unit. Perhaps, if I survive this war, in the years to follow, I may look back with deep gratification at having been a part of this organization, but more likely, of having served with great teammates.

The General continues to study us, but he eventually nods his head as if satisfied by our explanations.

"Sir, I took this camera from a dead Viet Cong tax collector," I tell the general. I hold out the camera to present the Nikon for him to take. "There is film in the camera that may have some intelligence value. I've been hauling it around the past five days, and I am tired of safeguarding it. Can you see that it gets to the proper parties?"

He takes the Nikon from my hands and starts walking back to his jeep. "Get something on that bare head, first chance you get," he barks back at me before climbing into his vehicle.

"Will do, and Sir," I shout to the General. "If possible, I would like to get that Nikon back."

Thompkins and Whitman instantly shove me on the back, although, I doubt the Brigadier heard my final remarks.

Though it is near supper, and I am famished, sleep prevails over all other bodily needs. I dreamed that Tillman shook me, over and over to say goodbye, but I just did not have the strength to wake up. It is not until next morning, when Thompkins shakes me that I can pry open my eyes.

"Time for eggs, pancakes, sausage, bacon, hash browns, chip beef on toast, and biscuits," Bert Thompkins explains, grinning with that long and generally austere face of his. "And of course, a bucket load of coffee."

I sit up to a loud growl from deep within my belly. The jungle boots and wet socks that I had not taken off once the past week are still on my feet. Some dry mud caked to the bottom of my boots came off during my sleep and rest scattered across the bottom of the blanket.

"No need to shower just yet," Thompkins adds as he moves to Whitman's bunk. "It's raining cats and dogs outside. You'll have plenty of time to clean up when we get back." That said, he flips the bunk over, with Whitman in it.

Baby Face leaps off the floor, startled and staggering, as he searches for signs of imminent danger. Others break into laughter. I feel for the terror Whitman suffers, but I too break into laughter, perhaps louder than the others; it is after all, Whitman.

We return through the ongoing, heavy downpour after a hearty breakfast. Once ponchos are removed and left to dry, the others return to their bunks to read, write or listen to music. Tony, Bert, and Baby Face wait on the rain to abate, before heading to the shower.

I, on the other hand, strip off the filthy clothing that I have worn and slept in for nearly a week. My stench is overwhelming. A bar of soap in hand, I run yelling and screaming out the back of the hooch and into the rain, buck naked, like some crazed lunatic.

Sometime during or since that mission to the gorge, I have lost some of my provincialism. Whether it is because of the exposure to the near naked Montagnard tribesmen, or perhaps because of four days of having crossed mountains and overflowing streams through heavily patrolled Indian territory, that I now joy at life to a point, of unabashedly appearing in the open without clothes.

Whitman soon runs out, naked and with equal exuberance, but no sooner turns to griping, "Oh crap! This rain water is ice cold." Tony follows and finally, our most dignified member, Bert, joins. We carry on like a bunch of delinquents playing in the rain, albeit totally nude. We stomp on standing puddles, splash at each other from those very pools, and look up toward the heavens, arms spread out to the sides and mouths open to catch the falling rain. Thompkins attempts a Scottish Highland dance but ends slipping down on his bare ass.

Sergeant Claude Hooper in CCT 1 happens to drive by soon after. A pale looking, somber lieutenant with black glasses is riding shotgun, and what looks like a canvas suitcase, is on the officer's lap. Hooper watches us lathering up in the rain. A curled upper lip and a sneer of angry contempt shows he is not pleased with our antics. He mutters something to the officer, but continues on without a word to us.

It occurs to me that Hooper has not spoken to us since that initial meeting weeks earlier. He has become as elusive as Prattchet, but then, who cares.

Tony surprisingly chases after the vehicle, but soon stops as it disappears into a curtain of falling water.

"Damn it, Hooper, we need to talk," he angrily yells out through that hard downpour.

Loud thunder sounds, and lightning flashes above us. I flinch hard, almost dropping to the soggy ground. The noise and sight have my heart pounding. For some bizarre reason, I feel vulnerable to the storm. My nakedness has me suddenly feeling far more exposed to a lightning storm, than I was atop that mountain overlooking the gorge. I hurry inside for my towel, running through guys standing, watching, and laughing at us from the doorway.

The other three quickly follow, and just in time. "Got company," Cooper points to a vehicle's approach. A Brigade Headquarters' jeep is coursing its way through the heavy downpour toward our compound. The vehicle drives past us, and heads directly to the HQ hooch. Cooper sticks his black-haired head and his shirtless upper torso out the back door for a view of the visitors. He is instantly rewarded for his curiosity by a sudden squall of wind and rain that hoses him down.

"We at least had the intelligence to take off our clothes before playing in the rain, you idiot," Whitman chuckles at Cooper's misfortune. "But since you are now wet, why not stroll over to HQ and find out who's paying us a call from Brigade and why."

"Screw you Whitman," Cooper snaps back. He heads for his bunk to read the July 22, 1969, *Stars and Stripes*.

"Back at you buddy," Baby Face grins as he continues ragging Cooper.

"Boys, boys, please, your language," Talmadge intercedes, faking shock at their coarse language. "We have children in our midst," he adds, pointing at Red.

"Screw you too, Talmadge," Red retorts.

"Hey guys!" Cooper hollers. He springs to his feet, fully animated by an article in the military paper that he holds. "Two Americans landed on the moon, day before yesterday. There is even a picture of one stepping down on moon dirt for the first time ever. Can you dig that!"

"Yeah, right," Red states, but moves next to Cooper to read over the man's shoulder to verify the improbable claim.

"Why they want to go up there?" Talmadge begs to know. "Vietnam is much prettier and far safer."

"To confirm whether the moon is made of Swiss cheese or not," I laughingly answer, though, like Red, I, too approach Cooper, looking for confirmation of such an implausible claim.

Undaunted by all the commentary and skepticism, Cooper continues to relate the event. "An Aldrin and an Armstrong landed using something called a lunar module, with barely enough fuel to return to their Apollo Spacecraft. They were on the moon for close to a day."

Silence pervades. Faces convey that all now contemplate at a magnificent, scientific achievement of sending and retrieving a spacecraft to the moon, and the courage of two Americans to risk all for the opportunity to venture to grounds outside their own planet. A sense of pride overtakes us, as if we, had a part in that spectacular achievement.

"Oh, darn!" Whitman suddenly laments, bringing us all back to a place where no scientific achievement can safely retrieve us from, where only time and a bit of luck can accomplish that feat. "Too late, Coop," he continues. "The jeep has left."

"Can't imagine anyone being here about a mission," Tony now speculates out loud, watching the vehicle disappear into the rain. "They would have called, and what kind of tracks would they expect us to find in this weather?"

Thompkins steps forward with a possible or perhaps a wishful explanation. "Maybe they are here to deliver orders to ship Nieman, Hooper and Prachett back to the World," he offers pulling up his trousers. "Wouldn't that be just dandy?"

"Coop, good buddy," Baby Face cries out, "I want that paper when you finish with it."

"Screw you, Whitman."

A short time later, Nieman runs in, out the rain. He walks straight for me, exhibiting a perturbed looking face. But, before he can get a word out, Thompkins intercepts him.

"What did Brigade want?" Bert demands to know. "Were they by some chance here to complain about your treatment of us?"

No reply is offered to either of Thompkins' sarcastic questions. Nieman doesn't even shy his head away from the man as he generally would when listening to someone speak to him. Instead, he snarls while he casts something at me. I catch it before it strikes me; it's a new boonie hat with the 173rd emblem patch sewn up front. There is no joy on Nieman's face when flinging the head gear, and I suspect a verbal reprimand is soon to follow, which I give a rat's ass about.

"Hey guys!" I scream, waving the headgear joyfully about and preempting or at least delaying Nieman's chastisement. "Check this out."

Thompkins snatches the hat out of my hands. "Well, I'll be damned. That General must have felt sorry for your ass or was impressed by your bullshit, enough so to award you with his token of appreciation."

"Is there a Congressional Medal of Honor that comes with that hat?" Whitman chuckles.

Nieman takes back the hat from Thompkins and throws it once again at me, looking angrier. "In the future, any intel you gather in the field, any intel," he screams at me, "is to be turned over to me or to Sergeant Hooper. Any intel, do you hear?" he once again shouts. "Sergeant Hooper and I will decide if that intel is worth turning over to S-2, not you."

Tony approaches, sporting a curious look. "There must have been some good shit on that camera for you and Hooper to get so pissed. I guess LJ stole the thunder with Brigade that you boys thought you might take for your own. What did S-2 find on that camera's film?"

Nieman now focuses his anger on the team leader, "This is not about garnishing credit, this is about procedure."

"Don't give me that bullshit about following procedure," Puteoli unexpectedly goes off on Nieman. "You and Hooper have no idea what proper procedure is, and tell that son-of-a-bitch I want to talk to him about his failure at procedure for extracting a team once the mission is complete."

Nieman heads for the door without offering further discussion, far angrier than when he first arrived.

"Hey!" I yell. "What about my camera?"

It rains and rains. There is no letup in the precipitation. It comes down in many forms: torrential, hard, light and even a super, heavy mist, but it comes down nonstop, day after day and night after night. For two weeks, moisture descends from the heavens, obscuring vision, at times to a mere foot or two, but never allowing sight beyond one hundred feet. The rice paddies in the valley below us are not visible, much less the heights behind them. I have not caught sight of either, since the seasonal showers commenced.

Tony had remarked that the monsoon season can last several months. "The worst is likely yet to come," he had offered, which dampened spirits.

A gloomy mood prevails in the hooch in the days that follow. The constant greyness of outside and the lack of a visible sun affects us all. We are confined to the inside by the rain, venturing out only to eat or to use the latrine. The sound of rain hitting galvanized roofing, which initially offered a lulling sound for good sleep, is now an irritant, reminding us we are prisoners of the weather.

There is nothing left in the hooch to read that has not been read and passed around. No one plays at cribbage, spades or hearts. Those that had an interest in multi-player card games have returned to the World. Cards are now used by the interned for playing solitaire. Bickering also prevails, at times approaching open physical confrontations, most of which involve Baby Face, and Red or Cooper. The fabric of our comradeship is unraveling, and if Tony is correct on the duration of this season, I question whether we can survive it.

How locals accomplish anything under such prolonged and devastating weather conditions is a wonder. This constant downpour has to be a severe hindrance to any and all forms of human activity. But what about all that run-off? How do the Vietnamese deal with the deluge? As this is an annual event, they must have developed ways to protect their homes and themselves from the oceans of rain water accumulation. But there is nothing that I have seen that looked like flood water management or control. Homes and businesses must surely be inundated with water. Lucky for us, LZ English is located on high ground, and Dog Patch sits on a knoll on that high ground.

The constant rains at least prevent our being called out on missions. Tracks wash away in the rain and helicopters pilots cannot see through downpours. We are grounded, and we are left struggling to find things to keep us occupied. I spend far too much of my time trying to peer through the curtain of precipitation for a glimpse of the paddies below or the mountains beyond. It is a futile effort, but one that spares me the ongoing bickering and dull discussions of others.

Our laundry lady shows up with our clean uniforms, weeks late, but a welcome sight, nonetheless. She is an unattractive woman with buck teeth, but of good disposition. The wife of a poorly paid RVN soldier, she supplements his meager salary by doing laundry. Today, she braves ongoing showers, holding up a broken umbrella of bamboo and wax paper construction and a loaded laundry bag over a shoulder. Two children, a boy no more than eight and a younger girl accompany her. The small girl holds a good, cloth umbrella over her and over the boy, that struggles with an equally loaded laundry bag on his shoulders. By their soaked clothing, one can deduce that the umbrellas are meant to keep the laundry bags and their freshly, starched contents dry, more so than themselves.

Talmadge is the only one of us that hand washes his uniforms. They go on him wrinkled and smelling of mildew. No one complains, for everyone knows his money goes to his family. On this singular occasion of the laundry woman showing up with her children, Talmadge takes the opportunity to entertain himself and the kids. He makes his way to greet and amuse the young pair. While the rest of us pay the mother and hand her new batches of filthy clothes, Talmadge has a go behind small ears, extracting delicious treats for the amazed pair. Not so much as a sing-song word is offered by the kids for the offerings, but then, broad smiles on happy faces offer more than mere words can ever express.

Our Tennessean returns to sit at his bunk, quite content with himself.

"Carl, where did you learn to do your magic tricks?" I ask him while stowing my clean laundry. "You're darn good at it."

He lays his head on his pillow and stares up toward the rafters at nothing in particular, before explaining. "I worked at a construction company after Pop died. Every pay day, after work, I would bring the money that I made home to Ma. I would keep just enough to buy a candy bar for each of my brothers and sisters. You know," he suddenly perks up and smiles at me, "after a while, it got to be a game of sorts. They'd be awaiting me to come home those days. So, I'd hide the candy, and I'd tell them that I was robbed of treats on the way home. Then, I would pretend to find the stolen candy bars, mysteriously hidden on them and accuse them of having robbed me."

He says nothing else. He just lays back on his bunk with a simple, and yet, so humble a smile that I envy.

Life takes each of us down separate paths. Some of us journey through life along paths cleared and graded by those who cherish us, or through simple good fortune. Others, denied such opportunities by providence, are made to wander over rough, primitive walkways. One would think there would be an inherent advantage for those going down paved roads. Yet Carl Talmadge, relegated to back trails by his father's death, shows no detectable wallowing of self-pity over his life's path. He appears to suffer no less for his lot, and instead, he makes the best of the little things and thrives doing so.

I make my way to the front door of the hooch, teary-eyed at the Tennessean's misfortune in life and wallowing in grief at the pathetic, narcissistic life that I suddenly rediscover to be mine.

The rain finally lets up and stops, but only for brief periods of time. This intermittent halt between downpours, becomes the new normal, at least for now. But when the rain returns after a short interlude, it appears to come down that much harder.

During one of these early-on intervals, Tony Puteoli scurries over to the HQ hooch to have it out with Hooper and the Scout Dog Platoon leader. Tony has not, until now, had the opportunity to file a complaint of our being stranded far from the nearest American outpost and abandoned to fend for ourselves through days of enemy infested jungles and mountains to reach safety. Claude Hooper has not been around, and according to a now curt and ill-tempered Nieman, neither has Prattchet. On this occasion, both CTT vehicles and the deuce and a half are on the compound. Tony seizes the opportunity to vent his frustration on those in charge. He went intent on extracting a clear understanding concerning committing a team into an unsecured site with no conceivable means of withdrawing that team once the job is done. He has waited for this chance for weeks, and he went there openly displaying a poor attitude toward our leaders, but a determination to make them understand safety issues.

The interval suddenly ends, and the rain returns, so does a fuming, Puteoli. Tony heads for his bunk and plops himself on top.

No one expected him to have any level of success with his demands. The best anyone expected from the front office was a, "We'll take it under advisement."

Our NCOIC, Claude Hooper, is far too concerned with impressing Brigade with his new ideas for tracking to worry himself with tried and proven, standard operating procedures. Though all choppers are grounded by the weather, Hooper feels it necessary to continue stoking Brigade's imagination with his ideas, until the weather allows for their implementation. Nieman, who has been by-passed for the NCOIC position, but continues to perform those very functions, is too resentful to care what happens to us.

"Any luck?" Bert Thompkins asks.

"Nope! Hooper only said that we got back safely, so why all the belly aching, and claims we lack balls and spine," he mopes. "I threaten to go to S-3 and gripe to them. He said that I would find myself a grunt before I knew what had happened. Thought hard about taking swings at that piece of shit."

"Had he slept out in the rain, with enemy patrols crawling all around, he would have a different attitude about this matter," I throw in my two cents.

"That bastard needs fragging," Baby Face injects his disappointment.

"By the way, I just found out that Prattchet rotated back to the World days ago," Tony suddenly recalls. "The new platoon leader for the Scout Dogs is stuck in Cam Ranh Bay. Hooper has been in charge of the entire enchilada all this time.

"That Fat Ass?" Whitman cuts loose on the man once again. "He has no idea what Scout Dogs do, much less care for the danger they endure each day. That jerk never bothered to inquire or even show concern for our disappearance while we skulked through enemy terrain to Kon Tum. If he cares less what happens to us, why would he give a shit about them? We are all going to die here, because of that clown's incompetence."

"Have you noticed how much weight Hooper's put on since he got here?" Cooper pipes in to change the discussion to suit him. "He looks ready to pop out of his fatigues."

"Did they say anything on whether my radio has come back from repairs?" I inquire.

"Didn't get a chance to ask," Tony answers. "But I did see Nieman playing with your Nikon camera, and your VC 9mm is on Hooper's desk, serving as a paper weight."

We all resume our routine at nothing that we were engaged in prior to Tony's return. Talmadge has a go with his sling shot at a fat, wet rat scurrying across the joists. Red and Whitman, startled by the bearing striking the metal roofing, yell, cursing him once again at a lack of prior warning. Thompkins picks up a worn copy of *Stars and Stripes* lying on Whitman's bunk, and unfortunately, Cooper follows me to my corner of the hooch.

"L J, got an idea how to get your camera back," he claims. "Next time Nieman comes over, follow my lead."

Cooper has been in a feud with Nieman for weeks. He considers himself a Cherry for not having been out on a mission, and he blames Nieman for that. While I have a deep vested interest in the Nikon, I am leery at going along with Cooper's undisclosed plot.

Later that day, Nieman enters our Hooch. Though he comes through the rain and without a clipboard, he wears that authoritarian, mission assignment face. We all take stock at what he is about to say.

"Team 2, prepare for a week-long outing," he starts.

"No can do," Baby Face immediately butts in. "Our swimming trunks and goggles have not yet arrived. Can't see tracks left behind under feet of muddy water without them," he continues to snickers and outright laughter.

Nieman turns and snaps at Whitman, "Well, you're not doing the damn war effort any good just laying on your ass around here! So, if you're finished with your bullshit, I'd like to continue," he snarls.

"Small units of VCs have been engaging paratroopers up north with nighttime hit and runs," he continues. "Tomorrow, Team 2 will be driven as far as possible to one of those units. There, you will be readily available to locate those indigent people responsible for the nighttime shootouts."

Tony speaks up. There is a controlled, yet angry undertone to his voice. "How are we to track in rain?" He continues with a series of questions deliberately meant to disarm and agitate Nieman. "What the hell you mean as close as possible? Is my team's radio back from repairs and is there a plan for getting us out at the end of that week?" He demands to know of Nieman, before getting at the meat of his suspicion. "Is this about my chewing Hooper out?"

Nieman is taken back by the series of questions, as I suspect was intended by Tony. His eyes flash right and left in their sockets as he thinks. "Red and Prince will not be going," he states, buying more time to formulate answers. "There are no roads leading to the precise location that you are going, and you go without a radio. The precise location is on the map in the office. When you are calm and ready to see where you are going, come up front. And yes, this is punishment, but not of my doing."

While everyone contemplates what has just been said, Cooper uses the opportunity to head Nieman from the front door. "Nieman," he hollers at the man. "After lunch, L J and I are going to Brigade HQ to check on the whereabouts of his camera. Can you suggest, who might be the proper party for us to ask?"

CHAPTER 15

What sounds like an angry ocean comes to my ears. In spite of a hard falling rainstorm drowning out most sounds, ocean waves pounding against a coastline, now seep through. For ten miles, we rode north on Highway 1, but now the road trends to the north east, bringing us closer to the South China Sea. That harsh crash of surf against beach, as wave after wave slams the shore, evokes a sense of helplessness against the wrath of nature. It is a continuous pommeling of water against earth that gets louder and louder, until even the sound of receding sea water is discernable.

Bert Thompkins rises to look for the source of those sounds at his rear. He is instantly forced to retake the shelter of his seat by hard, stinging rain.

Tony, Baby Face, Bert, and I huddle next to the cab of CCT 2. We have done so for some time, and we are soaking wet. We brought no ponchos with us, having deemed them useless for where we are going and for what we are expected to do. Talmadge and Cooper are inside the cab, trying to stay dry.

It has rained hard the entire way, often limiting road visibility to just feet. We had hoped to arrive at the first leg of our journey by eight, but travel through this hard rain has been painstakingly slow.

The rain temporarily slackens and visibility improves. A tall bunker along the road comes into sight. "Coop, let us out next to that bunker," Tony shouts over the rain. "That's our jump off point."

Cooper pulls the truck next to a massive two-level bunker, capable of holding a full squad of soldiers. We gather our gear and climb out.

A sudden and unexpected view to the west awes me. I rode on the vehicle's side bench, facing east, and I am totally unprepared for the sight that now greets me. Some three miles due west, the mountains loom; between them and us, lies a vast inland sea created by flood waters. Scattered about that ocean of water, on the few high points of land, are four, small, farm villages. Cut off from each other by flood waters, the farm shanties resemble small native isles in the midst of a sea.

Tony shouts up to Grunts manning the bunker, "Which way to Bravo Company CP?"

"Over at the base of that mountain," a Grunt shouts down, pointing west. "You can't get to it walking straight there."

"So, how in the hell do we get there?" a confused Thompkins demands to know.

"See those two dead trees three hundred yards down?" the Grunt points to the southwest at what looks like grey sticks protruding out the water. "Go to the tree on the left. Wilson and Bradley will direct you from there." He then adds in passing, "Watch out for deep holes under the water and don't deviate from my instructions."

Thompkins, the tallest of our group is first to jump into that inland sea. The brown water immediately reaches his groin. "The bottom is pretty soft," he yells back.

We proceed to wade through water on our way to the dead-looking trees. Mere yards from where we started, the water rises above our waist, and the bottom gets mushy. Our going is suddenly that much harder and our progress slows.

"Don't deviate from my instructions," Baby Face mocks the Grunt while struggling against the high water and soft bottom. "A boat would be of greater help than that slug."

Thompkins cries out before disappearing under the water. He back peddles, cries out and slips under once again, before finally making it back up. "Found one," he calmly states, water dripping off his chin. He then proceeds around the unseen hole, cautiously feeling his way with a left foot.

It is a treacherous journey that we are engaged in to reach the trees. We had no idea the difficulty of the trek prior to jumping into the water. Worse, I suspect we have little idea of the true danger that we course through.

The water eventually reaches chest level. We are constantly forced to detour around what Thompkins determines to be holes. For some time, we struggle at moving through water with weapons held above our heads. Muscles ache and burn from the strange and unusual means of locomotion required to propel us through high water. Exhaustion soon shows on faces, and the trees look just as far as when we first started. To add to our woes, the rain now returns with a vengeance.

"Can't see shit in this rain," Thompkins calls out, blinded by heavy splatters of rain. "You guys see the trees?"

Whitman at the rear yells back, "What?"

"Tighten up," Tony hollers. "There are no snipers about. Bert, keep moving straight."

We struggle for what seems an eternity. A look of helplessness and despair are added to the exhaustion on everyone's face. Still no sight of trees and the water level is now at the base of my neck.

Bert glances up at his watch to check the time. "Oh crap," he hollers. "My Timex has water in it."

"It's five to eleven," I shout, checking the Seiko, above the water.

"Oh, hell no," Whitman shouts from behind me. "We've been at this for over two hours?"

"And, we have no idea where those trees are," Bert adds. "Can't see more than a foot with all this splashing rain."

"Whitman, hand LJ your weapon," Tony has to shout the order to be heard, and then hands me his. "Squat down. I'm getting on your shoulders," he tells Baby Face. "I want to find where those two suckers are."

"There's going to be one serious blanket party once we get back," Baby Face announces while handing me his M-16 and hat. "Only question is, if it's for one crazy-ass European, or both him and our fat ass sergeant." Having spoken his mind, Baby Face disappears under water and shoots up his arms.

Tony takes firm hold of the hands and climbs Whitman's shoulders. "Two o'clock, eighty feet or so," he shouts down to Bert. "There's a rope tied to the upper branches from one tree to the other. I think I see two guys on a mound of dirt at the base of the tree to the right."

Eighty feet, in most cases, is nothing to traverse. It can generally be covered at a walking pace in under a minute. But, when you are pushing water, neck deep in it, and blindly feeling for deep spots with a foot before proceeding forward, it can take a considerable amount of time.

"This is bullshit," Baby Face whines while taking back his weapon and hat. "There has to be an easier way to get to that CP. Can't imagine having to haul food, ammo and supplies in this manner."

"The trees are just one step of our way to the CP," I add. As soon as those words escaped my lips, the implication on others hits me, and just as quickly sympathize at the disheartening frustration those words evoke.

We finally reach the leafless, stump of wood thirty minutes later. The tree sits on a mound, although that mound lies under brown water. But, for the first time these past two and a half hours, we stand in less than knee high water.

The rain continues, but the added height allows us to see the other tree sixty feet away and two dark shapes huddled underneath.

I find myself wanting to get back into deeper water. The rain and wind are cold against those wet parts of me now above the water.

"Wilson, Bradley, can you hear me?" Thompkins calls out.

"They're gone," one of the Grunts at the other tree hollers back. "We relieved them an hour ago. You the dog people from English?"

"Yeah!" Tony hollers back. "But we left the dog back at home."

"Good thing," the voice from the other side shouts back, "cause, you have to cross the ditch holding tight to the rope. The water flow in there is a bitch! Lost a guy from third platoon last week when he was swept away. Your weight and the flow will take you under for ten to twelve seconds, so don't loose it. Hold tight to that rope and scoot across as fast as you can."

"What ditch is he talking about?" Whitman asks as we all search the inland sea for it.

It is the first time that I see a difference in the water. Between us and the opposite tree, a thirty-foot-wide ribbon of fast-flowing water, apart from the rest, speeds to the northeast across the stationary waters of the inland sea. It is only visible by the flow and quickness of that current. Nothing but brown water shows in that rapid flow. Whatever may have been lying about to be washed away, is by now in the middle of the South China Sea on its way to the Philippines.

We sling weapons and secure hats in preparation to cross. "This is bullshit," Baby Face mutters as he slings his M-16. "Bullshit I tell you. My congressman will hear about this."

"Do you even know who your congressman is?" Bert asks. He takes hold of the rope without waiting on a reply. Moving hand over hand along the rope, he proceeds into the water and across an unseen ditch.

"Don't let go of that rope for any reason," Tony cautions Thompkins.

This is not a new exercise for us. We all trained to hang and move quickly on parallel bars at basic training camp. We learned to move swiftly across those bars, while a madman of a drill instructor, screamed, sweet words of encouragement. What is different now, is the fast-flowing water underneath that just last week, took the life of a paratrooper.

Bert's weight soon carries him down into chest level water. Shortly afterwards, he disappears under the murky water altogether.

The rest of us pensively watch. We watch for what seems a lifetime until his hands and then the rest of him return above water near the opposite side.

"L J," Tony calls out. "You go next. I'll cross last to make sure Whitman does nothing stupid. Warn Bert to be on the lookout, just in case."

"Hey, I take exception to your remarks," Baby Face states, looking mildly amused, which results in further cautioning from Tony.

I work my way across the rope with little effort, at least until my feet enter the fast flow. Feet, legs and torso are soon swept up by the powerful surge of rushing water. A deep breath, I hold tighter to the rope, close my eyes and hurry under the fast current. It seems forever that I move one hand over the other to work myself across, but I soon pop up and climb out the water.

Bert and I are soon joined by Baby Face and Tony. We sit on the muddy mound with the two Grunts, catching our breath.

Baby Face starts a discussion with a short, thin, black soldier that has been watching us quietly. "What's your name? He asks the soldier.

"Jones," the soldier replies with an unexpected deep voice for someone his size. "Luther Jones."

"Luther, I bet half the black soldiers in this army are Joneses," Whitman quips, "and nearly all are from Mo Town."

"It could be worse," Jones smiles, playing along. "It could be Smith, from Podunk Town," he adds to laughter while he points at his partner.

"Luther, you got a dry cigarette?" Whitman begs of the soldier.

"Got Camels," the grunt says as he leans forward to offer us all a cigarette.

"That works for me," Baby Face, our only smoker, rejoices at taking one. "So long as it is not one of those Picayune brand cigarettes. They'll make your head spin faster than a drag on a joint."

"Where you from, Jones?" I ask the friendly paratrooper.

"Rochester, New York," he answers.

"Volunteer or draftee?" Bert wants to know.

"I got drunk on graduating high school," he says all smiles. "A bunch of us bar-hopped that night. I ended up slugging a bartender at our last bar when he demanded ID's. Next day, a judge gave me a choice, a year at Attica or two in the Army, so you could say that I volunteered."

"You know," I chuckle, "judges recruit far more volunteers these days than recruiting sergeants."

We spend a good half-hour recovering from our meager three-hundred-yard journey. The pair of young Grunts do not mind, they are pleased to have company.

Tony eventually gets us back on course. "How much further to the CP?" He asks of the senior member of the pair.

"You got a mile plus to go," the soldier answers. "You've humped the worst part already. There are no holes or ditches left to negotiate, and the water is only waist to chest high." He and Tony stand for a better view through the rain. "The CP is four hundred yards south of that old church steeple," he adds. "You should get there in a couple hours."

"Couple of hours to cover what should only take minutes," Whitman protests while taking to his feet. "Hell, Lynden Johnson will hear from me about this."

"We've had a new president the past eight months," Jones smiles as he corrects Whitman.

Baby face is now back in the water with the rest of us. The water is at chest level. "So, who's the new tenant at the White House," he calls over his shoulder.

"Richard M. Nixon," Luther Jones cries through cupped hands to be heard over the rain.

"Do you think he'll get us out of this shit?" Whitman shouts back at Jones.

"Sure, hope so," Jones hollers back. "I just got here and have eleven months before I DEROS back to the World."

Rain continues to come down hard. It pelts heads and stings faces hard. What doesn't strike us, splashes hard on the water, marring our visibility to twenty feet, and often less. I start to worry that the water level will continue to rise in this downpour. Exhausted and burdened with wet clothing, supplies, and equipment, an extra one to two feet of water can drown us all. After all, Jones' partner, Smith, claimed the water would only be waist to chest high, and it is now at our necks.

We struggle on, wading through high water for what seems hours since leaving the ditch. An occasional sighting of the old Catholic church steeple near the base of a mountain, serves as more than a beacon to guide our way.

The ground under our feet eventually begins to rise, barely detectable at first, but it rises. Even the rain starts to cooperate by slackening. Soon after, our destination appears in sight; it looms a distance ahead. Three large tarp tents and dozens of make-shift lean-to shelters scattered around those larger tents come to view. We head for one of the larger tents that appears to serve as the unit's CP.

Strangely enough, I find it harder to move through knee high water than the much deeper water. Perhaps it has to do with our hurry to exit the mire that gives it that feel. But, the more we wade our way out, the colder it also starts to get.

It is just past three in the afternoon, when we finally emerge, and I am freezing cold. I have been immersed in water for seven hours. My uniform is soaked, and I am colder this day than any winter I ever experienced. As we approach what appears to be the CP tent, my body starts to shake. Something is wrong. I cannot stop shaking. No matter how hard I try, there is no stopping the muscular spasms. I cross my arms, I hunch my shoulders for warmth, all without success at alleviating the chills. Once inside the tent and out of the wind and rain, I realize that my body is failing to generate any appreciable heat. A sense of panic overtakes me.

Thompkins stares hard at me. "What the hell is wrong with you?" he wants to know. His words draw the attention of the others, and that of the staff inside the tent. They all look at me with puzzled but concerned looks.

"Can't stop trembling, and I am very cold," I fretfully answer.

The captain in charge of the unit approaches and examines me closely. He is a short man in mid-twenties, of stocky build and bull dog appearance. "The mess hall tent is behind us. Get your ass over there," he unceremoniously orders. "They have hot coffee. That should help warm you up. I'll have Robertson, our medic, drop by and give you a look-over, just in case."

There is no hot coffee. The remnant of coffee from lunch has been dumped. The two cooks are now busy preparing supper and coffee will not be available until then.

Serving tables are lined up across the middle of the tent, splitting it in half. The cooks are busy preparing the meal at one side of the tent. I find an empty corner on the opposite end to sit and to wait to die.

A medic eventually shows up to attend to me. I am on the verge of dangerously falling asleep, when he makes his way over to my corner and squats directly to my front. He reeks of grass, but gives me a quick visual inspection and then places a warm hand against my cheek and forehead. "Hyperthermia," he tells me. "Strip those wet clothes off and wrap up in a blanket till you warm up."

"Hyper what?" I struggle to ask.

I must be giving him a strange look, for he suddenly seems taken back and somewhat angry. "Hyperthermia," he replies. "Don't worry about a translation, just do as I said."

"All I have is a poncho liner," I finally manage to squeeze out between shakes.

"Then wrap up in that," he replies, looking highly pissed by the duration of our discussion.

"It's been under water the past seven hours," I tell him. "It's got to be soaking wet," I struggle to add, frustrated at his failure to comprehend my problem at having nothing dry.

"Suit yourself," he nonchalantly states, stands and heads out through the flap in the tent.

I weigh the medics unsympathetic, drug-induced advice against just sitting in that corner, shaking and waiting on death. I struggle to untie the poncho liner from my butt pack. The darn thing must hold a gallon of water and requires hard wringing just to get some of that water out. Then it's a matter of my stripping down and wrapping myself in the wet blanket, assuming the shivers cooperate.

Tony shakes me awake; Bert and Baby Face look on. "I see your shakes are gone. Get dressed," he orders. "Cook says we can chow here after his guys eat. Shouldn't be long now. They're serving spaghetti with meat sauce, so get up."

"LJ looks to have gone Montagnard on us," Baby Face quips, once he sees me stand and drop the poncho liner.

CHAPTER 16

Chatter box Whitman returns, sporting a fresh pack of cigarettes. He rejoins us after eating his spaghetti meal with Private Luther Jones and Specialist Fourth Class Wilbert Smith.

"Found us a dry place to sleep," he eagerly relates, while taking a drag on a cigarette. "Smith suggests we bunk down in an old, wooden warehouse that's inside their company's perimeter. No one uses it to sleep. There is plenty of room and it is nice and dry," he continues.

"That building looks totally out of place out here," Thompkins injects. "What's it for?"

"No one knows who built the thing much less for what purpose," Baby Face continues to relate the intel that he gathered on a place to quarter. "Smith's best guess, is that it was built by the French decades ago, sometime during their colonial period."

Bert looks hard at Baby Face with a curious and yet challenging look, "If it is as comfy as a Howard Johnson, why don't the Grunts use it.

"They're leery the building may be targeted if they use it to quarter on a regular basis," Whitman answers. "They prefer sleeping out in the open in their two to three men fortified lean-tos; harder to hit smaller targets. A few things are stored there, like boxes of C-rations and an occasional prisoner or two. So, what's your problem?"

"How about rocket and mortar fire while our asses are in there?" a dubious Bert Thompkins protests.

"Let's go check it out," I suggest. "It stands, and there appears to be no sign of damage. We can risk it for a few nights."

"The cooks are going to kick us out of their tent at any minute," Tony adds. "We've no place to sleep, so we'll check it out."

It rained hard all through that night. Nonstop thunder and lightning accompanied that downpour. Had the enemy attacked in the darkness, their assault would have been masked by the atmospheric discharges and rumbling. No matter though, we slept the sleep of the dead.

I woke to a painful muscle cramp under the left rear shoulder. I bolted upright and stretched and stretched until the knot eased and the pain subsided. Seven hours of wading through high water, stresses muscles unaccustomed to heavy or regular use.

Sunlight or what little greyness filters down through a dreary overcast, shows through the open doors of the small warehouse. It comes through, like an uninvited guest, an annoyance to slumber that offers an undesirable sight of the outdoors and a portent of the day yet to come.

My Seiko has six forty-three. The others are yet asleep, so I decide to rejoin them. But before my head hits the fanny pack that serves as a pillow, I spot her.

She sits on the ground, legs stretched forward, shackled to a six-by-six support column at the opposite side of the warehouse. Her back is to the beam and her hands are chained behind the post. Her black, pajama-like pants are filthy with mud as is her khaki-colored blouse. Long, jet black, silky hair, dangling from a slumped head, conceals all facial features.

I rise to check on the prisoner, recalling that Baby Face had said prisoners are sometimes kept here. Why I want to check on her, I have no idea, but it has little to do with any humanitarian interest. Perhaps it is to see if she lives, but more likely, to see what a female, enemy combatant looks like up close. As I approach, she turns her slumped head toward me, glaring viciously at me like some wild animal's warning not to encroach further. She is a beautiful young woman, in spite of a gnarled face. I edge carefully closer, alarmed by her hostile disposition, but even more intrigued. Six feet from her, she lifts her head and gives a sing-song dissertation that reminds me of the RVN, MP officer's gruff voice, more so than the ever so pleasant voices of Vietnamese women. She ends that dissertation, by spitting at me.

This is a land of extremes: a beautiful land, but one of grave danger, a land of very friendly people and those that want nothing more than to take your life, even when shackled. I smile at that thought, which must have agitated her further, for she starts spitting at me like a crazed llama. Feeling unwelcome, I decide to return to my warm poncho liner. But before I lay down, visitors enter the warehouse.

Two National Policemen walk in and head straight for the female captive. Both wear the standard issue tiger, camouflage fatigues for their kind, and the one leading the way is some ten to fifteen years the senior of the other. The eldest walks to the prisoner's front and steps in between her outstretched legs. He shouts down at her with greater venom than she had employed against me.

She refuses to respond to whatever he demands of her. Instead, she brings her knees up to her chest and looks up at her interrogator, but without speaking.

A furious policeman bends, and with his left hand lifts her up by the hair. A hard blow to her abdomen soon follows.

The captive flops forward from the blow, but quickly raises her head and shoulders. Mouth agape, she gasps and waits on air to replenish her emptied lungs. A second blow leaves her more stunned and in greater need of air.

Shock at the treatment of a defenseless woman, I start to rise, but a voice from behind stops me.

"L J!" It is Tony. "Let it be. This is not our country, and it's what they do to each other."

Tony, of course, is right. These people have been killing and torturing one another for decades. If the policeman had been her prisoner, she would have put a bullet though his head by now. I still do not like what they do to the young woman; from the looks on the sleepy faces on Bert and Baby Face, neither do they.

Aware of a judgmental audience witnessing their handiwork, the policemen unchain their captive from the post and drag her away.

A hot breakfast of pancakes and hot coffee consumed, courtesy of generous Bravo Company cooks, we return to the warehouse. First order of the day is to clean weapons and gear. Silt from the brown water has set into every nook and cranny of our rifles and equipment. Weapons require a thorough cleaning to ensure their safe and continuous operation. Afterwards, each cartridge from each magazine has to be ejected and all cleaned of silt.

Finally, our web gear and fanny packs are cleaned, which we beat against support beams to shake the dirt and dust off. By the time we finish, it is lunch time.

The rain ceases as we start back to the warehouse. Tony peels off to check in with the Bravo Company CO while Thompkins, Baby Face, and I return to our shelter before the rain resumes.

"I'm telling you that shit was not ham," Baby Face complains. "I've eaten many a ham sandwich, and what those cooks call ham, tastes more like fifty-year-old spam."

"It's call luncheon meat," Thompkins explains. "It may be fifty-years-old, but at least they fried off some of the fat, and the melted government cheese on the bread made it tasty. It wasn't bad. Almost tasted like a grill cheese sandwich that I used to get at Borman's Drugstore, back home."

"You know, I have a craving for a milk shake," I add to their food discussion once inside. "It's been months and months since I had one."

"Hey, L J," Whitman calls out. "Your girlfriend is back," he points to the female captive, once again chained to the support post.

Something is askew. Her position at the column is far different from earlier this morning. Her head and upper torso slump right, and her legs are sprawled to her left.

We approach her, drawn with curiosity by her strange posture, and wondering if she is alive. Thompkins steps directly to her front and squats for a close look at her.

"Holy crap," he says out loud. "Her face looks like a giant marshmallow. Can barely see her eyes for all the swelling. Those bastards used her as a punching bag."

The prisoner's head stirs at his voice. She makes a feeble effort to lift it in an attempt to see her visitors.

Whitman takes out his canteen and squats alongside Thompkins. He unscrews the top of the canteen, but before he can offer her a drink from it, she gathers her strength and spits a bloody spittle at him.

"That is one hardcore, ass bitch!" Baby Face shouts as he takes to his feet and backs off. "To hell with her. She deserves what she got."

Thompkins also rises and backs away, but unlike Whitman, he retains a sympathetic look. "From the looks of her, I suspect she gave up nothing to her two hosts and that party is likely just starting." He offers those words with a dry demeanor that evokes a deep sense of pity for the captive, at what she must yet endure.

Tony returns and so does the sound of heavy rain. Behind him follow the two, unpleasant National Police in ponchos. Puteoli halts near the door to watch the pair make their way to the prisoner.

The policemen appear angrier than ever. They scream and intentionally manhandle the prisoner, slapping her head and kicking at her legs and torso. Once satisfied, at whatever purpose intended, they jerk her arms high behind her back. They raise her up by her hair, unshackle her, and drag her limp body to the doors. But just as they exit into the rain, she turns a puffy face to look back at us.

Terror shows in those damaged eyes. I see it as clearly as those around me have surely seen my fear at the close of a track or shortly after a firefight. Her terror is a sight that evokes a painful level of anxiety within me. I find my stomach knotted as if I am the one beaten and being dragged off. I am, however, confused with her purpose of glancing back at us. Is she hoping for our intervention? If so, why did she spurn all earlier assistance?

Tony continues to watch her dragged through the doors to outside. He does so for several seconds afterwards, as if in deep reflection. "They are going to blow her brains out," he speaks as we approach. "The two sons-of-bitches warned the captain to expect a single gunshot. She is a VC communist party, political officer. She cut the throat of a man who refused to join her and her VC friends. She did it as an example to others that might hesitate. She pretended to be a grieving family member when Grunts unexpectedly showed up and surprised her, but the wife of the man she murdered, gave her ass up."

"What a fucked-up place," a dismayed Thompkins declares. "I don't know whether to feel sorry for the stupid bitch or gloat at her getting her just reward."

We are awakened by an exchange of small arms fire. It is dark outside, but just an hour or two before sunrise. We flee the warehouse as a precaution of the building being targeted by heavier ordinances. A light rain falls as we take up defensive positions, a short distance from the building.

Gunfire continues, as flares pop and drift down to light the sky, but with no effect at exposing the enemy through falling rain. Red and green tracers race across the darkness against one another. Fortunately for us, the exchange of weapons' fire is at the opposite side of the company's perimeter. It is, nevertheless, a spectacular display of competing colors that in little time turns lopsided, all red, and just as quickly, ends all together.

Soon after all flares die, come the loud voices, screaming out instructions and queries in the dark:

"reload," "check ammo," "have they gone," "anyone hit," "did we waste any?"

Two of Bravo Company's platoons are dispatched to the base of the mountains at the crack of dawn. They will act as a blocking force while three squads start house to house searches to flush out aggressors that may linger nearby.

We attach ourselves to a nine-man squad searching the area nearest where the enemy fired from during the night. There is little likelihood of finding tracks, but it's why we were sent, and we are bored at just seeing the inside walls of the warehouse. The two, murderous Nationalist Police hook up with us as well.

The sun makes a short-lived appearance at the eastern horizon. It shows itself through a light drizzle, before retreating behind low hanging, grey clouds. Our squad of Grunts find the expended casings left behind by the enemy. They proceed in single file toward the nearest homes and buildings, some two hundred yards away. The church with its tall, pointy, wood shingle steeple with a brass cross turned green, stands at the southeast corner of that large cluster of buildings.

Tony has us on line to the right of the Grunts' column. We move guardedly not expecting anything, but prepared just in case. Fifty feet from the nearest home, we sprint between it and the adjacent brick and mortar house, then hurry forward to secure the street at the front.

My mind goes into a tail spin at what I see. It is a sight that I would not ever have conceived to encounter in this war-forsaken land. I find myself in the midst of what the French Colonial period must have looked like in Vietnam. The smell of fresh bread baking in the air adds to my sudden bewilderment. I almost expect to hear an accordion playing, and to hear Maurice Chevalier singing.

The houses we shelter between are of two-storied French design, resembling older homes of a Montmartre District of Paris I once saw in a travel magazine. There are dozens of these brick and plaster homes, with a few single-storied dwellings scattered about, but all painted light yellow or faded pink or lime green. A few of the buildings have businesses on ground levels and living quarters above. They display signs identifying their specialty: boucher, boulangere, and marchandises séches. Large balconies at the living quarters above, with their cast iron hand rails, protrude over brick sidewalks along the street. Loads of colorful, potted flowers are visible on balconies and behind iron gates that lead to courtyards paved with flat stones or bricks. But of greater awe, is the narrow, winding street running past the front of these homes and businesses; it is paved with cobblestones. To my left, the glistening wet, stone road climbs slowly up toward the mountains, before curving and disappearing behind homes two blocks up. To the right, the road bends and disappears around the small French, country-style church at the end of the block. The scene presents a glimpse of a small French town; a sense of home that must have eased the hearts of homesick colonials, so far, far away from their native land.

Baby Face turns to me, wide eyed and grinning. He shrugs his shoulder. "L J, this ain't Kansas," he whispers.

I quickly nod and return to scanning the area for movement, remembering that this indeed is not France. The area is void of locals. After last night's gunfire, they remain timidly indoors.

Grunts can be heard entering homes at either side of the road to our left. The locals appear accustomed to the drill after a shooting and open their homes for inspection in hopes of a quick return to their daily routine.

A slight crimson streak on the yellow wall of a home opposite, catches my attention. I signal the others attention to it, fearing the enemy may actually lurk nearby.

Tony dispatches Baby Face and Thompkins to confirm the streak. Their boots clatter on the cobblestones, forcing Tony and I to hurriedly scan the upper floor windows for movement. Baby Face deems it necessary to stick a fingertip into the gooey mess, before both nod, confirming the finding.

Our team leader orders us to stay put and heads for the squad of paratroopers at the top of the road. He returns with three Grunts and the pair of executioners.

Whitman is soon moving cautiously along the sidewalk toward the old church. At the corner of the home nearest the church, he finds a splotch of blood and points with alarm toward the church.

We all retreat a short distance back up the road to confer on a plan of action. One of the three paratroopers is sent to bring the rest of the squad.

"There are three entrances to that abandoned church," the paratrooper's squad leader commences. "There is a door out back that leads to the sacristy, one on the east side that opens to the baptismal font, and of course the front door."

"You know your way around a church," Thompkins speaks out low, amazed by the young soldier.

"I was an altar boy for four years," he grins at our cover man.

"Does this mean that you have a plan or not?" Tony anxiously demands to know. Our leader has not been himself, since the young woman was led out to be executed. For some reason, Puteoli has taken that event harder than the rest of us, in spite of, or perhaps because of, having cautioned me against interfering in the locals' business. He now cast angry eyes at the two National Police, a look that makes the pair uncomfortable.

"Yeah, I do," the young squad leader answers looking as annoyed by the interruption as Tony to the slowness of the ongoing process. "Heard you boys don't get your hands dirty, so leave the lifting to us. We'll take care of things," he insultingly remarks before continuing. "Two of my boys will go in through the back, three through the front and four through the side. If things go south, we may require help. Think you can handle that?" he asks, looking at Tony.

"We'll follow your three men through the front door," Tony snaps at the man. "We've been in more shit than all your guys put together, so don't fret your little, altar boy mind about us."

The paratroopers perform a simultaneous entry into the abandoned church. We follow right behind through the large, teak, front door. There is little light inside, but three human forms stand out in the dim interior. The soldiers enter, aiming weapons, screaming, "don't move, get your hands in the air," at the three figures.

The commands to terrified Vietnamese are all in English. The trio fail to comprehend anything other than the harshness of the loud voices and the weapons pointed at them.

Hand signals and gestures to raise hands soon follow. They finally comprehend and shoot arms into the air. The floor where they stand is littered with bloody rags.

A shirtless, stocky, Vietnamese male sports a fresh, gauze bandage taped to his right side, just above the hip. He wears an angry, defiant look. A second male, taller and of slender build, has his left armed wrapped above the elbow with an equally fresh bandage. He expresses discomfort at having raised his arms. The third member of the group, a woman, looks on horrified, especially with the National Policemen.

The three are shoved toward the light at the side door by angry Grunts. No consideration is given to wounds, as the prisoners are herded past the door. The two males contort their faces in pain at the rough handling, but the woman just looks to be terrified. Once outside, the three are padded down. The tall man has ten rounds of ammunition in his shirt pocket. The stocky man has nothing but a bad attitude that earns him a smack across the face from a policeman. The woman, on the other hand, has pockets loaded with gauze, a pair of scissors, vials of drugs and a hypodermic needle.

"Looky here, Walters!" A paratrooper doing more groping than searching of the female cries out. He holds two vials of medicine up for all to see. "No wonder you can't get your clap treated. This VC whore has our entire allotment of penicillin. Here," he yells out, and tosses one of the vials to a paratrooper guarding the shirtless man. "Get Robertson to inject you with some of that shit."

We are soon heading off with prisoners in tow. Six of the paratroopers remain behind in the church, searching for weapons possibly stashed there by the two males. Three Grunts lead the way to an RVN camp at the southeast edge of the inland sea, where the prisoners are to be interned.

It is a trek of a mile that brings us once again to the flood waters. The RVN camp looms on high ground at a distance the other side of murky water. Lucky for us, a rice paddy berm sticks out the water by just inches. It is our path to their encampment, without getting our feet wet.

Our three escort paratroopers lead the way in single file along the top of the dike. The shirtless tough guy follows with arms bound high behind him. The older policeman is next, and behind him the tall prisoner, the younger policeman, and the female in that order. The team, with Tony directly behind the woman, bring up the rear.

A large gathering of RVNs await us. They stand on a large wooden platform built over the edge of the water, along-side the berm. All wear smirks that have the prisoners now moving tentatively. One particular RVN soldier stares suspiciously up to the heavens, as if checking on the day's weather. He is a behemoth of a Vietnamese, five ten in height and weighing in at thrice the weight of his peers. But what has the prisoners alarmed is a thick, four-foot piece of bamboo, with slits at one end that the Goliath holds. He rests the bamboo on his shoulder, much like a baseball player resting a bat while waiting his turn at the plate, but turns and smiles at the shirtless prisoner, as the three Grunts walk past.

The once defiant prisoner halts and takes in the scene before him. Other than jumping into the water and risk being shot as attempting to escape, the only means past that wooden platform is the berm. The old policeman shoves the hesitant man forward. A second shove has him scurrying to get past Casey and his bat.

A whistling noise sounds, followed by a nasty thwack. The bamboo slits spread open as the pole catches the prisoner squarely across the back, flinging him into three feet of water. The RVN soldiers scream with laughter at the unfortunate fellow's suffering, while the old policeman fishes him out the water by the hair. Two, long, deep gashes, where the splints of the hard wood pinched and gouged flesh, show on the man's back and arms. The unfortunate fellow appears ready to collapse from the blow. No mercy is offered, as he is hauled back by the hair onto the walkway. He is instantly shoved forward and collapses at the feet of three paratroopers.

There is no surprising the remaining two prisoner as to their fate. As his cohorts laugh and jeer at the pending victim, Casey now takes a batter's stand in preparation for the tall captive. The RVN soldier even shakes his fat ass to louder laughter from his fellow soldiers.

I have been a witness to violence inflicted on hapless humans by their own the past months. But this event, while humorous to the RVNs, I suffer with repugnancy. A compulsion to end the vicious shenanigans torments me; after all, these dirtbags had nothing to do with the trio's capture. But I am restrained by Tony's words of earlier that it is what they do to each other.

A more hesitant, second prisoner refuses to budge. The young policeman pushes and shoves at the tall man, but without success. Harsh words and a hard slap against the wound to the left arm, finally has the captive precariously inching forward, favoring his arm. He slowly approaches the strike zone, but once there, he makes a sudden dash for the safety of the other side.

That sickening whistling sound resonates once more, as does that sound of bamboo striking, ripping and tearing at flesh. The poor man is sent flying into the water by the force of the blow. He emerges from under the water, his back arched in pain. Perfect scissor-like gouges against the back and sleeves of the shirt show as he stands, blood oozing through those cuts. He falls to his knees; the laughter from the platform rages on as the man repeatedly attempts to stand, only to fall back to his knees. The old policeman is unable to reach the poor bastard's head to pull him out. Instead, he screams and aims his weapon, at the man's head.

I suspect the policeman will likely execute the prisoner where he kneels. Fortunately, and to the dismay of the RVNs entertainment, he stumbles to his feet and staggers out the water.

With a horrid tragedy averted, I take a deep breath, as the woman starts to wail a god-awful noise.

Casey is back in his batter's stand, waving his fat ass to amuse his fellow soldiers, but which pisses me off.

The younger policeman has the woman by the blouse and attempts to pull her around him and toward that bamboo pole. The woman drops to her side and takes refuge in a fetal position, wailing louder at the suffering that awaits her.

Without the slightest remorse, the young policeman lifts the hysterical woman to her feet and shoves her forward to the strike zone.

Anger snaps into my head. I yank back the bolt of my M16, chambering a round, fully prepared to pull the trigger. At or about the same time, I hear three other bolts, lock and load for action. The RVNs also hear. The laughter on the platform ceases, and Casey stands upright, eyeing us with grave concern. A standoff of sorts ensues for several long seconds. The whimpering and moaning of two males and a woman's cries are all that sounds.

"Hey man," one of the three paratroopers timidly calls out. "What the fuck you guys trying to do, get us all killed?"

Tony steps around the young policeman and leads the terrified woman past the platform. A fuming Casey and his disappointed cohorts watch as we file past.

CHAPTER 17

Captain Blake, the stocky CO of Bravo Company, calls for us the following morning. We suspect it has to do with yesterday's near catastrophic event with the RVNs.

"Got a call about you guys," he starts, moving closer to us. "Brigade wants your team back at English," he speaks, looking highly disappointed. "Don't mind saying so, but I like having you guys nearby. But it's my fault that you are being recalled. I reported that we would not be hit anytime soon after yesterday's apprehensions of the three VC. It turns out Brigade agrees. They want you where you can be readily accessible."

The captain shakes each of our hands in appreciation for our assistance. We happily accept his handshake, perhaps in appreciation of his compliment or perhaps because the meeting had nothing to do with yesterday's events. After shaking Tony's hand, he hands him a sealed envelope for our commanding officer.

A cup of coffee gulped down and biscuit in hand, we proceed through a light shower to the inland sea. We are most apprehensive at having to venture our way back across chest high water to the two dead trees and then the road beyond.

Six hours later, we sit at the side of the road to Bong Son and LZ English. We are wet, exhausted and famished, but eager to return to a hot meal, clean clothes, a dry bunk and of course, cold beer. A three-hour, hard hump along an empty, muddy road lies yet ahead. At least it is not raining, although that is not likely to hold for long.

"To hell with my congressman," Whitman now gripes. "My lawyer is going to hear from me to sue someone's ass. Does the army think we are ducks or have gills?"

No one bites at Baby Face's gripe. We are far too exhausted, and a long road lies before us.

At a quarter to six, we trudge past the gates of English through a deluge. With fifteen minutes left before they finish serving supper, we make a bee line to the engineers' mess hall. We dump weapons and gear at a table and make a mad rush for a tray at the serving line.

I gulp down an individual carton of cold milk and let out an "Ahh," of utter satisfaction. But as I start to chow down a fried chicken thigh, a captain with an engineer emblem on his collar enters and watches us, but soon approaches our table, screaming.

"What the hell do you mean bringing weapons to my mess hall," he screeches at us. "Weapons are not allowed in my mess and I don't give a damn about what excuse you deem warrants violating my rule." He halts his silly tantrum to glare at us, as if expecting one of us to step into a well-laid trap, of offering a viable excuse. No defense is presented, only surprised looks which aggravates him to no end. "Get the hell out of my mess hall. Now!"

We scramble for weapons, and fried chicken and a serving of German chocolate cake off our trays and hurry outside.

"Who the heck was that guy?" Thompkins cackles.

"Never saw the man before," Tony replies. He casts what is left of a chicken leg to a small dog with a cork screw tail that follows. "Based on the engineer emblem and railroad tracks on his collar, I would say he is one of our bosses."

"Why did he come down hard on our asses?" I ask, annoyed at a lack of appreciation for the work and risks we endure.

"Maybe you should have handed him the sealed envelope that Captain Blake gave you," Thompkins advises Tony. "That was darn good chicken. Wouldn't mind a second serving of it."

"In that prick's mood, he would have just torn it up without reading what it says," Tony replies.

It did not take long before word reached the front office that we were back. Nieman hurries in out of the rain to inform all four of us that we are wanted at the HQ hooch. We have no time for hellos to teammates; only time to remove web gear, before the frantic man shoves us out the front door.

We stand at attention before a new, second lieutenant. The name written on his fatigue jacket is Lewis. He is seated behind a desk, staring and studying us and our filthy, wet uniforms, while Sergeant Hooper stands, apprehensively behind him. The boyish-looking, brown-haired officer seems more like one of us than some tough guy wannabe, with thick glasses from Mississippi. But then, there is the question of why he calls for us, and why such urgency?

"I got a call from my commanding officer about you guys," he finally starts, softly but authoritatively, and takes to his feet for emphasis of what is yet to come. "My immediate boss of less than a week just finished chewing my ass!" he suddenly screams at us. "I have been here five days, and I have been handed my butt, because of the four of you. I do not like it, and I am not happy."

Tony casually steps forward and extends the sealed envelope to the officer. "Sir, the chow line was about to close. We haven't had a hot meal in a week," he lies, which the rest of us, nevertheless, think a great move on this occasion, "and we had no idea we were committing an infraction."

Nieman boldly steps forward from behind us, "Sir, I believe this is more about you than the violation of a rule no one has ever heard." With the lieutenant's glare now focused on him, Nieman tempers his speech and cocks his head back and to the side, "The captain does not like having trackers or, for that matter, scout dogs, attached to his company of engineers. He has made that clear since he took over command of that company. Lieutenant Prattchet caught hell over nothing from that man."

The lieutenant proceeds to open the envelope and read the letter inside, while we stand waiting on him. He stops reading, and curiously looks up toward Nieman, "If that is the case, it would help to understand why."

Nieman shrugs his shoulder, "Best guess, you have a direct line of communication to Brigade for field instructions. He is likely jealous or insecure with that."

"Speaking of Brigade," the lieutenant appears to recall earlier instructions, "They want a team over at LZ Uphill. They've called about your whereabouts twice today. Sergeant Nieman will drive you there as soon as you gather your equipment."

"Sir!" a frustrated Tony barks. "We've just arrived. We have humped the past nine hours, two thirds of that time through chest high water. We are tired. Our weapons, munitions and kit need cleaning, and a good night sleep wouldn't hurt. Just what the hell are we expected to do at Uphill that can't wait."

"Where have you been that takes nine hours to get from?" the lieutenant asks.

"Sergeant Hooper sent us to a unit in the field, as retaliation for having complained over a prior mission. We had to wade through chest high water for hours to get there, and some of us ended suffering hyperthermia in doing so," an angry Puteoli replies, his eyes on Hooper's.

"Lieutenant," Nieman pipes in, saving a terrified Claude Hooper from having to offer an explanation. "It's dark and it's raining. The road between here and Uphill is flooded at several points. If we attempt to drive through standing water in the dark, we are most likely to end up stuck or in an accident. I recommend we wait till morning. It will give them time to prepare and to rest. I'll get the other unit members to assist with cleaning their gear."

"Thank you, sergeant," the lieutenant speaks while returning to his chair. "I appreciate sound advice. I'll notify Brigade that the team, less dog and handler as per sergeant Hooper, will head out in the morning. You men are dismissed, and I suggest you avoid all contact with our captain for the near future."

"Sir," Hooper finally ventures to speak as we step through the door. "What was in that letter? I hope they caused no problems at their last assignment?"

"A Captain Blake is giving me a heads up that he has recommended the four for the Army Commendation Medal along with several of his men," he replies.

"He can't do that," Hooper objects.

The monsoon season starts to wane. The sun shines each and every day across the country side for longer periods of time. But with the return of the sun, comes the unrelenting heat, and with all that water lingering across lowlands, comes high humidity. Conditions are once again, unbearable.

"This remind you of home?" Whitman quips, teasing me about the sauna-like effect outdoors.

"More like that track with Lieutenant Harbor and his dismounted platoon," I respond, knowing he does not like talking about that event.

"Thanks for reminding me, cocksucker," he angrily replies, as I expect he would.

We have been loitering about LZ Uphill like a group of vagrants for a week. It has not been a difficult assignment, as no missions have been called. We bunk with MPs, which means no smoking grass, but some serious night time drinking. Best part is that they have their own bar and club. The alcohol is free, courtesy of bribes taken from soldiers apprehended with contraband, who do not want to be reported to their superiors.

But we are restless. The inactivity allows for ugly memories to surface, and there is just so much friendly teasing and bantering, before things heat up. A change of pace or venue is needed. That change is suddenly provided when Tony, bearing Red and Prince, approach, making the team whole.

Prince leads Red into our temporary quarters, tail wagging, happy to see us as we are him. "Here," Red removes a radio pack from his back and hands it to me. "No extra battery," he adds. "Prattchet failed to forward the requisition order for additional batteries. Coop says it was deliberate, his way of saying bye, and "fuck you," trackers.

"Whoa, you silly dykes," an MP sergeant hollers from the back of the hooch. "We don't allow dogs in our sleeping quarter. We don't want that thing pissing and crapping or bringing in fleas where we sleep; so, get it out."

"This soldier," Puteoli angrily responds, pointing at Prince, "has a fifteen-thousand-dollar bounty on his head, put there by Señor Charles. That is fifteen big ones more than is on your sorry ass. We are not going to leave him outside, so suck it up."

Tony's temper as of late suffers a short fuse. His diplomatic demure has gone south. I feel it my responsibility to step in and help smooth things. "Sarge, I recall you getting wasted and pissing all over the floor, just two nights ago. Our tracker dog, Prince, has better sanitary habits than you, you drunken cunt." Somewhere through that short discourse, I too managed to lose my temper, and from the look on the six-foot two brute, he has also.

A runner enters the hooch before I can drop the radio to get my ass kicked. "The major wants to see ya'll. Grab your gear, you got work."

"Most convenient, L J," Baby Face mutters. "Most convenient indeed," he adds laughing loudly while gathering his things.

"It sure is," I remark. "That MP is lucky the runner came in time to save his fat ass."

Thompkins laughs loudest. "Serves you right, you Little Shit."

Whitman, being one not to be easily sidelined continues as we head outside, "You know, Red, I don't appreciate having a five-thousand-dollar bounty on my ass, while your canine companion has one three times that amount."

"Guess Charlie doesn't think as much of your skills," Red replies.

Major Schneider opts to ride with us to our drop-off. Perhaps, like us, after weeks and weeks trapped indoors by rain, he suffers cabin fever. "It may be nothing," he shouts over the propeller wash. "A mech platoon was following up on a booby trap installation gone bad. Two VC bodies were found, and blood trails led away from the site. A Lieutenant Harbor requested trackers for assistance, just in case they lose the trail."

"Oh crap," Whitman softly mutters, more to himself than anyone else. "Harbor and his Cub Scouts again," he adds, turning an anxious face to cast his gaze outside the transport.

We fly between a carpet of shadowy greenery and a low, blackish-grey ceiling. The monsoon rains are not yet finished in the highlands. Lightning from a fast-moving group of ominous clouds to the southeast, makes the trip eerie.

Though this sounds like another maybe…perhaps… iffy… mission, that lonely, orphaned mood sweeps over me. Once again, I am engulfed feeling sorry for my current lot in life. A terrible sense that no one exists at this far fringe of the world, not those in the Huey transport, nor those that await the transport's arrival, engulfs me. Only I and those with metal on their collars that sent me to this desolate nowhere, exist. Not even fleeting thoughts of Talmadge's positive disposition with his unfortunate life, alters dark spirits, as my mind constantly reverts to whether anyone, other than myself, truly cares for what may happen to me.

The Huey commences a sharp descent to a clearing in the highlands. My old companion, fear, shakes off the self-inflicted doldrums and has me back to reality. Body and mind quickly assume the stress, anxiety, and alertness associated with the role of a tracker.

We leap clear of the Huey and take a knee at the edge of the clearing. We watch our lifeline to safety quickly disappear. Thunder suddenly rumbles overhead. It starts to our left and rolls across a dark sky in a matter of a second. We search the sky for the source, as if expecting to see something nature never intended for human eyes.

A whistle from across a field of knee-high grass, draws our attention. Three grunts wave to us from the tree line the other side. By the time I and the others reach them, Lieutenant Harbor joins the gathering.

He quickly examines my face, then Whitman's, likely recalling us from when his green troops opened fire on us. Apprehension shows on his face, and he wastes little time relaying instructions to us.

"We are going to get hit, and hit hard," he starts, as his anxiety now spreads like a highly contagious disease. "Major Schneider radioed. He spotted a large force heading this way after they dropped you off. He has ordered artillery on them. My platoon is hunkering down here to face them. We are setting up a crescent defensive line in the trees behind me. We do not have number superiority to cover our rear. So, they will try to outflank us. My right flank is on a sharp slope, one not easy to traverse. This grassy field is where they will likely try to outmaneuver us. The end of my left flank is fifty yards inside those trees. I need your team there," he points to an area in the trees, "to keep them from getting behind…"

A supersonic, whistling roar, suddenly screeches overhead. All flinch and start for the ground. It is a startling sound, even though expected, and one with far more lethal consequence than nature's overhead tantrum. That screeching roar is quickly followed by others, one after the next, in quick succession. Whump, whump, whump, whump sounds as artillery shells tear into a nearby ridge. The ground shakes, stomachs tighten and hearts skip beats with each whump. Earth, wood and smoke rise, lifted above tree tops by a relentless pounding of explosions, until that entire ridge disappears under clouds of black and brown debris.

We race to the area Harbor assigned us, as the pounding continues. Sixteen feet inside the tree line, we drop to the ground and set up a defensive line facing the clearing. Thompkins, I, Red with Prince, Tony and Baby Face lay hidden, deep among trees, watching and waiting, but praying no one shows. All the while, artillery shells hammer at the enemy's approach.

The explosions get louder and louder. The bombardment is marching closer and closer to Harbor's line. Each exploding shell shakes the ground where I lay on my belly, and each appears far closer and more violent than the last. Sounds of wood snapping and trees crashing to the ground now mingle with each powerful detonation. I turn, to look behind me, expecting Harbor's troops running for their lives ahead of the shelling. But as I glance back, the barrage ceases.

The rumble of thunder is again evident. It continues at a far distance, and sunlight now shines upon the clearing beyond the trees. Tree limbs continue to creak, crack and fall, but in short time, only the occasional far rumbling of thunder is heard, and soon after, nothing at all. An eerie hush ensues; the sort of silence that prickles at the skin and raises the nape hairs.

The hush continues for several long minutes. I take a deep breath of moldy air, confident that the assault has been thwarted. With the element of surprise gone and their ranks undoubtably thinned by the shelling, it seems only prudent that the enemy would turn tail and head back to their safe mountain retreats. Thompkins seems to concur with my unspoken assessment. He gives me a quick nod. To my right, Red, looks far more terrified than I could have ever demonstrated. His entire body appears to tremble, even though the shelling has ended.

It suddenly occurs to me that those safely in the rear will demand an engagement with the enemy. They will call for pursuit, or at the minimum, a body count of the damage inflicted by the artillery. Careers are made through body counts, the higher the number to report, the greater the opportunity for recognition. Some order for action will be forthcoming. Dangerous commands for lowly Grunts to risk all for the sake of someone's promotion to major, colonel or perhaps general will be issued.

Chaos suddenly erupts to my rear. An uproar of rifles and machine guns, spewing hundreds of rounds per second, sprinkled with explosions from grenades and detonated claymore mines violate the silence.

The enemy is at Harbor's line. Stupidity, courage, but likely a lack of communication, has NVA and VC throwing themselves at the Grunts. That kak, kak, kak sound joins staccato bursts of M-60 machine guns and M-16 rifles. Harbor's troops are holding their own and dishing out a steady supply of gunfire.

The clamor of firing and explosions nears as the flanks of the crescent shaped line are engaged. The sounds of battle get louder and louder. I shoot another glance over my shoulder to where the nearest commotion emanates; tracers bounce among trees, crisscrossing the arena of death, and explosions kick up dirt and debris to darken an already dim interior. The enemy searches, blindly, testing for a weak spot at Harbor's line, and shortly, they will have a go at the far end of his left flank.

A Vietnamese voice sounds to our far right. It gets louder. There is a strain and tense quality to that voice, as if urging or hurrying others to dangerous action. Five soldiers in North Vietnamese uniforms soon show at the edge of the grass clearing to our front. They run left, eager to get at Harbor's rear. With the exception of the man leading the charge, the rest are kids, fresh off the Ho Chi Minh Trail. Their uniforms are clean, and weapons and equipment appear brand new. A four second burst of M-16 and Carb-16 fire sends the five sprawling to the ground. They lie where they fell, likely, not knowing what killed them.

As I look to the bodies in the grass, the enormity of our heinous action seeps into my mind. Some eight decades of combined life lay wasted amid the grass. In a matter of only four Mississippi, years of struggle to survive and thrive are violently terminated. Five beings, cast into an arena of killing, will never return to their World, their families ignorant of their whereabouts, much less their death.

A sense of shame takes root. Even though I know that it had to be done, I question what we just did. I feel as if I had taken a sledge hammer to a wondrous, marble statue of antiquity, denying others, a thing of beauty.

Tony waves at us to crawl further into the trees and undergrowth. All gladly follow those instructions, if only to put distance from the evil we wrought. We crawl backwards, six to seven feet further into the murky safety of trees.

The firing at our rear wanes. An occasional kak, kak, kak is instantly retaliated by bursts of M-60s and M-16s, and afterward, the thumps and explosions of M-79 grenade launchers.

Premonition or logic, moving further into the shroud of the trees pays off. Minutes later, six, fast moving Viet Cong, attired in khaki shorts, black shirts and sandals, charge along the tree line. They halt by their dead comrades, but quickly shift their focus to the trees where we lie. The six move into the woods, but take a knee, feet inside, and proceed to scour the darkness for those responsible.

Silhouettes with weapons peer into the trees for what seems forever. The six are but feet away; so close, I think I smell them. One seems to stare straight to where I lie, but fails to fire. *How is it that he does not see me or hear that pounding in my chest?* Another shadow turns his head, cocking an ear, as if to pick up on any faint sound. The finger at my trigger aches, as I fight against the urge to shoot.

Someone to my right suddenly fires. The rest of us instantly join the new round of killing. A deafening fracas of automatic rifle fire echoes among the trees, drowning out the racket to our rear. The firing is up close, and exceeds those four Mississippi required to terminate the NVA in the clearing. It goes on and on as both sides light up the woods with clamorous munitions. A VC to my front releases a stream of green tracers straight in my direction. I fire until only my red tracers show and the firing ceases all together.

I continue to lay, checking the prone bodies to my front, studying each for signs of movement. My skin crawls. I feel a need to rise and run away, not out of fear but to burn off overpowering energy coursing through veins. As the seconds progress, I give myself an apprehensive pat down, convinced that at such a close range, a bullet must have bitten into me. Nothing awry, a glance to the left and right has troubled faces glancing back.

Thompkins rises behind the trunk of a thick tree. He fires a single shot at a prone figure attempting to raise his Kalashnikov, and then into each of the other five Viet Cong bodies.

"You there," someone to our rear hollers. "Lieutenant Harbor wants your RTO. Now!"

I crouch my way to join the loud mouth who, to his surprise, has succeeded in drawing a burst of enemy fire. He in turn, leads me, stooped low, further into the trees to where Lieutenant Harbor waits. The officer waves for me to hurry to him. A medic stands, tending to Harbor's left arm, cautioning him not to move.

"Need your radio," he winces, as the medic prods around a six-inch splinter of wood protruding from the arm. Harbor snatches the hand set, raises the volume and calls a fire base for artillery support. "Damn, Doc, that hurts. Can't it wait? I've got calls to make."

"No time to be gentle," the medic calmly replies, while continuing to prod at the wound with a blade of sorts. "Got a hell of a lot of others to tend to after you, and this thing needs extracting before it breaks up and leaves smaller splinters in your arm. Good thing the wood is green and not much bleeding." That said, with the fingers of one hand, he spreads the wound wide, while Harbor cringes and eventually screams. The medic then pulls out two inches of bloody wood with the other hand.

"I'm commandeering your radio," Harbor blurts out, eyes closed, yet grimacing. "Both my radios are done for and this is our only link to the rear."

"No extra battery," is all I can think to say. Harbor moves off with my radio and the Medic now treats a bullet wound to the calf of a Grunt.

"Can do, Sir" Harbor transmits over the radio. "We can hold for the forty-five minutes to an hour till you get here.... Five wounded that I know of, and maybe three dead.... I can use a Medivac to get the wounded to a hospital.... Yes Sir."

Whump, whump, whump, the shelling resumes. It is loud and nerve-wracking, though this time, it marches away from the platoon's line.

"Doc, check with Sergeant Arroyo for other casualties," Harbor hollers over the detonations. "Medivacs will arrive within fifteen minutes."

"You there," the medic calls to me. "Help these three to the edge of the clearing," he points to three walking wounded, one of which he just finished treating. "Make sure they take their weapons with them, and come back with one of your buddies to help with the non-ambulatory cases."

Gunfire breaks loose once again. A tree, feet from the head of the medic is chiseled by the enemy's fire. I drop to the ground. "Get up; take these men to the clearing," the medic angrily orders. "They weren't aiming at you and the Medivacs are on their way."

There are far too many dead. Eleven is a small number by most accounts, but when you drag out six bodies from inside the woods and place them alongside five dead NVA in the clearing, the quantity of corpses makes a head spin and a stomach taut.

Four of us stand like statues, not a word passed among us, just staring at the horridness we produced. They are all dead, and not so much as a minor scratch on any of our team.

Grunts that dragged out the six went through all the clothing, seized all weapons and munitions, and tagged all eleven with a camouflage stick to signify each corpse has been counted. The dead, they just lie, uncaring that their bodies are violated with graffiti for the sake of a correct body count.

Harbor approaches, and shakes us from our statuesque appearance. "We killed a lot of them, but they made us pay a high price doing so." He pauses and lets out a loud sigh. "The CO will be here in ten minutes with third platoon," he speaks, wiping at damp eyes. "I have been ordered out to deal with this flesh wound. The arriving transports will see you back to Uplift."

"I'll get Whitman," I volunteer. It is my chance to put some distance from the carnage, and I want nothing to delay or hamper our departure from this place.

Baby Face is a short distance up along the clearing. He stares down to the grass at his feet; the muzzle of his weapon hangs at his side. "Brandon, move your ass, we're leaving."

He doesn't flinch. Baby face continues staring down, as I approach. "Did you hear me?" I ask, but suddenly realize that he is gazing at four dead Grunts lined-up in the grass.

"Do you recognize this guy?" he asks, pointing his weapon to a dead kid at his feet.

It is his somber voice that makes me look at what I try hard to avoid seeing. As expected, I am horrified by the egregious sight. Someone's child is looking up with only one eye. It is a lifeless thing; the spirit and the very essence of it having been snatched from the living creature that had once been him. The left eye is gone and so is part of that socket and the temple on that side. What is left of that side of his head is a grotesque sight of hairy, mangled flesh and exposed bone. His own mother would initially fail to recognize him, never once thinking anyone would dare do such a dastardly thing to her child.

Who exactly am I expected to recognize in this lifeless corpse, a future night visitor? "Damn it, Whitman, let's go," I yell, tugging hard at his shoulder, wanting to now put distance from this dreadful spot.

He shrugs off my grasp. "Remember him, L J?" Once again, he asks, fighting back tears, while maintaining vigilance over the boy.

Baby face is deeply affected by this one corpse. It is a far different behavior he now exhibits from his standard happy go lucky attitude. His insistence has me looking back down for yet another look. I shut my eyes and reply, "No, I don't."

"He tried to kills us," he explains. "I was on the verge of smashing his brains out, when Harbor stepped between us."

My eyes are drawn down for a third time. I see now what Baby Face had discovered. My eyes water and a thick lump in my throat makes it difficult to swallow. I suddenly feel a tingling numbness spread down to the tips of my limbs. I recall having contemplated killing the kid myself.

The guilt over that brief event, months ago, and what now lies at our feet, rips at me.

"LJ, I'm scared," Whitman confesses. "I just turned twenty, and there are so many things I yet want to do, things that I've dreamed doing. I don't want to end up like him with my dreams forever lost, and I'm scared that I will. I just want to go home to Seattle and do all those things that I've always wanted to do," he adds, as tears roll down chubby cheeks.

"Come on Brandon, let's go home," is all I can think to say.

CHAPTER 18

We are lethargic. We sit or lay on bunks, motionless and quiet, deep into our own dark thoughts and oblivious to the non-stop yapping and laughter of three new Cherries.

Perhaps, like I, the others of Team 2 are counting and recounting the eleven dead. I have done the math, from the average, to the mean, of the likely percentage of life that I took. Yet it changes nothing, and only draws me further down a dark hole. The enemy dead remain broken receptacles of once vibrant animated beings. Not even disappointment and anger over the dead Grunts, lessens the shame of my part in their killing.

I force myself to rise and walk to the weapons rack to deposit my clean M-16. Baby Face sits at his bunk staring at, through or far beyond the back door. Red, whom I remember annoying us with a bombardment of questions about boonies and firefights, sits at his footlocker, cradling his forehead in his right hand, the elbow of that arm resting against a knee. Thompkins watches me, with tired, somber eyes that plead for forgiveness, an indulgence that one sinner cannot extend to another. Puteoli lays in his bunk, his right arm over his eyes. All the while, the new replacements huddle, laugh and talk nonstop by the front door.

Nieman enters the hooch. He bears mail and a small package. Cooper and Talmadge, and our three new additions to the unit are the only ones that show interest.

Two letters are deposited on my bunk. Nieman throws the small package on Tony's bunk, but hurries back to me, "One's from Tillman. Well, you going to read it?"

Like a zombie carrying out a high-priest's command, I return to my bunk, open the letter and start to read. Tillman writes that he stopped to visit Cardona before heading home to his wife and his new posting at Fort Dix. Cardona, it seems, has not fared well and has not been able to transition back to life at home. He writes that he sympathizes with Cardona. He also feels out of place, like a stranger in his own country, but that he at least has a wife to go home to. He also confesses that he wrote to me, because I would understand the reason for his cutting off all future ties to us.

"What does he say?" Nieman begs to know. Tony rises to join Cooper and Talmadge as they converge on me to hear what Tillman wrote.

"He says that he has to move past this war, before it destroys him," I answer, holding out the single page for Nieman to take. That said, I return to the bunk and my counting, but just momentarily. It seems I have given little thought to what happens, if by chance I come out of this war physically unscathed. Since that day on the beach, I have felt that we were all aboard Charon's ferry, crossing the river Styx, the token for the crossing paid for by an army quartermaster. I have been so embroiled in such sinister thoughts that there has been no time for serious considerations of a DEROS or of returning to a civil society.

Tillman's guarded, yet explicit, words now have me commiserating on wounds other than to flesh; wounds that may be beyond Freud's ability to heal.

Once the letter has been sufficiently passed around by those hovering near my bunk, they head back to their little corner of the hooch, having discovered nothing in Tillman's letter to lift their spirits. Tony opens his package and withdraws a cassette and a letter, and Cooper comes back to show me pictures from his Rest and Recuperation trip to Bangkok, Thailand.

Coop's pictures are mainly of him at bars, groping scantily clad young women with small breasts and little to no ass that sit at his lap. Three pictures, likely at the front of the roll of film and taken far earlier, catch my attention. They are of us, here in the hooch smiling and laughing. One is of a smooth skin cherub face sporting a monstrous smile, while holding a Pabst Blue Ribbon beer can. It was a picture taken a life time ago, a time before who we are today.

"I've never seen so many half-naked girls in my life," Coop brags, forcing me back to reality. "The city is full of them. The very name, Bangkok, Thailand, oozes with sex," he adds, dragging out "oozes," as if savoring memories.

A woman's voice faintly sounds. It softly wafts through the air like a gentle spring breeze, sweeping the winter doldrums away. Tony has Cooper's cassette player and is trying to listen over all the talking and laughter of our three new members. He turns up the volume to hear over the jaunty yapping of our Cherries. A sweet, yet powerful voice sings *Greensleeves*.

"Keep it down!" Talmadge admonishes the trio. "That's his sister singing at her college recital."

Greensleeves is a song known to us all. An ancient English tune, it is a song that now pulls at hearts, yearning to revert to the innocents of who we once were.

As the applause dies, the heavens allow an angel's voice to float down to mere mortals. Tony's sister now sings, *Ava Maria*. It is a song that I have heard in church at ceremonies, though those occasions now escape me. It matters not, for the voice has me at a pew, sitting alongside my family at St. Bernard, feeling out of place.

My eyes unexpectedly water. I close them, as the music carries me away, deeper and deeper into a festering hole. Fearful of breaking down and blubbering, I open them wide and take a deep breath. Despair strikes me, as the curtain rises and exposes my environment and all its wickedness of which I am a part. The body tenses tight. I gasp at short breaths. The realization that my soul is damaged beyond repair sinks deep. I grasp that I am doomed, to be relegated to merely look up, as those not sent here to kill, frolic among the heavens. That angelic voice only teases at what I might never attain, driving a stake, through my anguished heart. I want to jump up, to run out, to search for salvation or hope, but dread drawing attention to newly found fears.

A long, hearty applause offers a break to the music. It allows me an opportunity to rise without drawing anyone's attention. As I make my way to my web gear, the angelic voice sings out in Italian, a sound so sweet it must have been meant for God's ears and for those pure of heart, "*O mio babbino caro.*" I pull out two fragmentation grenades from an ammo pouch for no conscious reason, and pocket them, desperately needing to put distance from music not intended for ears of those forever lost. As the lyrics "*Andrei Sul Ponte Vecchio,*" sail across the vitriolic air of my Hades, I hear the cries of a man. I scramble for the door, fearful of others seeing the rivers of tears flowing down my cheeks. I sprint through searing heat, down the compound's long drive to the main road and then the half mile to the front gate without pause.

Thompkins and I are on punishment duty. We have been for close to two weeks. In the mornings, our team lays out practice tracks for Team 1, and in the afternoons, when not cleaning the latrine or raking the hard ground around the compound, Bert and I nail boards to posts and plant a forest of signs that warn of dogs or identify the two units at Dog Patch. My offense is for leaving the base without authorization, in spite of calls to halt by MPs manning the gate, not that they would have dared to physically stop me. Bert's crime is of having threatened a Cherry with his M-16.

"What purpose does this sign serve?" I ask, from high atop the kennel's berm. I shade my eyes from the sun to gaze below to the perimeter wire and then to the green rice paddies while waiting on a reply. Lacking an answer, I lean on a shovel, sweat dripping off my shirtless torso, to watch a somber-faced Bert, pack dirt around the posts supporting the sign.

"Guess it warns to stay back and go away," he finally replies.

"Yeah, but no GI in his right mind is going to risk the steep climb way up here, read the stupid sign and break a neck going back down," I assert, disappointed by his poorly thought-out reply. "We have planted near a dozen of these things where we were told, and most of the locations are just outright ludicrous."

"L J, do you know the names of our Cherries?" He straightens, looks me in the eye with a face far more haggard than my Uncle Alfred's.

I am taken aback; not by his appearance or the query itself, but the fact that I cannot recall their names. The trio has been with us for two weeks, and I can see their childlike, innocent faces as if they are standing before me. We have shared the same roof, eaten at the same mess hall table, and breathed the same hot, muggy air, yet no name pops to mind. Hell, I have seen all three naked under our open-air shower, how is it I can not remember their names. "The one you wanted to waste is named Dawkins; I think. I have no idea about the other two."

"Hawkins, I believe," he corrects me.

"So, why did you threaten Hawkins?" I pose the question whose answer is yet a mystery to the rest of us.

The man returns to patting down dirt around the post, but shortly, straightens his tall frame, looks across the paddies toward the mountains and answers. "Red was on his locker, crying to himself after that last mission. Hawkins, if that's his name, sneered at him and mockingly pointed him out to his two pals. That piece of shit hasn't the right to disrespect a brother tracker, especially," he angrily adds, "him being a Cherry. I would have pulled the trigger had Tony not begged me to wait until his cassette ended. Claimed that by the time the ruckus over a killing ended, it would be days before he could get around to finish hearing his sister's recital." He gives a quick chuckle and looks at me. "You missed it. You were gone by then, out the front gate without so much as a weapon."

I promptly correct him. "I had two frags, in my pocket," to which we both laugh.

He takes on a somber, thoughtful look, giving rise to expect a serious question. "That was a very stupid thing to do, and you are not stupid. So why go out without a weapon?"

Thompkins had exposed what drove him to nearly kill a fellow tracker. It seems only fitting that I reciprocate, at least, a partial disclosure. "I needed to be around regular people, civilians, going about their daily lives. I had to get away from the army, if only for a few minutes."

"Bert, L J!" Tony calls from the other side of the dog pens. "Get that shit stowed and grab your gear."

There is a high level of anger in his tone, not directed at us. His wrath has again taken a turn for the worst, this time, since learning that a Cherry is to serve as Team 1's leader. He and Claude Hooper have argued vehemently and regularly over the dangers of a rookie with no combat or actual field tracking experience heading a team. He advocates for Talmadge, who at least has experience, but Hooper has dug in his heels, declaring he intends to personally train the new leader, and mold that team into an efficient combat group.

In the mornings since that initial announcement, we lay tracks, intentionally designed by us to make Team 1's task pure hell. We take them through thick brush, steep heights, across ditches and cesspools of standing water, and plant fake booby traps. We even backtrack and go in circles to confuse them. At the end of the day's track, we wait on a tired bunch to stumble into our ambush.

By the third morning, Sergeant Claude Hooper had his fill of the field training. He proclaimed that he and Nieman were of the opinion that the new leader is properly prepared to do the job, but insisted the field training continue, but of course, without him.

"Come on, get a move on," Puteoli yells out. "I want to put distance from these assholes."

Thompkins and I run to HQ to return hammer, nails and shovels. As we approach, we hear loud argumentative voices coming from inside that office.

"Two of the five are gone in four weeks," I hear Hooper explain, "and one, we can work with," he continues. "We can ship out the other two once new replacements start streaming in."

"Getting Team 2 out of the way is instrumental in having Team 1 top dog on all mission calls," Nieman chimes in. "They are now set to go."

"Brigade has been notified of our positioning Puteoli's group on that new firebase," Hooper expounds. "That will serve to transition those trouble makers out of the unit, and allow us to do things our way."

"Therein lies my problem!" I hear the lieutenant squawk, thinking he is coming to our defense. "I told the two of you that all communications with Brigade are to go through me."

"We had a narrow window to get this done," Hooper haughtily replies. "With no missions the past few weeks, Brigade doesn't care what we do, so long as we have a team ready to go when a need arrives."

"Besides," Nieman injects, "you have deniability, if things don't work out."

I watch the sun sink beyond the horizon. On this particular day, it descends on its daily celestial exit from view, behind a far-off range of dark, jungle highlands. A spectacular mural of orange-red, the color of the inside of a blood orange, is displayed above where it slowly disappears; a reminder to all who gaze, of just how precious and wonderful, its rays are. With a final curtain call, it splays the sky with a deep violet, and allows lesser stars to shine.

A sense of abandonment strikes me as the sun disappears altogether. This impression lacks that imminent death feel, and confines itself to a sense of desertion by someone close, and of being relinquished to tedium until its return. To add to the loneliness and woes of being temporarily forsaken, the temperature now plummets.

"L J, get your ass down," Thompkins cries out. "Do you want some sniper to get lucky?"

"Does it really matter," I answer, as I step down.

"Tony, you and Bert DEROS in four weeks?" Whitman asks for confirmation. With but a brief pause and no reply, he continues, "L J and I are clearly the two trouble makers, so who then is the one that they can work with?"

All eyes soon pounce upon the shadowy face of Red, sitting with his back against the inside of the perimeter trench. Prince also lays at the bottom of the trench, resting his head on the handler's lap.

"I don't know why they would think that," Red sheepishly defends himself. "Maybe because, I'm the newest on the team?"

"You Benedict Arnold," Whitman calls out as the rest of us break into laughter.

"What worries me most, is what appears to be Hooper and Nieman taking total control over Lewis," I speak, speculating over a possible future problem for us all. "I had hoped he would be one of us."

"You can lay that idea to rest," Puteoli scornfully speaks out. "He threatened to send us to the brig, if we refused to come out here."

Thompkins wastes little time checking us back into reality. "Guess we'll be here for the next four weeks."

"Least, we have three hot meals each day and big guns to cover our ass," Benedict Arnold chimes in, as shocked faces snap toward him. "What?" he asks with his broad shoulders hunched about his ear lobes. "What did I say?" he repeats, dismayed by the glaring looks at what he thought was an innocent remark. The poor guy continues to search faces for an answer to the nature of his sudden blasphemy. His eyes finally settle on mine.

I feel compelled to play at Tillman and resolve Red's concern. "My team leader, when I first arrived, was kicked off the unit a few months before his DEROS. He was shipped off to a firebase, probably not unlike this place without a name. Three hot meals and heavy artillery to do his shooting were among his last words to us. He died at that outpost during an enemy assault."

"Yeah, and this place looks like it couldn't withstand an assault by a flock of my uncle's chickens," Thompkins injects. "A single RPG round can take out this side of the perimeter."

"You think that's why these artillery guys posted us on this side?" Red, suddenly frets and wants to know.

"If we are going to be stuck here for four weeks, I think reinforcing this wall with four to five rows of sandbags, and even constructing a hard bunker to shelter in is called for," I suggest.

Puteoli nods, "I'll talk to the captain in the morning, and get us sandbags and a couple of those steel engineer..."

"Way to go Monsieur Trouble Maker," Whitman interrupts Tony.

"If Charlie comes knocking, you'll be thanking me," I reply.

Our attention quickly migrates. A most rancid odor wafts up in the cool of night to assail olfactory nerves. "Oh, sweet Jesus, who cut the cheese," Thompkins snarls.

We all turn to Whitman, who emphatically disavows the release of the inhumane stench. We finally settle on two yellow luminous eyeballs, sheepishly looking up from the bottom of the dark trench.

"You feed, Prince, pork steaks from c-ration cans?" Thompkins, who is nearest Red, demands of the handler.

"Why not?" he answers. "Everyone else turns their nose at that crap, but he loves the shit," he adds, reaching down to pet his canine, but just as quickly pops up and stands with a horrid, sour face.

"That's why," Thompkins angrily points out. "Didn't anyone tell you not to feed him that crap? He's going to be farting all night long." Bert stands up and negotiates his way around legs and equipment to put some distance from the flatulent canine.

"Those farts qualify as an illegal gas agent under the Geneva Convention," Whitman offers in a most serious tone.

"Mr. Charles is not a signature of that treaty," Bert chimes in while settling his ass down. "But just the same, it would be cruel and inhumane to use Prince's farts against the enemy."

"By the way, anyone know the names of our three new Cherries?" I ask, not having forgotten my and Bert's apparent lapse of memory and wondering if the others had as well.

"Tad Moore is Claude's anointed team leader," Whitman replies, surprised that I would be inquiring. Of course, if anyone would have the answer, it would be our social butterfly. He suddenly rises to put distance from yet another silent, but toxic fart. "Mel Janson is Zeus' handler and Theodore Wilkens, the visual tracker."

"Wilkens, huh," Bert remarks with a chuckle. "Close enough for government work, I suppose."

Four days have passed since our arrival at a firebase without a name and only a number for a designation. Thompkins claims that the number, cold and lacking of civility or compassion, is based on the elevation of the mountain peak. Nevertheless, the days fly, and our budding bunker the boys in the artillery unit have taken to calling the Alamo, is taking shape.

Our exile to this gulag, has proven highly beneficial to the team. A general calm and a cheerful attitude has evolved among the five of us. We do not anticipate being called out to a mission from such a desolate location, and are free to do what we want, within the confines of the firebase. We are clear of all frustrations and politics at Dog Patch, and time and isolation has allowed us to build closer bonds.

I feel as if I have been submerged in a tub of scalding water, and risen to have all the vileness of the past eight and a half months washed away. Even nighttime visitations have lessened, allowing me to wake, refreshed and full of vigor.

Heat during the day gets testy, atop a jungle mountain stripped of all foliage, but cool evenings and chilly nights make it all worthwhile. Brandon Whitman has found a means of enhancing those fantastic evenings. He has cases of beer secretly smuggled on each resupply ship. No one knows what power he wields over chopper crews to get it done, and certainly, no one complains. As the sun disappears from sight, we retreat within the walls of our Alamo in progress, talk and laugh the night away with beers in hand.

On the seventh day of our exile, the artillery boys get wind of our brew. They approach, *en mass,* after a supper of mystery meat stew, hoping to get at a can or two from our stash.

"A dollar a can," Whitman tells them, hoping the five hundred percent mark-up will discourage them and send them packing. When they angrily protest the exorbitant price, Brandon merely shrugs his shoulders and blurts out, "Carrying charges." But to Brandon's amazement, the young artillery men are cash flush and dish out the military scrip as if it grew on trees. As it turns out, there is no place for these boys to spend wages, and army pay days do not cease, merely because one is out in the middle of nowhere.

Two days later, the captain in charge of the firebase and his two underling officers come to confirm the rumors of beer on his two acres of mountain top. "Yes, Sir," I confess, while the commander examines the thick rising walls to our fortress under construction. "We need the empty cans to hang on the perimeter wire. We intend to place small rocks inside the cans to rattle and alert us, should the enemy try to crawl through the wire. Their contents are merely lagniappe."

The trio soon help themselves to cans of our lagniappe. Tony, who has recovered from his festering anger with the front office at Dog Patch, entertains the artillery officers by detailing the work remaining to complete the Alamo.

One of the officers, a second lieutenant named Leech, informs him that he is leading a squad at nine on a patrol, and asks if we want to join him. "We are going into the nearby trees to check for signs of enemy incursions. I do it every three days to see if we are being watched," he proudly announces.

I had forgotten that we were still in a combat zone. My mind has been caught up with filling and stacking sand bags during sunlight hours and the nights in drinking and conversing. The request is in line with what we do, and I know what Tony's response has to be.

At precisely nine the next day, we wait on the inside of a flimsy barb wire gate set between two unmanned machine gun emplacements. The walls of the gun bastions are of a single row of sandbags, five course high that a toddler could easily negotiate. It has been over a week since our arrival, and the only defensive improvements made anywhere to this firebase has been the groundbreaking and the ongoing construction of the Alamo. We wait on Lieutenant Leech and his make-shift squad to go out on patrol, all the while, highly appreciative that no attempt to overrun the camp has occurred.

"Dear Lord," it is Thompkins, who points to a motley crew led by Lieutenant Leech. "LJ, does that vision bring to mind a spectacle from months earlier, or what?"

I focus my attention, from a gate capable of only signifying a boundary to the firebase, to where the tall cover man's finger points. Nine soldiers led by Leech saunter down to where we wait. None wear web gear or shows bulges in pockets to indicate extra munitions. Some, as the RVNs support when searching for mortar tubes outside LZ English, carry their rifles atop their shoulders, as if axes or shovels.

Lieutenant Leech sees the ghastly concern on our faces and approaches Puteoli, "Is there a problem, Sergeant?"

Tony looks to the patrol before answering Leech. "You patrol every third day, at precisely this time of the morning, with your men dressed and equipped exactly like that?" he inquires.

"Well, pretty much," the lieutenant reluctantly answers. He turns his attention to inspecting our combat ensemble down to our bulging, canvas, ammo pouches. "But I don't think the enemy is so brazen as to attack us so close to our camp."

"Charlie watches for routines before they strike," Tony instructs the second lieutenant. "They are masters at surprise tactics, waiting for that perfect opportunity to hit an unsuspecting unit."

"But there has been no sign of the enemy to date," Leech offers an excuse.

Tony Puteoli's diplomatic overtures at dealing with officers has returned. His mannerism for cajoling men with metal on their collars into accepting his recommendations as if they themselves had conceived the idea, is back. "I agree that being random with the days you patrol and the time that you head out to be an excellent notion. Making sure your men carry enough ammo in the event of an engagement is also a great point."

A half hour later, we pass the flimsy gate looking like a Grunt unit on patrol, although, only looking like one. As Whitman leads us into the jungle, further than the artillery men have ventured to date, fear begins to take them, making them ready to be molded into a fighting unit. They dispense with their gripes of possibly missing lunch and other senseless chatter, to hear our instructions. They start to communicate with hands and fingers as taught, although their use of the middle finger initially prevailed. But the further into the nearby jungle we proceed, the more fear takes hold of them, and the more willingly they accept our instructions. They soon take to silently gliding past trees and shrub, searching the brush for anything out of kilter. Four hundred meters from the basecamp, the halt sign cascades down the column and students are taught to form a perimeter of eyes. Tony and Leech are eventually called forward. I follow in the event the radio is required.

Thompkins takes a knee and scans the area. I thought that I detected a faint smile, just before he turned his attention away from us.

Brandon Whitman stands looking down at his feet and pressing hard against his left temple. At his feet is a heaping pile of human feces.

Leech hurries and squats before the shit. I see shock on the man's face as he closely examines the pile, and for a brief second, I thought he was going to reach out and touch the damn thing. Instead, he looks up at Tony, and mouths the words, "Still warm."

Tony moves alongside Leech's left ear. He cups a hand between the man's ear and his mouth, to relay information. Leech nods and both take to their feet.

I spot a poorly concealed wicked look on our visual tracker's face and Thompkins, appears to struggle to stifle a laugh. A quick look into a nearby bush reveals white, c-ration, toilet tissue, peeking from deep in that shrub.

Whitman's turd serves its intended purpose. The patrol continues lapping up at any tidbit of knowledge dispensed by the team and are left hungering for more. Minutes after our return to base camp, the turd and immediate area around it are obliterated by thousands of dollars of army munitions.

The next day, the perimeter starts to get a face lift. Sandbags are filled and stacked with earnest to add rows and courses to the outer defenses. By the end of the second week, we set up empty beer cans beyond the fence for target practice. Whitman prizes the two best shooters with two cans of beer each. The artillery men rise to the challenge, and by the fourth patrol, Thompkins admits to Leech that his artillerymen have become far more skilled on patrol than any Grunt unit he has worked with.

Time flies by. Our tenure atop a firebase with no name is soon to expire. In three days, we return from exile to a land froth with ambitious and mindless leadership. To add despair to our little time remaining, Tony receives written denial for an extension and travel orders for him and Bert, accompany the rejection. "I think I know how the citizens of Mudville must have felt," a downcast Red offers that night.

Our last evening on that firebase is one the artillery men will long talk about. The head of the kitchen fries chicken using a family recipe handed down to him by his grandmother in Savannah, Georgia. All admit to being the best chicken they've eaten, although only the captain appears curious as to the means employed to get fresh poultry way out here. Our stash of beer rests in five, large, army kitchen thermoses. They are iced down, all courtesy of Whitman's ingenuity and generosity. It is a fitting goodbye tribute to the artillerymen who took in an orphaned team as one their own.

Leech with the other two officers, approach with cold beers in hand. It is the captain that first speaks, "You got to tell me how you fenagled getting ice out here," he tells Baby Face.

"Sir, if I told you, I'd have to kill you afterwards," Whitman answers to jovial laughter.

"I don't know whether I will miss you men, or your beer, but mind me, I think both will be sorely missed," Leech speaks to nods from the other two officers.

CHAPTER 19

Arrival in the Republic of Vietnam is a shock to the senses. The land, the people and language, and the culture are unlike anything experienced by eighteen or nineteen-year-old Americans. The place has new arrivals thirsting for greater exposure to the exotic sights, sounds, and smells of the place. But the army did not ship healthy, young males to partake in an adventure of the wonderous nature of the region, and one is soon exposed to the ugly reality of why he has been brought here. A countdown of remaining days before rotating home commences shortly after that first, dreadful exposure to reality. It continues with faithful devotion until those days can be easily counted on the fingers of a lone hand.

Whitman, Red and I watch a reluctant Puteoli and Thompkins pack their meager personal belongings. The others are on a mission. They were gone when we returned from exile. One extra uniform, socks and briefs, hygiene products, a cassette tape and several pictures are stowed in olive drab, canvas valises.

Our DEROS brothers are catching a flight to the Air Force Base at Phan Rang at four this afternoon, for an early morning flight back to the World. In two days, they will disembark a plane loaded with the betrayed and the disenchanted. They will arrive at a place that will shock their senses and will have them feeling like a convict, stepping through the gates of a prison after a twenty-year incarceration. Just how does someone returning home, transition back to civil society after witnessing and being a part of the bloodletting of this war? The realization of going back, to partake in that new adventure, altogether different from what one has had to acclimate to the past twelve months, makes a short-timer, suddenly anxious and fearful of returning home.

Whitman and I suffer differing trepidations. We await travel orders to Phan Thiet, where our new unit, a mechanize, infantry battalion is headquartered. Red, the lone member to remain a tracker, appears the most forlorn. His linebacker's shoulders appear to sag.

Claude Hooper enters our hooch for only the second time since his appointment as NCOIC of our unit. Amid a hail of invisible, flying daggers, he walks straight toward me, a sickening grin carved into his face. He holds out papers for me to take. Realizing that I have no intention of seizing the papers, he flings them on my bunk. He proceeds to do the same at Whitman's bunk, wearing a jovial face that begs for a fist.

He heads for the back door, but halts at the threshold. A slow turn back, and with a silly grin worthy of a Ringling Brothers' clown, he gives us an impudent salute, followed by a girlish flap of fingers alongside an impish, crouched head, teasing and gloating at a goodbye. He exits, laughing and joins a solemn Nieman in the cab of CTT2.

"How can you not help but love that man!" Thompkins proclaims to a slow to build, but prolonged heavy laughter. "I'm going to miss that fat bastard."

"Let's get some breakfast," Tony suggests.

"Yeah!" Whitman hollers. "I've a few words to tell that engineer captain, before I leave this shithole."

"Best save that for the last meal here; otherwise, we'll likely find ourselves eating our meals in the brig," I warn.

"Why are you getting your panties all bunched up?" Whitman sarcastically quips. "You and I are out of here at eight tomorrow morning."

It is hot as Hades and only midmorning. Puteoli and Thompkins pace the floor like expectant fathers and fidget with any loose item that come in contact with their fingertips. I suspect they will continue burning nervous energy for the next four and a half hours, when we drive them to our small, army runway, at the other side of English.

Whitman stands to block Thompkins, "You mind. You're driving me nuts with all this stomping. Why not stroll over to the front office and wish our backbone of humanity, Lieutenant Lewis, goodbye?"

"Get out of my way you little shit," and with that, Thompkins goes around Whitman, but not without bumping him.

"Consider yourself lucky," Brandon yells out to Bert. "Fate will likely have it that L J and I get to within a day or two of DEROS, before snuffing out our lights."

"Thank you, Brandon Whitman!" I voice my protest at being included in such a gloomy prospect.

"Let's head out to lunch before someone gets hurt," Tony chuckles. "The chow line should be open by the time we get there."

All agree, for it is something to do, other than pace or watch those doing the pacing.

We are halfway down the knoll our compound sits at, when a jeep, with Brigade HQ designation, suddenly turns barreling up toward Dog Patch. It halts at our side. A major in the passenger seat and a captain of rangers in the back, both in their twenties, fail to return our salute. "You men trackers?" The major asks.

We nod, unable to mouth words as minds race to search for a conceivable reason for the inquiry and visit by a major and a captain.

"Grab your weapons and gear," he orders. The jeep shoots up the rest of the way to Dog Patch, without our having the opportunity to pose a single question.

Salutes are dropped as we watch the vehicle drive to the HQ hooch. We plod back, no one stupid enough to continue on to the mess hall in challenge to an order from a major, and all engaged in speculation at the mystery of what has transpired to warrant such visitors and orders.

As we gather our things, the major hurries in as if there is no tomorrow. A sheepish looking Lieutenant Lewis is sucked in by the wake of the man's rush, and the captain with a ranger patch on his sleeve follows close behind.

"Sergeant Hooper is missing," the major starts. "He was let out of a LOH he and your other sergeant were riding. Hooper got out for a close inspection of markings on a trail. Gunfire erupted and the LOH crew had a knee jerk reaction and withdrew, abandoning Hooper."

Seeing and sensing an icy reception, and lack of concern among his audience, the major pauses to examine unmoved faces, before resting dark, worried eyes on an apprehensive lieutenant.

Lewis stands by the front door, slouching, as if waiting on a scolding that he knows is coming.

"The LOH crew eventually circled back, wondering whether Hooper had accidentally discharged his weapon when he disembarked. They were unable to locate him by then," he adds, now looking far more curious at our reception to his words, than we had when he ordered us to grab our gear. "Look, I don't know what the hell is going on here, but I need you men out there, finding Hooper or to at least establish that he was on the right trail of our missing teams." He halts, but continues to study mute, uncaring faces, searching for a means to break through that empty façade that we wear. "As you know," he baits his hook, "we are desperate to get word on your team and the two ranger teams that went in with them."

Puteoli bites. "Sir, we know absolutely nothing of the mission Team 1 is on, much less that they are lost or that Sergeants Hooper and Nieman went searching for them."

"Well now you know, so get your asses in gear," a visibly angry major interrupts.

Tony steps toward the officer, wanting no further interference until he has said what he wants to say. "Sir, I and our cover man are due to catch a flight for Phan Rang this afternoon. Tomorrow morning, we fly home. My extension request was denied by Lieutenant Lewis and Sergeant Hooper. The team's visual tracker and RTO have been transferred out of the unit by Lieutenant Lewis. They fly out for Phan Thiet tomorrow morning to join an infantry battalion. The team you now seek to search for Hooper doesn't exist."

Like the masochist who nearly got his ass kicked by an MP sergeant at LZ Uphill, I step forward to inject some payback of my own. "Sir, Lieutenant Lewis and Sergeant Hooper posted us to a firebase out in the middle of nowhere, the past four weeks. They wanted us out of the way while they showcased untested, tracking techniques. Team 1, the model of that pending disaster, consists of green trackers and only one member of that team has any combat experience. The team leader lacks both combat and leadership experience. Our protesting those facts got us sent out to the middle of nowhere and now kicked off the unit."

The major glances at Lewis who stares down at the floor. By now the officer realizes that he is dealing with an organizational catastrophe. He shuts his eyes for several long seconds, deep in thought. "There is an urgent and desperate need of your help," he suddenly restarts, having a sense of what he has to deal with. "The other tracker team and two ranger teams were sent in to track down an NVA counter intelligence unit. That is the enemy's version of a tracker team, and they have plagued ranger teams sent into the mountains. Our three teams ran into a heavy firefight yesterday morning, and there's been no word from them since."

He has my attention and that of the others. The idea that Cooper and Talmadge, and the three others, whose names again escape me, are in peril, pains me to no end.

"I have two ranger teams waiting to act as your support. They are biting at the bit to get in there and find their missing friends."

"Sir, we need an infantry platoon for support," Bert adds to the conversation. "Rangers are trained to glide through the jungle like ghosts, and just gather intel. Like us, they are trained to avoid firefights with the enemy. Just how are they to deal with the enemy, should we choose to go, and should we get into a firefight?"

"Don't underestimate my rangers," the captain replies. "If I send a team in to pluck an enemy officer from the enemy's rank, they will return with one."

"Look, I realize you men have transfer papers and that I have no authority to counter those orders," the major continues. "Hooper may hold the key to locating your teammates and the rangers. The lives of those boys, if still alive, may be in jeopardy. They don't deserve to die over what goes on here." He steps closer to Tony to preempt further opposition. "In the event, this outing goes beyond your scheduled flight time, I will have air transport on standby to get you and your cover man to Phan Rang. That, I can promise you."

Tony turns his head to us, and shrugs his shoulders. The decision, after all, rest with all, but Red.

I nod. The idea of Talmadge and Cooper in danger calls for all we can do to bring them back.

Whitman grabs his things and heads outside to the deuce-and-a-half without being told. "Well, looks like Coop finally got his Combat Infantry Badge."

Three Huey transports descend, simulating to land to deposit us in a clearing in the mountains, but then swoop off to another similar site, miles away, only to repeat the process. They finally take turns, going in and dumping us in a small narrow opening between hills, while big brothers, with their lethal mini-guns, cannons and rockets, scour the ground from above.

We lead the way toward the general area Hooper was last seen, but only after an on-board debate with the ranger captain that argued he and his men should go first. We locate the trail at the very spot Hooper disembarked, a quarter of a mile from our drop zone. The trail is cluttered with sandal prints, but only one set of jungle boot markings. Crushed grass, upturned stones, and bent and broken twigs dangling from bushes, show some clumsy person wearing boots went down a steep wash-out; Hooper is our guess.

Shooting Hooper in a friendly fire incident, teasingly crosses my mind. Afterall, it was his foolhardy implementation of pretentious, self-promoting ideas that have recklessly endangered friends. Unfortunately, he may possess knowledge as to their whereabouts, and surely, these thoughts are only whimsical fantasies, or a transient notion.

The midday heat and humidity are as stifling as ever. Sweat burns at my eyes, and the horrid air sits heavy in my lungs. I realize that once we start down that dried-out drainage trough, things will get far more repressive, but I also realize that it is but the first leg of our journey to finding Cooper and Talmadge.

Ten minutes of struggling to maintain steady feet down a steep gully strewn with rocks and boulders, Whitman abruptly signals a halt and a secure-in-place sign. A second later, he points two fingers to troubled eyes. He follows that signal with a lone digit aimed at the bottom of the wash-out, where fallen trees rest in a pile, much like Pick-Up Sticks. Anxiety strikes our expedition. Tony relays the signal to the ranger captain, and with a sweep of the hand, informs him to send in men to investigate.

It requires four, long, angst minutes for three rangers to crawl on their bellies to the log jam. They spread out along the fallen trunks before venturing a quick peek inside the maze of timber. Gunfire suddenly breaks the silence, followed by angry voices of two rangers. "Cease fire, cease fire, you Dumb Fuck."

A familiar voice cries out, "Oh, thank God!"

My stomach suddenly gets a queasier feel. The opportunity for a friendly fire mishap is lost.

The rest of the team sent down, scurry to Hooper's location. One pissed ranger captain leads the way. They hurry to where a ranger writhes in pain with a shoulder wound.

The second team soon trails past them to the bottom of the ravine and sets up security. We follow, but only to a few feet above the pile of timber, where we shelter and cover the rear.

"Bless you for coming to get me," we hear Claude thank the men at the log jam.

A peek back, shows him painstakingly rising from among fallen tree trunks. There is a wince of pain in his voice as he sits on a log. "I thought I was a goner," he speaks to no one in particular.

It is not what I had hoped for, but I nevertheless, take some satisfaction from the suffering he appears to endure.

Hooper swings his legs over the log he sits, but not without further discomfort. "I think my ankle is broken," he whines to those tending to the shoulder of the wounded ranger. "How are we getting out of here? Will it be long? I need to have this ankle checked out."

We hear the constant chatter of our NCOIC from below. His voice continues to be a source of great irritation, not only for me, but others.

"How were you able to locate me?" he posts that query to the officer.

The captain rises from aiding his ranger. He wears a hard scowl on his face, "We didn't!" he snaps at Hooper. "They did," he adds, pointing an angry finger toward us.

A shock and angry look sweep our sergeant's face, once he spies us. He had not expected to ever see some of us again; and yet, here we are, credited by an officer for having located him in this vast jungle terrain. Resentment and disdain at our betrayal of being the ones to come to his rescue, produces a pronounced snarl to his face. He glares at us with such contempt, that compels us to turn our backs on the wretched man.

"I'd advise you to find a new attitude and fast, Sergeant!" the captain admonishes Hooper. "These men have volunteered to be here. I'm starting to get a clear understanding of why they hesitated doing so. You are one walking cluster fuck!"

That said, the captain turns to his men, "Get them on their feet. Got to get to the extraction point before an entire enemy regiment descends upon us, as if things couldn't get worse."

Red and Prince take point on a dry creek bed that offers a gap among trees and bushes. The dry bed mirrors the direction of the trail high up on the slopes. The handler and dog lead our group toward an opening in the jungle, less than a mile away that is our extraction point.

We trackers wear the happiest grins possibly ever exhibited by a team while in the midst of Indian country. The ass-chewing Hooper got was far more satisfying than any friendly fire incident could have been. But with time, the heat and humidity, along with the danger of our current station, brings us back to reality, and to trepidation and stress.

Halfway to our destination, a stench permeates the air. Alarmed by the odor, we creep, cautiously onward. As we do, the smell becomes more distinct. In short time, we take a knee, far too reluctant to go further. Tony warily signals the captain forward.

It is a distinct foul scent that fills the air; a stench whose source is instinctively recognizable, as is the aroma of hot bread, baking in an oven, although this smell stokes, only deep, imbedded evolutionary fears. Cardona once described the odor as a bit sweet and the rest, pungent putrid. On this hot afternoon, only the putrid part of rotting flesh stands out.

Tony points out for the captain, what has us not wanting to proceed further. What looks like a large black creature, lies in a heavily trampled clearing. It is a creature we think to recognize, but pray we are dead wrong.

The officer shoots a worried glance at Prince, before signaling a team forward to investigate.

I watch the rangers advance in relays. My stomach is tight and my muscles so tense that I long to follow them, to do something physical to ease that strain on my body; but instead, I just watch, along with the rest of my team, dreading what I suspect the rangers will discover.

They mask their noses with hands as they approach the black animal. A quick glance down at the unfortunate creature, they hurry past, but abruptly freeze as they come face to face with what lies among nearby trees and bushes.

The captain pushes past his rangers. He halts, his torso jerks back, and soon, his chin sinks into his chest. He cradles his forehead in his left hand, but not long, before spinning around to direct his boys to set a defensive perimeter. Afterwards, he turns back and reverts to cradling his forehead, as his chest heaves violently.

I tend to attribute a far older age to those here than the late teens and early twenties which we are. The work and responsibility we engage in matures us and takes a toll on appearances. The emotional consequences of stress and fear gives us an older appearance than those men far older at home. So, it's difficult to remember that the man silently weeping to my front is but in his early to mid-twenties.

I rise and move forward to where the captain weeps for a preview of tomorrow's nightmares. Like a moth to a flame, I am drawn to view a sight the mind pleads not see, but which the legs openly defy.

Zeus is on the ground. His poor body is riddled with bullets, and his head is missing, likely taken as proof for a hefty bounty. I close my eyes tight, till they hurt, recalling the big, friendly creature, before mustering the courage to continue forward to look at what lies in the bushes. I take a glance and shut my eyes tight. A snapshot of what lies between the creek bed and trail is forever chiseled into memory. It will fester in some recess of my soul, to suddenly spring forth, like an unwanted visitor that stalks you into your sleep.

I once thought that eleven bodies piled in an open field a large number of dead. Perhaps that was due to the shame at so much killing, of which I had taken part. But, as I now gaze upon nine dead bodies, clad in OD fatigues, their left sleeves with the unit designations taken as bounty or trophies, I construe this to be a far greater carnage.

I turn my head aside, wanting to avert my eyes and attention, no longer capable of dealing with the gruesome spectacle, only to come eye to eye with those of the ranger captain. He is at a radio, struggling to maintain some composure, but turns away lest the sight of anger and pain in my eyes cause him to lose that struggle.

Behind me the rest of the team is up and moving, drawn by that flame that drew me. I contemplate halting them, sparing them from one more egregious image to terrorize their future. But how do I tell them that Carl Talmadge, along with Zeus's handler, Melvin Janson, lie among the corpses. They will insist on seeing for themselves.

Prince abruptly halts and raises his head. Like a small statue, his entire body freezes, aimed toward heavy foliage far to the right of our little clearing.

I look, but find nothing of danger. Beyond the trees and shrubs of that area, I spy what looks like sections of the trail on a slope. A sharp left curve in the trail, as it skirts around that rise is as far as I can see. I continue searching, now scanning every rock and tree that may harbor a sniper or someone hiding and watching, and yet, nothing.

Just as I begin to think that Prince has issued a false alert, I spot bare, muscular legs, pumping fast from around that bend in the trail and coming our way.

I offer no warning to others of what I see. Anger and a vengeful desire to inflict pain on those responsible for the death of a poor boy from Pigeon Forge, directs my actions to the detriment of all logic. Quick bursts from a weapon set on automatic is my response to the sighting. Four, five or six short firings bring down the owners of those legs.

A chaos of action and weapons fire now envelops the area. I reload a full magazine and continue to fire, aiming at anything that appears to move along that trail, and there are no shortages of targets heading our way. In time and amidst a blur of movement and noise, I find the ammunition pouch on the right of my web belt empty. Spent magazines lie at my feet in the sandy creek bed, at where I have not moved since I started firing. I take quick stock of my immediate surroundings. Others have taken refuge behind trees, rocks and shrubs and are fully engaged with the enemy, while I stand, openly exposed in the dry creek.

As I reach for a full magazine in the left pouch, I spot dozens of heads appearing higher up on the slope of the hill by the trail. One of those heads has his upper torso visible. He shoulders a rocket propelled grenade launcher, and takes aim, directly at me.

I scamper to the safety of a large tree. A hard dive behind that tree, then, a rocket swoosh sounds, ending things.

CHAPTER 20

"LJ...L J! I know you hear me. Get your bald-headed ass awake. I'm flying back to the World tomorrow, and this is my last day to visit. You're not going to skate free of saying goodbye like you did Tillman, and I know you're faking it. You just love having these nurses hand wash your cock and balls, but it's time to give it up."

"Soldier, I've cautioned you about using vulgarity in my ward. Another word of profanity and I'll have you barred from here. Am I making myself clear?"

"Yes Ma'am, you are. It's just that the doctor suggested I talk to him. He told me that he may be listening, and some swearing is how we generally communicate."

"I do not care," a woman's cross voice replies. "That language may be suitable for some Bangkok brothel, but not my ward."

"Well, Ma'am, what do you suggest I say to him?"

"Sing, read or recite poetry to him, I do not care," that angry female voice continues. "But one more filthy word out of that mouth and I'll have it washed out with soap, and afterwards, you thrown out. Clear?"

A slight indiscernible mumble sounds.

"What?" The woman demands. "Are you comprehending what I am saying?"

"Yes, Major."

The sound of footsteps moving off, and then another set, along with a loud thumping noise, approaches my left ear. "L J, you do not want that old dried prune anywhere around your balls," the voice whispers. "Tell her you want one of the young, Philippine nurses to scrub your groin." That annoyance continues at tormenting my solitude, "If asked, which one, tell them Lieutenant Garza. She is the hottest nurse on this ward."

There seems no getting rid of the unwanted guest. So, I struggle at opening my eyes against better judgement, if only to tell Brandon Whitman to go away and leave me the hell in peace.

"Hey. Hey! Hey Major!" I hear him suddenly scream. "His eyes are opening!"

I see a blur of a silhouette standing alongside my bed, perhaps Whitman. It is a dark shape of a man in pajama bottoms with a crutch under his left armpit. He backs away to safety, as a flurry of people converge at the sides of my bed. Apparently, there will be no returning to my solace.

"Can you see and hear me?" a man's anxious voice inquires. "Talking may be difficult for a short time, so just blink or raise an arm if you can."

Both mouth and throat are as parched as the Sahara Desert. My tongue feels stuck to the roof of my mouth so talking is indeed difficult, if not impossible. I blink, or think I blink.

"Excellent!" The doctor boldly states. "Now, can you tell me your name?"

I try to speak, but only a low, gurgling groan emerges.

"Blink for me if your name is Cory Lejeune," he now asks of me.

A nurse with the rank of major approaches, as I blink. She wets my lips with a cool, damp cloth. She then forces the end of a straw past my lips. With the other end plugged by a finger, she allows a trickle of syphoned water, trapped in the straw to quench the dryness.

"You haven't had much need of your mouth and throat the past three weeks," the doctor explains. "We have fed you intravenously and through a nasogastric tube. Your palate, esophagus and stomach will have to be reacquainted to nourishment." The man pulls up a chair, sits, and commences to toying with my fingers. "You are in a military hospital at Long Bien. We performed surgery to remove shrapnel from the top of your shoulders," he continues. "Those healed nicely. Of upmost concern, has been a head injury. Concussion caused your brain to swell and that swelling resulted in your being in a coma the past weeks. The surgery to reduce the pressure appears successful. If you are up to it, we are going to run some tests to make sure everything is functioning properly."

"Doc, how long will these tests take?" I hear Whitman ask from behind the crowd of medical personnel.

An orderly, suddenly aware of the nearby pest, starts to usher Whitman away.

"Come back later this evening," the doctor at my side barks at him.

A battery of tests is administered over the next three hours. Most of the tests are related to sensory perception and muscular movement and coordination.

The medical staff appear pleased with themselves at the fast recovery progress which I demonstrate or perhaps with their success at retrieving me from a vegetative state.

They take pleasure at lecturing and showing other medical staff their guinea pig. At any rate, they are delighted, and I am regarded as a celebrity.

Shortly before two in the afternoon, an attractive, olive skin lieutenant, my age, with what could pass as a slight oriental appearance to her otherwise Spanish face, wakes me from a brief nap. She sticks one end of a straw in my mouth, while the other end rests in a mug. Beef broth is introduced to a palate starving for flavor. It shoots down to an empty stomach, far too quickly, leaving only a salty taste behind. At times, I drink and swallow so fast I gag on liquid.

"Slow down," the lieutenant orders with a smile that exposes the bright, white enamel of her teeth. "I have some strawberry yogurt for you when you tire of this."

"Yogurt, what is that?" I ask, after one of my many chokings.

"You don't know what yogurt is?" she asks, smiling in a manner indicating she teases rather than having a genuine curiosity at my ignorance.

"No Ma'am," I reply with a playful look of my own, emboldened by my newly acquired celebrity status. "I have heard it mentioned, but I'm unfamiliar with what it's like."

"It's creamy, like sour cream, but just as sour. Fruit adds sweetness to it," Lieutenant Garza tells me.

"Can't recall that being a food staple back home in Louisiana."

"I will be right back with some for you to try."

Why yogurt, and why does it require fruit to sweeten it? Plain vanilla ice cream would be far more preferable than some unfamiliar dairy product, but I lack the inclination to disappoint the pretty lieutenant by asking for something other than what she prescribes. Besides, I always enjoy trying new foods and she seems eager for me to have the cream.

There are other nurses like Lieutenant Garza that work in this large ward of some forty beds. Young, female Philippine citizens, trained as nurses at the expense of the U.S Army, now fulfil their end of a contract by serving as army nurses, but none are as attractive as the exotic Garza.

Twenty minutes after being spoon-fed a dairy product turned rancid, while desperately struggling to not barf or otherwise humiliate myself with nurse Garza, I discover the true purpose of that yogurt. It explodes past my sphincter before I have time to adjust for the sudden urge.

"Orderly!" I yell out. "Orderly," I repeat, praying for assistance from a male attendant.

An hour after a bland supper of oatmeal, with small chunks of banana for taste, they have me walking, barefoot and in my hospital gown, from one end of the ward to the other.

Lieutenant Garza explained that this is not a test, but rather exercise, for muscles that have been dormant for weeks. An orderly is assigned to make sure that I not fall, which I deem unnecessary and somewhat degrading; though in fact, my gait initially resembled that of an old man's walk.

Thirty minutes later, I am heading to my bed, when I hear that familiar voice from behind, "Gone Montagnard, have we?" I look back at Whitman, as he points to the rear of my hospital gown.

I reach back with my left hand and feel ass. I close the gap of the gown, feeling the warmth of humiliation course throughout the body. No one said anything about my exposed rear until now. I recall the old major watching me walk, but I assumed that was a clinical observation. The leers from the other nurses in the ward, should have alerted me, but I was too busy showing off for Lieutenant Garza, to pay heed to their peeks and smirks.

"Well, buddy," Whitman continues, while I carefully mount the bed to minimize further exposure, "never thought to go trolling for nurses by baring my ass as bait. Any bites, other than that old biddy?"

"You do realize the major is likely in her late thirties or early forties?" I venture to inform rather than ask.

"That is still twice my age, but if you want her to test out little LJ, be my guest. Me, I'd hold out for Alicia Garza."

"So, you heading out tomorrow?" I inquire, hoping to divert his attention to a less vulgar discussion.

"Yeah, catching a military flight to San Antonio, Texas. I'll be there three to four weeks, for therapy, before they give me an early release.

"Where and when were you hit?"

Whitman pulls up the lone chair between me and the empty bed on my left. He lowers himself into the chair and sits quietly for longer than I have seen him be silent. He stares down at his feet as his eyes glaze over.

I and the others tagged him with the nick name of Baby Face for a reason. But now, all that I see is the haggard face of a man, of someone who has experienced far more horrors than anyone should ever have.

"You and I, along with a ranger were shipped by medivac directly to this hospital," he commences to explain. "Took two rounds to the hip, shattering it. Needed two operations to remove lead and bone splinters and to fit the pieces back together. I've got to wear a silly girdle-looking thing till it fully heals," he chuckles and wipes at his eyes. "Doc said it will leave me with a sexy limp. You on the other hand, we all thought you were a goner. That firefight was one hell of a hullabaloo, but we kicked some serious ass. Shit flew everywhere, but there you were, standing in the open, blasting away like John Wayne. Then, one minute you're diving for cover behind a tree, a split second later, an RPG round explodes and has you changing direction in mid-air. Strangest thing I ever saw, you flying about like a rag doll. But I got that bastard that nearly got you."

"Talmadge is dead," I declare, not knowing if he is aware or perhaps to confirm my own memory of that day, "so is Melvin Janson."

"Yeah," he suddenly sighs, and lowers his eyes. His chest commences to heave, and he covers his mouth with a hand squeezing so hard a lack of blood flow turns the immediate area pale white.

I wipe at moisture from my own eyes, and with a squeaky and shaky voice ask, "and the rest of the team?"

"Not sure," he whimpers, but only to buy time to wipe tears off his face and to take a deep breath to compose himself. "Tony and Thompkins are okay, back in the States by now, I guess. Red and Prince are fine; they're probably back at Dog Patch, putting up with all of Nieman's bullshit. Hooper's ankle was indeed broken," he continues, with a smile threatening to emerge on his face. "The rangers were pissed and indicated they would seek to court-martial his ass over the friendly fire incident, although, I suspect that he will catch a lot more hell over the loss of Zeus, should he return to Dog Patch."

"And the others?"

Whitman wipes his cheeks. He appears forlorn and embroiled in dark festering memories. Seconds pass before he dares to speak, "No idea about Coop and the other two Cherries," he whimpers, but just as suddenly and surprisingly, he forces a cheerful look. "Look at us, bawling like babies. You'd think we should have done this when the shit was flying all around instead of now."

"There wasn't time," I force a smile as I reply. "But we have a lifetime ahead of us to do just that."

"Hey, almost forgot," he announces. He digs into his pajama bottom pocket and produces a piece of paper with a telephone number and an address in the state of Washington. "You can get in touch with me there," he says and hands me the paper. "It's my parents place, but they will pass on any messages. I'm thinking of doing some travel when I get to the World, maybe Kissimmee, Florida and Pigeon Forge, Tennessee."

An orderly at the ward's light switch, dims the room, prompting at Whitman to depart. "Guess that's my cue," he says and rises. He looks down at me for some time with a far distant gaze, as if suddenly recounting all our time together and all the ordeals we endured. He passes a hand across his eyes and steps closer. "Got to go L J," he sobs, and sticks out a hand for me to take.

I took that hand, still wet with his tears, fully cognizant that this was the only time that we had offered each other a handshake of friendship. I finally released his hand and watched him hobble away.

That was the last time that I saw or communicated with any of my brother trackers. A small band of young men, we bonded tight while suffering through life and death tribulations. Their failure to have stayed in touch is as much a mystery to me, as my own reluctance to have reached out to them. Perhaps as Tillman wrote in his last and only letter, we had to put the war behind us. We had to forget our time in Vietnam, as essential to staving off or at least keep at bay, the demons that came home with us.

I left the war zone, an altogether different person than the naïve, prodigal son, who sought redemption from petty sins and searched for a purpose to life. Returning home, forever scarred, was not what I had ever intended. Yet, unlike Newsome, Talmadge and Melvin Janson, who never aged past those youthful days of 1969, I had the opportunity to return to a nation, ignorant and indifferent to what they sent us to do and endure.

A half century would pass before I dared to consciously evoke memories of the war and the brothers who suffered it with me. For decades, I agonized through a self-imposed exile from those who once stood side by side with me, to bear alone vile, triggered memories that only that family from long ago can comprehend. Now, like a masochist, I revel in the conscious memories of those days and the world that revolved around that long ago group of boys. But as in all the horrific nighttime episodes that plague my sleep, the vivid images that I have of them are forever frozen as nineteen and twenty-year-old boys.

Ingram Content Group UK Ltd.
Milton Keynes UK
UKHW012207140423
420199UK00002B/54